# Bound for the Holidays

An invitation too hot to pass up.

*Ties That Bind Book 1*

Angela Clarke finds herself bound for the holidays, literally. Not by one, but two gorgeous men—a powerful executive and one sexy cowboy.

Angie expected to spend Christmas alone, not in the arms of her new boss after the office party. Their attraction is hot enough to melt ice, and his wicked promises alluring. What he's offering she has only fantasized about.

To her surprise, the night not only involves silk scarves and a set of handcuffs, but one tall dark cowboy.

Ryan Tyler has never thought twice about sharing his women with his best friend—until Ryan touches Angie. She stirs something deep inside him. But it's too late to stop the decadent night from unfolding. What starts as hot sex with a warm, willing woman turns into something more. After tonight, Ryan knows he'll never be satisfied with just one taste.

Could his fantasy lead to something lasting, or will it only be one night of pleasure?

*Warning, this title contains the following: explicit sex, graphic language, ménage a trois.*

# Bound by the Past

Breaking the rules—to heal a broken heart.

*Ties That Bind Book 2*

Years of neglect and disappointments have molded Jessica Evans into a strong, independent woman, determined to live life by her rules. The only place she's willing to relinquish control is in the bedroom. Even then, it's only on her terms.

A safety net of multiple partners keeps anyone from getting too close. That is, until one sexy cowboy throws a snag in that net, big time. Not only does Wade Peterson make her body burn, he's crossed the line. The damn man wants to marry her.

For Wade, sharing her with another man is almost more than he can bear. But if he pushes too hard, he could lose her for good—something he refuses to allow to happen. Jessie's rejection isn't the end of it, not by a long shot. He's back, and he's hell-bent on seducing her right back into his wicked arms.

Then her past comes back to drop a bomb in her lap, and Wade sees a part of her he didn't know existed—and another obstacle that could drive her to discard her only chance for love.

*Warning, this title contains the following: hot, explicit ménage sex, graphic language, and one sexy-as-hell cowboy.*

# Look for these titles by
## *Mackenzie McKade*

## *Now Available:*
Six Feet Under
Fallon's Revenge
A Warrior's Witch
Lisa's Gift
Lost But Not Forgotten
Second Chance Christmas
Black Widow

*Ties That Bind Series*
Bound for the Holidays (Book 1)
Bound by the Past (Book 2)

*Wild Oats Series*
Take Me (Book 1)
Take Me Again (Book 2)

*Print Anthologies*
The Perfect Gift
Beginnings
Midsummer Night's Steam: Sins of Summer

## *Coming Soon:*
Merry Christmas, Paige

# Bound by Desire

*Mackenzie McKade*

A SAMHAIN PUBLISHING, LTD. publication.

Samhain Publishing, Ltd.
577 Mulberry Street, Suite 1520
Macon, GA 31201
www.samhainpublishing.com

Bound by Desire
Bound for the Holidays Copyright © 2009 by Mackenzie McKade
Bound by the Past Copyright © 2009 by Mackenzie McKade
Print ISBN: 978-1-60504-298-5

Editing by Angela James
Cover by Scott Carpenter

Bound for the Holidays, ISBN 1-59998-387-7
First Samhain Publishing, Ltd. electronic publication: December 2006
Bound by the Past, ISBN 1-59998-945-X
First Samhain Publishing, Ltd. electronic publication: August 2008
First Samhain Publishing, Ltd. print publication: March 2009

# Contents

*Enjoy!*

*Mackenzie McKade*

# Bound for the Holidays

# Dedication

To my dearest friends Cheyenne McCray, Patti Duplantis, Katie Walo, Kendra Egert, and Julie Cummings. Thank you for your continued support.

# Chapter One

Angela Clarke blinked hard. The owner of *Silk Sheets* magazine did *not* just ask how good she was in the layout position.

Did he?

Of course, the crowd's loud laughter and the music didn't help her hearing. The employees of *Silk Sheets* were celebrating Christmas at the Hyatt Regency at Gainey Ranch in Scottsdale. Ryan Tyler had reserved the ballroom, served a four-course meal, hired a band and had a full service bar to entertain his staff. They were a rowdy bunch, eating, drinking and dancing at the company's expense.

The man in question leaned casually against the bar next to where Angie sat on a stool. An ebony curl fell across Ryan's broad forehead giving him that sexy, bad boy look. He radiated sexual heat.

Damn. You're good-looking.

She sucked in a breath and held it, trying to withhold her immediate response, *Hell yeah, I'm good in the layout position and I'd be happy to show you.* But his woodsy cologne was playing havoc with her senses. She clenched her jaw to keep the words from spilling out her mouth.

The bartender pushed another cosmopolitan in front of her, but she ignored him. Was her new boss making a pass or was it wishful thinking on her part?

Perhaps Angie just heard what she wanted to—an invitation into his bed.

She mentally shook the thought away, remembering her ever-blunt father's words, "Dipping one's pen in company ink is never wise, Angela. Keep your legs crossed and your mind on business."

She hadn't been the kind of child who listened to her father's advice, so why start now?

It was two days before Christmas and she was desperate.

The idea of spending Christmas alone with her tabby cat, Kitty, was not her idea of a good time. Her mother and father were basking in Hawaii for the holidays, while her two brothers had decided a skiing trip to Colorado sounded more fun than spending Christmas with their big sister in the deserts of Arizona.

Dark eyelashes hooded Ryan Tyler's sensual blue eyes. He cocked a brow, reminding her that he had asked that question—about being good in the layout position.

Fighting to keep a calm mien and obliterate the naughty thoughts swirling in her head, she attempted an unassuming smile that didn't quite feel right.

Truth was, she had it bad for the boss. From the first time he walked into the boardroom and took her hand in his, she immediately fell in lust, trapped in a state of hopeless intoxication.

The small blue Christmas lights that trimmed the ornamental copper railing above the bar didn't help. The soft, erotic hue added to the sexual hunger tightening her nipples as they rubbed against the clingy black evening dress she wore.

With a slow, drawn out glide, she crossed one leg over the

other. The hem of her dress rose to display a hint of her garter belt fastened to black thigh-high nylons.

His gaze stroked her legs, thoroughly.

*Yowza!* The heat in Angie's body erupted into a fireball. She resisted a show of feminine satisfaction, thinking it wise to make sure she understood his non-verbal actions correctly.

"Excuse me? Could you repeat that?" she asked breezily.

With a drop-dead gorgeous smile, he studied her. Desire dampened her panties. His dimples were too much to resist. But it was the fire simmering in his eyes that put her into meltdown.

Angie wanted this man. Fuck the consequences.

She'd find another job in a heartbeat, but never another man who made her nerve endings explode with white-hot sensation.

He moved a little closer as the noise in the room elevated. "Just how good are you at layouts, positioning art and text?"

*Dammit.* He wanted to talk business.

A moment of disappointment swamped her, until his gaze caressed her breasts, making her nipples harden to aching peaks. That "come-here-baby" expression, masculine and sexy, made her think of hot, sweaty bodies tangled in silk sheets.

She raised her martini glass, trying to retain eye contact and a suave appearance, when what she really wanted to do was undress him. Peel that light gray Armani suit right off his firm physique, before tasting every inch of his body. Instead, she raised her glass higher and proceeded to cram the straw up her nose.

*Well fuck.*

Heat crawled across her face. Talk about a moment killer. She expected laughter, instead he moved closer.

Inconspicuously as possible, she turned the glass and sipped her cosmopolitan. The tart taste of cranberry juice and lime touched her lips, wetting her now dry throat.

"Layouts?" She cleared her throat. "I'm the best." He took another step forward. Her rising arousal lowered her voice when she spoke again. "That's why you hired me, Mr. Tyler."

He sat his nearly empty beer bottle on the bar top. It wobbled and fell to its side.

It was true. The magazine had sent one after another of their headhunters in an attempt to seduce her from their competitor. The last job offer had clinched the deal. Ryan Tyler was paying out his nose for her expertise.

He reached for a napkin and gently brushed against her hand. Raw sensations sparked up her arm. "Ryan," he said, holding her gaze with his, as he intentionally bumped her hand once more before cleaning up the small beer spill.

The scent of his cologne, earthy and warm, subtly wrapped around her with his closeness. Her tongue made a slow path across her dry lips. She raised a brow in question.

The man's eyes dilated. "My name's Ryan—" Her gaze focused on his delicious lips as they moved. Damn, but she wanted to touch them with her own, feel their softness next to hers. "—Angie," he finished on a note of heat and promise.

Oh yeah. He was interested.

A night with the King of Sexy Magazines would be her Christmas present to herself. She couldn't think of anything she wanted more than to feel his naked body pressed to hers. The thought of his cock parting her pussy and pushing deep inside her almost made her moan aloud. It certainly left her wet and wanting.

Her thoughts were ripped away from her when the Senior Editor, Manny Garcia said, "Hell of a party, boss."

16

Ryan took a step backward and accepted Manny's outstretched hand and shook it. "Glad you're having fun."

The Hispanic man raised his beer into the air and laughed. "Sure am. Hey, I wanted to talk to you about the Krueger account."

"No business tonight. Angie and I were just heading for the dance floor."

Surprise made her eyes widen, quickly replaced with a soft smile of anticipation. A slow dance had just begun. In seconds she would be in his arms.

He held out his hand and she placed hers in his. Just the thought of touching him made her stomach clench with desire. For a moment she felt locked in his gaze, then oddly, he put a little distance between them by taking a step backward. That's when she looked about the room. It felt like all eyes were on them.

Rumors would be flying by the end of the evening. And they'd probably be right if she had anything to do with how this night would pan out.

Her right hand clasped in his left, he placed his other hand firmly at the small of her back, setting fireworks off in her head. That particular area had always been an erogenous zone for her. With the slightest pressure he commanded her, guiding her across the floor.

He held her close, but not too close for those interested eyes that followed them as they danced. On a turn she swung into him, their bodies pressed tight for only a moment and then too quickly it was gone.

She wanted more bumping and grinding—preferably alone and without clothes.

It was a ridiculous thought, but it felt right in his arms. Who was this man she would willingly give control to? He

17

moved so skillfully. Where he led, she would follow.

"You okay with this?" he asked, drawing her gaze to his.

Huh? What was he talking about?

"With what?"

"The fact that everyone in the company is staring at us, wondering if I'll take you home tonight." His voice took on a sexy, mysterious quality that smoothed across her skin like silk.

Excitement raced through her veins. "Let them talk." She flashed him a coy grin.

The pressure of his hand on the small of her back firmed. He drew her hard against him, chest to chest, hips to hips. His knee slipped between her thighs as they whirled around and around to the music.

She felt lightheaded when he put a more appropriate distance between them. Her mind—her body—was spinning and it wasn't the two drinks she had. The man intoxicated her.

"Should we give them something real to talk about?" He paused momentarily, before he asked, "Come home with me, Angie."

She missed a step. Her mind as well as her heart stilled. This time she knew she heard him correctly. Tonight she would be lost in one hot executive's arms.

*Merry Christmas, Angie.*

Ryan felt perched on the razor edge of anticipation. This woman turned his head like no other had. He never fraternized with his employees, and now he had propositioned one.

Not a wise move.

It had the makings of disaster. That was until she demurely said, "I'd like that." Her eyelids slid half-mast as she peered up at him through feathered lashes. Desire flickered in her blue depths.

His cock sprang alive, swelling against her belly. Her fingernails bit into his shoulders. He felt her inhale and the tremor that followed. He couldn't wait to strip her out of that little black dress, pluck the snaps of her garters and kiss every inch of her satiny skin.

As they twirled, his cheek found hers. Cheek to cheek, he inhaled her light perfume, sweet with a hint of citrus. "We can't leave immediately," he whispered. "I need to keep up an appearance for at least an hour or so. Mingle. Is that okay with you?"

"I understand," she murmured, sliding seductively against his bulge so that it grew even more prominent.

He released a soft, low groan. "Baby, don't do that unless you want me to take you here on the dance floor."

Her light laughter was bewitching. She teased him once again, by moving her hips across his.

"Witch," he muttered playfully. "Would you like an audience?"

Her eyes brightened. "No," she said, but her body language said differently, as she brushed against him once more.

*Oh yeah!* No doubt she would be a hell-cat in bed. He might even be able to introduce her to a few of his toys and other things he enjoyed. Like tying her to his bed, or maybe a little whip and chain play. He had all night to discover what turned Angela Clarke on.

The thought sent a rush of blood to fill his balls with a pulsing ache. He couldn't wait to be alone with her. A more immediate problem was how to contend with his raging hard-on.

Step by step, he guided her in the direction of the

restrooms. After the music ended he would make his escape, ease his rising hormones. Then make merry with his employees, until it was time to leave.

The song came to an end. He squeezed her hand gently. "Excuse me for a minute."

He hated to leave her standing alone, but he knew he wouldn't last long—not in his aroused state. Quickly, he moved toward the sign that designated restrooms. As he pushed the door opened, he was thankful that no one was about. Without delay he strolled into a stall and locked the door.

The material of his pants was stretched taut over his hips. He wouldn't make it through the night in this condition, not to mention how embarrassing it would be if he came before pleasuring Angie first.

With trembling hands, he slid his zipper down and released his cock. It sprang forth, eager for attention. He released the breath he held and wrapped his fingers around his shaft. With slow, measured pumps from the base to tip, he thought of Angie, remembering her beaded nipples pressed against her clingy dress. How would those nipples feel and taste in his mouth?

He didn't think it was possible but his cock grew firmer, his balls drew close to his body.

A slight tingle made his grip tighten and his rhythm increase.

Harder and faster, he thrust his hips forward, pushing his engorged erection through his fingers. He leaned his free hand against the wall and threw back his head as fire licked his sensitive organ.

Fuck! This felt good. Nothing in comparison to how it would feel when Angie went down on her knees, her beautiful mouth sucking his cock, the caress of her tongue, the warmth and moisture of her wet cavern.

Out of nowhere his climax slammed into him, rocking him back on his heels. A tremor shook him as he forced himself to remain silent and upright. Hand unsteady, he continued to pump his hand, up and down, until all his semen spilled into the commode.

Heart pounding, breathless, he gave himself a shake and eased himself back into his pants. With short, quick movements he tucked his shirt into his slacks. The door creaked, heavy footsteps sounded across the floor. Zipper in place, he flushed the toilet, unlocked the door and headed toward the sink.

Manny grinned over his shoulder, as he relieved himself in one of the urinals against the wall. "Enjoying yourself, boss?"

"What?" Ryan asked, as he pushed his hands beneath the automated faucet and activated the water.

"The party? You enjoying yourself?" The grin plastered across Manny's face was easy to read. It wasn't the party the man spoke of, but one particular woman.

Ryan pulled a paper towel from the holder, dried his hands and threw the wipe away. "Sure. I hope you are too." He was halfway out the door when Manny spoke again, but Ryan ignored him.

The scent of alcohol rose in the air along with an array of perfumes and cologne. Laughter filled the air and the band began another slow tune. He scanned the crowd, immediately finding Angie speaking to Joyce, a fellow editor and the gossipmonger of the group. Joyce was animated, her hands moving as she talked. Her gaze darted from him to Angie, as if she were looking for signs that they were a couple.

Betty Hodges, his secretary for the past three years passed by him, giving him a gentle nod. He pulled the aging woman into his arms. "Betty, what do you say I take you for a spin around the floor?"

She swatted him on the chest. A charming blush radiated across her wrinkled face. "What the devil has gotten into you tonight?"

It was true. He felt happy and excited about the prospects of his night with Angie. His cock stirred to life again and he thought it wise to refocus his attention somewhere else.

"Christmas spirit." He grabbed her hand and led her out on the floor. He gave her a spin, before pulling her into his arms.

The first thing he noticed was how differently Angie and Betty felt to hold. Angie had felt right, an extension to his body. The second was the musky perfume Betty wore that made his nose tickle. Angie's scent had stroked him with a hand of desire.

The older woman moved in and out of his arms easily. Her brown eyes sparkled, a dreamy expression filling them with moisture. Did she think of her husband, who had passed away several years ago? Had she enjoyed dancing much like Ryan's mother did?

Ryan knew that in established relationships romance, and in particularly dancing, died over time with men, but not women. He could make his mother smile every time by dancing her around the kitchen.

Too bad he wouldn't make it home for Christmas. Home was Manhattan. One thing he wouldn't miss this year was the snow, but missing his mother's pumpkin pie was a tragedy. And then there was his brother's first child, a son.

His thoughts were interrupted when Betty asked, "How come you're spending time with this old woman instead of that pretty little thing you were dancing with before?"

He kissed her lightly on the cheek. "Because no one can hold a candle to you, Betty. Where did you learn to dance like this?"

Her face beamed as he spun her around and back. "Jerry taught me. We use to go dancing every weekend. Well, until his knees gave out. Arthritis." She grew quiet.

Holidays were hard on people who had lost loved ones and were alone.

The dance ended, and he led Betty off the floor. She pivoted toward him. "Thank you, Ryan." Appreciation shone in her moist eyes. "I'm leaving now."

"So early?"

"I don't see well at night." She gave him a big hug. "Merry Christmas. I'll see you next year."

He watched her retrieve her sweater and exit, before he turned to the bar and ordered a glass of Chivas Regal. He put the cool glass to his lips and sipped. The scotch was smooth, the burn welcome.

"Do you have a pen?" he asked the bartender. Without a word, the tall man behind the bar reached beneath the counter and set one before Ryan. He extracted a business card from his coat pocket and quickly wrote down his cell number. He laid the pen on the counter top, slipping the card into his pocket, before he finished his drink.

He talked with a few more people throughout the night, danced a couple of times, even once more with Angie, making plans for the night. Before they parted, he pressed his business card into her palm.

"I'll leave first," he whispered. "Give me ten or fifteen minutes and then call me. We'll meet up down the street and you can follow me home. I'm not too far from here."

She appeared a little hesitant, but finally she said, "Okay."

He left her and walked toward the stage and climbed the

stairs. The party had been scheduled from six to eleven o'clock. It was now ten-thirty.

"Would you mind if I made an announcement?" he asked the band leader.

"Sure." The man handed him the microphone.

"I hope everyone is having a great time." Ryan's voice echoed through the speakers. His words were met with a roar of applause. "I want to thank everyone for a successful year. The bar will be open for another half hour. But I'll be leaving as I have company coming over tomorrow."

*Well shit.* The words came automatically because they were true. His long-time friend from Texas was to arrive tomorrow and he'd nearly forgotten, he was so bewitched by Angie.

Then a smile crept across his face. He had shared many a woman with Wade.

*Maybe...*

"Merry Christmas," he yelled to the crowd. As he stepped off the stage, he wondered if Angie would be interested in a threesome. That was, after he'd had his fill of his little blonde angel tonight.

# Chapter Two

The moment Angie pulled behind Ryan's Silver Hummer and followed him into the locked community of Gainey Ranch, she was second-guessing her decision for a night of unadulterated sex with the boss. In front of them loomed a one story ranch style home that had to be worth at least two million.

Just the elegant wrought iron gate which opened automatically had her admitting her anxiety level hit a new high.

What on Earth had she been thinking, accepting a one-night stand with her boss? She could wake in the morning without a job.

He pulled into the circular driveway and stopped. She eased up behind him, letting the engine of her Honda Accord remain running. When he stepped from his car, walked to her side of the car and tapped on the window, she turned the engine off and reached for her purse.

She cracked the door open. "Ryan?" Before she could explain why this arrangement might be a bad mistake, he widened the door and pulled her into his arms. Her purse slipped off her shoulder and she caught the strap in her hand.

With just a touch—a look—he erased all doubt and insecurity. He cupped her head and gazed into her eyes with so much intensity. His expression prickled her skin, giving her the feeling that she was on the pinnacle of being kissed like she'd never been before.

"*Shhh...*" he hissed.

With a feather touch he smoothed his mouth over hers, sucking first on her top lip and then the bottom, before parting them to slip inside. Languidly, he caressed her mouth from side to side, flicking his tongue against hers. She responded in kind, tasting scotch and spearmint. He thrust more firmly against her tongue, tilting his head to deepen the kiss, and their tongues began to duel.

Her fingers curled into the upper sleeves of his coat as she clung to him—lost in a valley of sensations. Arousing and potent, his kiss was like a drug.

She wanted more.

"Soft. Beautiful," he groaned, moving his lips lightly across hers.

The night air was crisp. A small breeze stirred the paloverde trees that dotted his landscape, along with an occasional saguaro cactus or two. An ocean of rose-colored gravel with a line of walkway lights trailed alongside the sidewalk leading to his front door.

Strong palms stroked her neck with a gentle touch before he broke his caress and his lips followed the path of his hands. Fingertips breezed over her collarbone, working the neckline of her dress down to expose more skin. His tongue followed, dipping into the hollow area and moving lower to place small kisses upon the beginning swells of her breasts.

"Oh my God." The words slipped from her mouth as she tossed back her head.

He didn't stop there. Instead, he proceeded to lavish her cleavage with hot, wet kisses that made her breasts heavy with need, her nipples screaming to be next in line for his attention.

The area between Angie's thighs was wet and ready. She needed him inside her now. But he took his time licking and nibbling on her skin, torturing her with long, slow caresses.

"Ryan, your neighbors." Just the thought of performing for an audience made her hot.

Without releasing her, he guided her to the front door, reached into his pocket, extracted his keys, unlocked the door and pushed it open. No sooner did the door slam shut than she was back into his arms.

In their heated frenzy, she briefly noticed they stood in a foyer that opened up to a spacious living room where a huge custom decorated Christmas tree stood at least twelve feet tall. The glow from the twinkling Christmas lights bounced off white walls and marble flooring. A hallway led from both ends of the room. Everything else was a blur as he kissed her again.

When his hands touched her thighs, she felt her dress rise and her purse slipped from her fingers, falling to the floor. "Ryan, please." Cool air swirled through her legs, stroking the dampness of her arousal. She released the breath she held, knowing she was one step closer to making a dream come true—making love all night long to Ryan Tyler.

*What the hell is wrong with you, Angie?* She was usually not the aggressor, but something about this man made her want to tear his clothes off, push him to the floor and fuck his brains out.

"What?" he asked, as his tongue slipped beyond her bra, getting closer and closer to a nipple.

"I need you inside me." She released the death grip she had on his coat and began to push it from his shoulders. Her plan hadn't been well thought out because in order to undress him, he had to stop touching her and that was simply unacceptable.

A cry of frustration pushed from her lungs.

He chuckled softly, making no attempts to hurry his seduction as his coat dropped upon the marble floor.

Excitement slid up her backbone. She wanted him to finish what he had started—undressing her. She knew it would be provocative to feel his palms sliding up her body, peeling off her dress.

"Dress. Remove it." Her demand was breathless with anticipation.

Achingly slow, he pushed the silky material up her thighs, past her waist and then over her head.

She was so caught up in the moment she hadn't noticed the large mirror hanging on the foyer wall until her reflection appeared inside it. She stood before Ryan in a black strapless bra, three-inch heels, black thigh-high nylons, a garter belt, a lacy thong and a look of pure lust on her face.

He took a step back and male appreciation washed over her from head to toe. "My God, you're beautiful." With a toss of his hand he slung her dress on the table beneath the mirror. As he approached, his eyes darkened with desire.

Again she found herself locked in his arms, another kiss of a lifetime placed upon her lips.

*Thud! Thud! Thud!* The door rattled with a pounding that startled her out of his arms. Heart racing, she tried to steady her breathing.

"What the hell?" Ryan growled, glancing over his shoulder. "It's almost midnight." He reached for the door as Angie dove for her dress.

But she didn't have time to cover up before the door swung out of Ryan's hand and the most gorgeous cowboy entered. Angie wondered if the man decked out in tight blue jeans, cowboy shirt and boots was another Christmas present for her to enjoy.

*Da-yum!*

The minute he saw her, dress clenched to her chest, a big Texas grin tipped his mouth. He released a whistle, and then touched the rim of his black Stetson. "Ma'am." Gaze pinned on her, he set his duffle bag on the floor before he said, "Evenin', Ryan."

"You're early." Ryan sounded a little gruff as he closed the door.

The cowboy took another assessment of Angie starting at her feet and moving up her body. "Nah, partner, it looks like I'm *just* in time." His southern accent was like warm chocolate on a cold morning.

Where Ryan was dark and sophisticated, this man was light and rugged. Golden brown hair, mustache and beard groomed neatly around his mouth, he was the persona of the wild-wild west. All he needed were chaps, spurs and a six-shooter.

Yee haw!

For a moment, she wondered what he'd charge for a mustache ride. Would that facial hair tickle against her thighs? With the wicked thought, her nipples tightened and moisture released between her thighs.

"Angie Clarke, meet Wade Peterson, who used to be my best friend." Ryan ran his fingers through his wavy hair. He glanced at her and she could see an apology in his eyes.

Wade jutted out his hand. When she reached to shake his callused hand she lost the grip on her dress and it floated to the floor. Heat flared across her face, as his big brown eyes darkened and he caressed her with his hot gaze.

His broad chest rose on a breath. "You've been holding out on me, Tyler. Is this filly saddled for two riders?"

*Filly? Two Riders?*

*Holy shit!* Was the man talking ménage?

Ryan shook his head. "Sorry, Angie. This redneck is from down south—*way* down south. His manners are a little antiquated."

"Never bothered you before to share," Wade grumbled, taking off his hat. He ran his fingers through his hair, then set the Stetson firmly back on his head.

Her stare flew from Wade to Ryan.

A mischievous grin played across Ryan's face as he shrugged. "What can I say? Wade and I have been friends for a long time—we share everything."

So Ryan Tyler was a bad boy. The thought sent chills of delight through her veins. Her deepest, darkest fantasy was a ménage, sandwiched between two men making love to her. Ryan made her body sing. What would the cowboy do to her?

"Well, darlin', whad'ya say? Are you willing to give us both a ride?" Wade's voice turned husky. His boots clicked against the marble as he approached. He placed his hand beneath her chin, drawing her gaze upward. Before she knew what was happening, he captured her mouth with his.

Where Ryan's kiss was gentle and coaxing, Wade's was not. He took what he wanted, invading her mouth with his tongue. He tasted of beer and masculine heat, throwing her off balance so that she leaned forward, falling against him. He wrapped his arms around her, enveloping her in his musky scent of sandalwood. Masterful and demanding, he swept his tongue through her mouth, and then bit her lip—hard.

Shocked and dazed, all she could do was stare at him when

he stepped away from her.

"Darlin'?" Wade asked. No beating around the bush with this man.

Angie looked at Ryan and could see the burn of desire shining in his eyes. The bulge in his pants was evidence that he wanted this to happen. Wade's telltale hard-on was just as impressive.

She was being offered a chance of a lifetime. All she had to say was—

"Yes," she blurted, before she chickened out. *Yes. Yes. Yes.*

Ryan couldn't believe his ears. Angie might be interested in a threesome, but the pink that dotted her checks and the hesitancy in her voice announced she'd never done this before. He didn't know if the tremor that visibly shook her was from excitement or apprehension. With a couple of steps, he was by her side.

He placed his hand on her arm. "Honey, are you sure?"

Without hesitation, she stepped into his arms, wrapping hers around his waist, tilted her chin up, and kissed him soundly on the lips. "I'm sure." Then she laid her cheek against his chest.

The moment was tender. Strangely, touching his heart and making him think of his family and home. His parents and siblings around the fireplace where stockings hung, and Angie curled up next to him on his mother's couch as they laughed together.

His mom would like Angie.

Ryan tensed. He didn't know this woman. But oddly he did. Call it intuition. Without a doubt, he knew she would want to please him, make this night heavenly.

"Give me some of that sugar," Wade growled.

For some unknown reason Ryan was reluctant to let her go. But he did, releasing her and stepping back to let Wade once again take Angie's lips with his.

Something twisted in Ryan's stomach, but he didn't listen to the nagging voice in the back of his head telling him to rip Angie from his friend's arms. Heat swarmed up his neck, radiating across his ears and face. It wasn't the fact that Wade outweighed him by ten pounds. His large frame swallowed up Angie's smaller one. But his own sense of control held him back from taking what he wanted.

Angie—alone.

The thoughts he was experiencing were irrational. Angie had agreed to the threesome. He didn't have a right to stop the inevitable.

"How about we rope this little filly to your bed and give her some lovin'?" Wade suggested, picking up his duffle bag and moving toward the hallway.

Wade was impatient to get started, and who could blame the man. Angie was a veritable treat. But he sensed something was needling his friend. He usually wasn't so restless—so blatant. The man could woo a woman as effectively as Ryan could, even better.

But not tonight—something was wrong.

"Rope?" Angie's voice rose in pitch.

Ryan didn't want to scare her now, but she needed to know how Wade and his tastes swung when both of them were at the helm. "Honey, have you ever dabbled in bondage and domination?"

Wide-eyed, she stared at him and then jerked her gaze to where Wade stood in the hallway. "No. But I've read about it."

The fact that she didn't turn and run made his cock grow even harder. "So you're willing to try a little bit of kink?"

She raised a brow haughtily. "I just agreed to a threesome. How much kinkier could it get?"

Wade and Ryan shared a knowing glance.

Perhaps it was nervous energy or they had finally succeeded in scaring her, because she took a step backward. "Okay. That doesn't make me feel good. What are you two going to do?"

Ryan slid his hand through her silky hair and cupped the back of her head to drag her against his body. "We're going to turn you inside out. Fuck you all night long, and then start all over again."

She fit perfectly against him, as the most seductive expression softened her face. "I think I can handle that."

"What about sex toys and whips?" Wade asked, leveling his sight on her. His friend enjoyed flogging women.

Ryan had to admit it thrilled him to envision Angie's sweet ass hot and pink with his touch.

The tendon in her neck tightened. "Uh...I don't know. Maybe."

"Good enough for me," Wade crowed as he disappeared down the hall.

Ryan added, "Honey, all you need to do is tell us to stop and it's over."

Her brows furrowed. "Stop isn't an appropriate word to use. I need a safe word."

The corners of his mouth twitched. "You have been reading."

"Red means stop? Yellows means ease up?"

He smoothed his hands up and down her bare arms.

33

"That's right. Now let me show you where the play begins."

# Chapter Three

The lights were dim as Angie entered Ryan's bedroom. His masculine scent and the woodsy cologne he used were prevalent in the air. The furniture was southwest style. His king-size bed was yellow pine with large bedposts. The smell of sulfur rose briefly as Ryan lit tea-lights along the mantelpiece, and Wade started a fire in the flagstone fireplace.

The mood was soft, sexy, and Angie couldn't wait to be touched by these two strong men. She drew her attention back to the bed and a wave of excitement dampened her panties. That was when she heard soft music begin to play in the background.

These men knew what enhanced a women's sexuality. Tonight her fantasy would come true.

*But what about tomorrow?* The little voice in her head rose, but she vanquished it. She wouldn't look any further than tonight.

Angie startled when she felt Ryan's palms on her shoulder. He leaned in close, his breath a warm whisper across her skin. "Lay down on the bed."

The clicking of her heels against the marble floor made her tense. It was really going to happen. The man who had wreaked havoc with her hormones would be hers tonight. Add to that a sexy cowboy and Angie couldn't ask for more.

Clad in only her bra, thong, garter belt, silk stockings and heels, she slinked across his dark brown velour comforter. It was soft across her skin as she lay upon her back.

"Fucking hot," Wade growled his approval.

Ryan remained quiet. Flickering shadows danced across his face, giving him a mysterious quality.

Both men began to take their shirts off at the same time. Angie's pulse leaped. They were amazing. Where Wade was hard muscle, obviously built from physical labor, Ryan was sculpted by hours in the gym. She couldn't wait to thread her fingers through the light covering of hair on their chests. Kiss where the hair swirled around their belly buttons, and then move down further with her tongue and mouth to taste them.

Wade started to take off his cowboy hat, but Angie said, "No. Keep it on."

His chuckle was deep and sexy. "You want a cowboy, darlin'?"

"Oh yeah. I want both of you."

Wade reached in his duffle bag and extracted a piece of rope and a small remnant of material that look like velvet.

"Lock your fingers together and raise your arms above your head," Ryan directed.

When her fingers folded together, her heart crashed against her chest. She was really going through with this?

Wade wrapped the soft velvet around her wrists before he looped the rope over it and fastened it to the headboard of the bed. She felt the strain of the muscles in her arms. A quiver slithered up her backbone releasing a flood of moisture between her thighs. Her breasts felt heavy, aching to be touched.

The bed moaned beneath their weight as both men sat on the edge, one on each side of the bed, and began to remove their shoes and socks.

What they did next, she didn't expect.

Each man cradled one of her feet, slipping off her heels, which they tossed over their shoulders. The shoes made a thud when they hit the floor. Their warm hands cupped her feet, taking away the chill. As if they had done this a million times, in unison they smoothed their palms over each foot from the toes up around her ankles and then back. Carefully, they stretched each joint, sliding them from base to tip between their thumb and index finger. Their touch through her silky stockings was wicked. When they pressed gently all over the soles of her feet she moaned softly. With feathered strokes they drew their fingers over her feet toward her toes then back up to focus on her ankles and calves.

She felt like a decadent piece of chocolate beneath the sun, slowly melting into their touch. Every muscle relaxed beneath their ministrations.

Each garter made a snapping sound as they disengaged them from her stockings. Then smoothly the two men drew her hose down her thighs, until the silky material slipped from her feet. Without a word, they used her stockings to secure each of her ankles to a bedpost at the foot of the bed. Spread eagle, her arousal flushed across her body as two sets of male eyes scanned her splayed body.

False concern flickered in Ryan's eyes. "Looks like we have a problem."

With a knuckle, Wade inched his Stetson higher. His eyes reflected the same heat of passion. "What's that, partner?"

"Our woman still has her thong on, and with her legs tied we can't remove it."

Wade dug in his pants pocket and extracted a folding knife. It made a sharp click as he opened it. "Looks like we'll have to cut it off."

Angie's breathing elevated. The way they looked at her and the smooth cadence of their voices made her pussy clench. They were unbelievably sexy. She squirmed, pulling against her restraints. She needed to be fucked now.

The scent of sandalwood filled her nostrils as Wade drew closer. His fingers dipped beneath one side of her thong. The material snapped, giving way to the sharp blade that slid across the material. He did the same thing to the other side, then peeled her thong from her heated body. Cool air touched her moist center.

Wade placed the knife next to her garter belt when Ryan spoke. "Leave it. I like how it frames that beautiful patch of hair between her thighs." Leaning forward, he placed a kiss upon her mound.

"Would you like to see what this lacy bra is hiding?" Wade asked Ryan as he slipped his knife back into his jeans.

"Oh yeah. Take it off." With Ryan's approval Wade's hands slipped between Angie's back and the comforter. His fingers worked expertly to unfasten her strapless bra. She gasped as it loosened and he removed it, tossing it aside.

Her nipples beaded, exposed to the air. Immediately, Wade fell forward to take one into his hot, wet mouth. His facial hair tickled her skin, causing her to writhe beneath his attention. Alternating from one peak to the other, he sucked, licked, and nibbled until her breasts ached and her nipples were sensitive and hard.

But it was Ryan's touch, the way his fingers stroked her pussy, that made her want to scream. She arched her hips into his caress, wanting and needing more. Slowly and teasingly, he moved across her swollen folds, circled her clit to drag out each sensation until every tendon in her body drew taut. She held her breath, loving the way her sex closed around his fingers when he inserted a finger, his thumb still teasing her clit.

With steady thrusts she rode his hand, pretending it was his cock deep inside her. Just the thought pushed her closer to climax. As the threads of her arousal began to seek fulfillment, he moved away from the throbbing nub.

"Ryan!"

Wade captured her cry with his mouth. As his fingers tormented her breasts, his tongue tasted and thrust. She released another cry that tore her hips from the bed when Ryan's tongue started to mimic what Wade's did, but between her parted thighs.

Her climax rose like an imminent wave and then washed over her, sending the flames of desire throughout her body. Over and over again, her inner muscles clenched and released, until she felt as if she would die from the exquisite sensations. She pulled at her bindings, needing something solid to hold on to—needing Ryan in her arms.

Wade sat back on his haunches. She looked down her length to see Ryan smiling up at her.

"Damn, Ryan. You should have seen her face. Friggin' hot, buddy."

Eyes hooded, like a predator, slowly and sensuously, Ryan crawled up her body. His slacks rubbed against her sensitized skin as he lay on top of her, their mouths inches away. "I plan to watch her come all night long." Then he pressed his lips against hers.

The unusual flavor of herself upon her taste buds was arousing, but it was Ryan's caress that had her melting all over again. The man's kiss was lethal. He left no place untouched, paying special attention to her lips and tongue as he sucked it deep into his mouth. Alternating the pressure, light and firm, his mouth slid across hers.

She hadn't even noticed that Wade had released her ankles, until she instinctively wrapped them around Ryan's clothed hips. The fly of his pants pressed into her folds, rubbing against her clit, driving her crazy with need.

When he broke their embrace and drifted out of her arms, she whimpered, soft sounds of disappointment.

Wade was unfastening the rope around the headboard and her wrists as Ryan rose to stand next to the bed. She pulled her arms down to her sides, feeling the burn from having them above her head for so long. A roll of her shoulders to ease the ache brought Ryan to her side. His fingertips danced across her skin, seeking out the tight muscles, massaging and easing out the soreness.

What was it about this man that made her body dissolve into a puddle of ecstasy? His touch was pure heaven. He knew exactly where to caress to make her burn for more.

"Thank you," she murmured.

Ryan nuzzled her neck and caressed the dip of her shoulders with his lips. "Kneel before the fireplace, baby," he whispered before he helped her to her feet. Dressed in only her garter belt, she walked toward the flickering flames and knelt on the thick oblong rug. The heat of the fire warmed her naked body, as it radiated deep into her skin. She stared up at Ryan and Wade and wondered what was next.

Ryan couldn't believe how responsive Angie was to his caress. She had tasted like honey against his tongue as her pussy tightened and sucked him deeper inside her.

Walking was difficult, his balls so full of blood they ached with each step he took toward his dresser. No doubt, Wade was in the same condition if the bulge in his pants was an indicator.

His friend's heavy breathing matched his own.

Wade's fists were clenched by his side. His simmering gaze stroked Angie as she knelt obediently before him. He obviously wouldn't last much longer.

For that matter neither would Ryan.

Angie's back was to Ryan as he rustled through the top drawer and found what he was looking for—a condom, a set of handcuffs and a silk scarf. When he moved in front of Angie, she cocked a brow.

"Put your hands behind your back," he instructed. When she did, he stepped around her and clasped her wrists in the manacles. Then he covered her eyes with the silk scarf and secured it. He nodded to Wade and they both began to remove their pants.

Angie licked her lips, a seemingly nervous response to not being able to see. He knew that restricting one's senses heightened the others. Her hearing would become more acute, but this was a game of silence. She would be more susceptible to their touches, and she wouldn't know which one of them stroked her.

When Wade moved before her, Ryan's gut tensed. It was the first time in their friendship that he didn't want to share a woman. Not any woman, but Angie. There was something special about her.

Still, he refused to voice his thoughts.

Instead, he watched Wade take his cock in hand and silently nudge Angie's mouth. She opened without being instructed. Blindly, her tongue flicked out, wetting the head of Wade's erection. The veins in his buddy's neck were bulging as he moved closer and pushed between her lips.

Ryan held his breath. He had never seen anything as erotic as Angie, on her knees, wearing a garter belt, handcuffs and a blindfold. Wade had both of his hands on her head, thrusting his hips, slipping in and out of her beautiful mouth. The soft whimpers and sucking sounds she made didn't help. The scene sent white-hot fire down Ryan's cock, and he had to grip his shaft tightly to choke off the roaring need to come.

When he could breathe again, he tore open the condom package and with shaky hands rolled the sheath over his shaft.

Suddenly, Wade's facial features twisted. He stilled, throwing back his head and squeezing his eyelids. A low, coarse growl rumbled from deep within his chest.

Angie drank from Wade. Her throat muscles moved up and down, as she swallowed and sucked. When he eased from her mouth, she licked her lips, now red and swollen.

Ryan lost it.

As Wade stepped aside, Ryan grasped her shoulders and guided her to the carpet so she lay on her stomach. With his feet he parted her legs, kneeling between them. Hands on her hips he brought her up on her knees, but her chest still remained on the rug. Then, without another thought, he entered her pussy with a single thrust.

She gasped. Her cheek pressed to the carpet.

*Sonofabitch!* Ryan almost came the minute her warmth surrounded him. She was tight, hot and wetter then he had expected. The submissive picture she portrayed made his heart pound.

His hips moved slowly, easing back and forth, trying to prolong the feel of her heat and the way their bodies fit together. He smoothed his palm across her abdomen, through the patch of curly blonde hair, until he found her clit.

"Ryan," she cried out as he pressed down on the swollen nub.

Taken back by her ability to recognize it was him in her body, he paused.

Her breaths were short, quick pants. "No. Please. Faster. Harder. Oh God, fuck me."

There was no way he could resist her plea. His hips slapped against her body, again and again. He took her hard. He took her fast, while his finger circled her clit.

A soft roar began in his head and intensified with each thrust. He watched his cock disappear inside her and then reappear to plunge into her once more. Black spots appeared before his eyes as his blood pressure soared. With a fiery rush his seed raced down his cock. He felt the explosion clear to his toes.

Angie screamed as she tensed and joined him. Together they found ecstasy.

Her body jerked with the tightening of her pussy, squeezing him and milking him of every ounce of feeling.

Spent, he slid to his side and drew her to him, face to face. With a tug, he removed her blindfold. She looked up at him, blinking as her vision adjusted. The sated expression on her face warmed him through and through. When she tangled her legs with his, he couldn't help but smile, before taking her lips in a gentle kiss.

For a moment Ryan was at peace. Then Wade said, "I want some of that."

Wade moved behind Angie, unfastened the handcuffs and tossed them aside. He joined Ryan and her on the rug, spooning her back and throwing his leg over theirs. As a threesome, they enjoyed the quiet moment, letting the crackling fire warm them.

When Angie yawned, Ryan smoothed her hair away from her face. "Tired?" The hands on the clock above the fireplace mantle announced it was almost two in the morning.

She responded with, "No. Happy. It's Christmas Eve. I love the holidays."

It didn't dawn on Ryan that Angie might have plans. A twinge of disappointment swept through him. He ran his hand over her belly. "You have family coming over today?"

Her silky leg slipped along his. "No. Mom and Dad are in Hawaii. My two brothers ditched me for a skiing trip. I thought I'd go to the movies or something."

"Why not spend Christmas with us?" he asked, hoping she'd say yes. "I'm having dinner catered today, so there won't be anything for us to do, but relax and enjoy each others' company for the next two days."

She sucked her bottom lip into her mouth, nibbling on it before she spoke. "I don't want to impose."

Wade rolled onto his back, a frown on his face. Ryan had never seen his friend so quiet after a bout of rowdy sex. He was usually the first one jumping in for more. When Wade pushed to his feet and moved toward the bathroom door, Ryan said, "That okay with you, Wade?"

He turned around when Ryan spoke to him. "Sounds like a great idea. I'm hungry," Wade mumbled, before disappearing behind the door.

Ryan helped Angie to her feet. "Hey, why don't you take a shower while I scrounge us up something to eat?"

Lightly, she moved her lips across his. "I'd love that."

"Since Wade's occupying this bathroom, why don't you use the one down the hall, second door on the left. There are clean towels, soap and shampoo on the counter. Let me know if you need anything else."

It was a beautiful sight watching Angie's naked ass walk across the room and out the door. Just as she disappeared,

Wade stepped into the room. He must have taken a whirlwind shower because his hair was wet and he wore a fresh pair of jeans.

Ryan crossed his arms over his chest. "Okay, Wade, spill it. What gives?"

Wade rubbed his eyes as if they hurt. "Nothing."

Ryan released a quick breath. "Bullshit! I'm not falling for that. Is it Angie?"

"Oh, hell no. She's great. It's just—" He paused. "Jessie."

"Jessica Evans?" Ryan asked. Jessie was a gal they had grown up with.

"I've been seeing her again. And, well, I asked her to marry me."

Ryan slapped Wade on the back. "No fuck! Taking the leap—"

"She turned me down." Pain splintered in Wade's eyes. He'd never seen this reaction in his friend over a woman. But Jessie had always been special to Wade. He forced a smile and released a heavy breath of sarcasm. "Better off. Now why don't you take a shower and I'll fix us something to eat."

Obviously, Wade was through talking. From experience, Ryan knew his friend wouldn't say anymore. And Ryan was eager to start where they'd left off with Angie.

# Chapter Four

The shower was refreshing. Beads of water trailed down Angie's skin as she stepped from the stall. A man's T-shirt lay next to a towel on the marble counter top. The shirt hadn't been there before. She smiled, thinking of Ryan. How he had made her body burn.

Grabbing the towel, she wrapped it around her and worked its warmth over her body. After folding the towel and setting it aside, she reached for the shirt. With a tug she pulled the material up and inhaled deeply. It smelled like Ryan, woodsy.

Since she didn't have any clothes and the thong she had now lay in ruins on Ryan's bedroom floor, she would have to go without. She had to admit that wearing Ryan's T-shirt felt good. Being loved by two men wasn't shabby either.

Although she'd been blindfolded, she'd known who'd touched her and when. Their scents were a dead giveaway. Not to mention the smoothness of Ryan's hands versus Wade's callused ones. There was even a distinct difference in the way each one touched her. Wade's caresses turned her on, but there was something about him that made her feel disconnected, while she came undone in Ryan's arms. Everything he did to her stole her breath and squeezed her chest with emotion. No one had ever kissed or made love to her like he had. He made her feel special—almost loved.

Angie knew that sounded silly. It was hard to explain—it just felt right.

The thought lingered as she opened the bathroom door. Decadent smells drove her into the hall, past the softly lit living room where the tall Christmas tree twinkled with the colors of the rainbow and a fire burned in the hearth. Her stomach growled as she padded barefoot down the cool marble floor.

The sight was something to behold as she entered the spacious kitchen decked out with every modern convenience she could think of. Both men wore blue jeans, no shirt. Ryan held a spatula, while Wade sliced mangoes into long strips.

She felt her eyes widen with pleasant surprise. "Both of you cook? Wow! You're every woman's dream come true. What smells good?"

"Sautéed scallops, cold shrimp, caviar." Ryan pointed to a large platter of oysters on the half-shell. "Oysters, fruits, cheese, vegetables, champagne...and you." His voice turned thick with desire. "Come here."

She went into his open arms, whispering, "Am I on the menu?" His hand slipped beneath her T-shirt, stroking her bare ass, and then he squeezed gently.

"Damn straight you are, woman. You're dessert." Wade moved beside them. "It's my turn." He took her roughly into his arms and devoured her mouth like a man thirsting for water. She was breathless when they parted.

The frown that crept across Ryan's face when Wade released her was hard to miss.

"Easy, boy." Ryan's warning was low and menacing. But Wade didn't appear to be affected. With two platters in his hands, he headed for the living room.

*God, I hope this doesn't turn awkward.* Since she'd never had sex with two men in the same night, in the same room, she had no idea what to expect. Although she did know this was one Christmas she would never forget.

*Maybe...*

No. This was a holiday fling. When the New Year rolled around and things went back to business as usual, Ryan would be her boss and she would be—what? Forever pining for something she couldn't have? Well, if that was the case, she was going to take whatever these two men offered for the next couple of days.

"You okay?" Ryan asked, handing her an ice bucket with a bottle of champagne, a corkscrew, and three glasses. Condensation dotted the silver pail he pressed against her chest. The chill made her nipples harden.

"Sure," she said, as she fumbled with the glasses. When she had them firmly in hand, she released a sigh of relief and followed Ryan out of the kitchen.

The food was set on an oblong coffee table. A white downy carpet lay before the fireplace and they each settled themselves on it. The scent of pine wafting in the air mingled with the scent of the seafood placed before her. The blinking of the Christmas lights from the tree streamed colors across the room.

Wade worked on the bottle of champagne, twisted the corkscrew around and around, and then he pulled. A pop sounded and the effervescent white wine spewed from the opening. The cowboy jerked the bottle to his mouth, drinking, before it could spill onto the rug.

Angie laughed, but the truth was it heated her loins to watch Wade sucking on the bottle. All she could think of was having his lips sucking on a certain body part of hers, while she gave Ryan head. She was dying to see the look on his face as she took him into her mouth and down her throat.

As Wade poured her a glass of bubbly, Ryan placed a

spoonful of caviar to her mouth. She opened wide and felt the salty eggs burst upon her tongue.

She licked a seductive path along her lips. "Mmm...more."

He gave her another bite, before Wade pushed the flute of champagne into her hands. The glass was cool against her lips as she sipped lightly.

The moment was sensuous, each of them feeding the other. It was one of the most erotic things she had ever done. Every piece of food conjured suggestive images in her mind. It must have affected the men as well, because their hot stares turned to her.

"Strip," Ryan said. As he unzipped his jeans, his firm erection pushed from its confines.

Grabbing the hem, she drew the shirt over her head. Without hesitation, Wade's finger moved swiftly to unfasten his jeans and pushed them down his muscular legs. In seconds they were all naked and seated on the downy carpet.

Ryan rubbed a slice of juicy mango on both of her nipples and then each man leaned over to take a harden peak into their mouths. It was a strange and wonderful feeling to have two men suckling at her breasts at the same time. Wade's facial hair tickled her skin. Arching into their touches, she pushed her fingers through Ryan and Wade's hair, holding their heads tightly to her.

Ryan released the hold he had on her breast. "Lay down."

When Wade moved away she knew it was time to play, and Angie was ready.

A shiver raced up her spine as Wade poured champagne in her belly button and Ryan lapped it up, tingles raced across her skin. The men each took pleasure in decorating her body with different foods.

Cool shrimp curled and hung from each nipple, her breasts again smeared with mango juice. Pieces of cheese and fruit dotted her stomach. Her belly button was now home for a scrumptious scallop. One by one they took turns plucking a morsel from her body, making sure they laved the area with their tongues.

When they made their way to her mound, Ryan said, "Open up, baby." On command she spread her legs, eagerly.

Wade held up a red cherry with its stem still attached. "This game is called hide-and-seek." He stroked her body with his heated gaze. "I'll hide it and Ryan has to find it."

Without hesitation, he separated her labia and pressed his finger and the cherry inside her. She felt the coldness of the fruit, the excitement of Wade pushing in and out of her pussy. Another finger was inserted, increasing the feeling of fullness. When Wade moved away, Ryan slipped between her thighs. Instead of using his fingers, he dipped his head between her legs.

Gently, Ryan massaged her pubic area with his fingertips before he lightly flicked his tongue over her clit, pulling it into his mouth as he sucked. She gasped. Her thighs widened, wanting more of what he offered. The slurping sounds he made were followed by soft growls that vibrated against her sensitive skin. Her fingers curled into fists. She strained into his touch. With long strokes, he slid his tongue from her clit all the way down the length of her slit and then back again. Then he penetrated her, thrusting deeply and stealing her breath.

"Oh God." With her fingers curled in his hair she pulled him tightly against her core. "More." The single word didn't accurately convey what she wanted. She wanted more of him inside her—his cock. Instead, he sped up licking, sucking and nibbling as she squirmed beneath him. He was driving her out of her mind.

Suddenly he stopped. "Problem," he murmured, against her sex. "It seems we have lost the cherry."

With a squeal she started to rise, but Wade held her down by the shoulders.

"Would you like me try?" Wade asked with a devilish grin upon his handsome face.

Ryan's eyes twinkled with mischief. "Perhaps you should. I believe it's buried pretty deep."

She couldn't help laughing. "You're both bastards. Now get that thing out of me." Angie had never had such an uplifting sexual experience. She couldn't remember the last time she had laughed during sex.

Wade's mustache and beard teased her thighs. The light prickle of hair was exciting against her inner thighs as he brushed his face against her leg. Brown eyes that had previously appeared wary, brightened as he gazed up her length. "Darlin' are you ready for a mustache ride?"

Angie was more than ready. She'd never been eaten by a man with a mustached and beard. "Oh yeah," she breathed.

"Hold on tight." With his fingers, he parted her flesh, placing feathery kisses that tickled her skin. He did the same thing to her clit and she jerked her hips. The experience was strange, but wonderful. "Like that, do you?" he asked in a sexy southern draw. Alternating strokes, he licked a long, slow path, and then flicked his tongue with quick, short licks across her clit, making her groan. When he buried his face against her pussy, his tongue penetrated her slit, she almost lost it.

*This can't be happening.* Her body tensed trying to fight the oncoming orgasm. Even still she couldn't believe it. She was naked upon her boss's living room floor with two gorgeous men feasting between her legs.

This was by far the best Christmas present.

Just before she reached the pinnacle, he pulled away, rising on his palms, a smirk on his face as he held the cherry stem between his teeth.

All three of them broke into laughter, tumbling on the carpet next to each other. The moment was spectacular.


Angie was beautiful standing next to the Christmas tree. She was adjusting the lights of the tree to change the strobe and color pattern. The soft glow bathed her body in different colors as they changed from red, blue, green, and then a mixture of the three.

"Leave it on the blue," Ryan suggested. The blue looked mysterious and chilly, just like Christmas in Manhattan. He thought of his family and how much he would have liked his mother to meet Angie. *Maybe next year...* He paused with the thought.

Wade loaded a CD into Ryan's sound system. The whine of some male singer's voice sounded. *Country music.* Ryan should have known that would be his friend's choice. The cry of a steel guitar joined in, causing Angie to sway seductively. Her hands went behind her neck, raising her hair, as her hips undulated.

Wade growled long and low. "Come here, darlin'." She went into his arms and he held her close. Their bodies slid against each other as they glided around the room. His hands caressed her back, moving to cup her ass, pulling her against hips. A lone finger slipped between the crease of her cheeks, and Ryan knew exactly what was on his friend's mind.

Hell, it was on every man's mind—breaching that sacred orifice. Ryan knew that Angie's would be the sweetest surrender.

He slipped behind the dancing pair, pressing his chest and

hips to Angie's backside. She wiggled her ass against his firming cock, making him smile. In the blue glow of the Christmas lights, the three of them moved together to the slow music.

Wade began to kiss her as Ryan nibbled and sucked gently on her neck. With a caress of his hand, Ryan wedged his fingers between Wade and Angie and captured one of her nipples between his fingers and rolled it gently. She whimpered, the cry soft and low. Wade's knee parted her thighs and rubbed her crotch. Ryan knew this because his friend inadvertently stroked Ryan's balls a time or two in his effort to stimulate Angie. Heat blazed up his neck. Surprisingly, he found the touch arousing and his cock hardened even more.

Angie's movements became more pronounced as she increased the pressure and friction of her body, bumping and grinding, against them. "Take me," she whispered. "Now."

When Wade stepped away, Ryan continued to hold her to him. She leaned her head back on his shoulder, her body swaying to the soothing flow of the music. He skimmed his hands down her stomach to her pelvic area. She was soft beneath his palms. With his fingertips, he massaged the patch of hair before slipping a finger further down to press against her clit. Her knees buckled, he tightened his hold on her.

"That feels so good," she hummed.

The way she moved, so sexy and uninhibited, set his libido on fire. He wanted this woman, more than any woman he had ever dreamed of. Sex had always been a game, something to fulfill a need, but with Angie—she had a way of involving his heart.

It scared the shit out of him.

Ryan pushed deeper inside her, working his finger in and out of her hot, wet core. A gasp made her voice catch. She turned in his arms, her eyes dark with desire.

"Fuck me, Ryan." Her tongue made a sensual swept across her lips. "I need you inside me," she said with an ache in her voice.

Their gazes locked in a fiery exchange. The pad of his thumb traced her lips. They were soft beneath his touch.

Such a passionate woman.

He replaced his finger with his mouth and tasted her hunger. Like always when he kissed her, her body softened against his. She clung to him as if she were drowning, drowning with need.

Angie humbled him. No woman had ever made him feel so much a man.

The moment was lost when Wade entered the room. Without missing a step, he pressed a condom package into Ryan's palm and spooned his body to Angie's back. His friend inhaled deeply, nuzzling her neck, as his hands skimmed down her waist, hips and thighs.

*Dammit.* A moment of disappointment crushed Ryan. He wanted Angie to himself, to lay her upon the carpet before the fire and take his time pleasuring her.

Stupid. Stupid.

Whatever had come over him, he needed to get rid of it quickly. What woman would want one man, when she could have two? By the gleam in her eyes, he knew she was looking forward to being fucked by both of them.

A stack of throw pillows were piled on the soft white carpet lying before the fireplace, courtesy of Wade. Playfully, he extracted a piece of garland from the Christmas tree and wrapped it around Angie's neck, weaving it around her body to secure her arms to her side.

"Up or down?" he asked Ryan.

Oddly, Ryan had turned cold the minute Wade had returned. But when he looked at her, he smiled. She wanted to reach out to him, cup his face in her hands, but she was a little tied up at the moment.

"Down. I want to see her expression," he replied.

Angie didn't know exactly what was going to happen, but if it included Ryan being inside her she was sure it would be delightful. She watched his taut ass as he moved toward the pillows, lying on his back and stuffing them beneath him so that his hips were raised approximately a foot. He spread his bended knees wide.

His fingers closed around his rigid cock, holding it straight up. "Come here, baby."

It was amazing how off balance she felt with no use of her arms. When she stood before him, he said, "Kneel between my legs." Wade helped her to accomplish the feat.

With his teeth, Ryan tore open the condom package and placed the rolled sheath on the tip of his penis. "Put it on me— with your mouth."

Angie's heart jumped. She'd never done this before—heard about it—but never attempted to sheathe a man with her lips and tongue. It excited her beyond belief. Sitting on her haunches to steady herself, she parted her mouth and leaned forward.

The taste of strawberries touched her tongue as she tasted the latex. Her head bobbed, trying to push the condom down with her mouth, but didn't get anywhere.

From behind her Wade chuckled. "It's a slow process, darlin'. Use your tongue and lips."

Carefully, she ringed her tongue along the ridges of the condom, moving her mouth at the same time. Little by little, the rubber inched down Ryan's erection, until he was deep inside her mouth. Then she began to rock to and fro, easing him in and out of her mouth. The hand he had around his cock followed her rhythm, sliding up and down. When she used the muscles in her throat to squeeze him, he tensed.

A visible tremor shook him. "Stop, Angie." He sucked in a breath through clenched teeth, as he shifted out her grasp. "Wade. Help her straddle me." He relaxed his legs.

Strong hands gripped her arms, still bound to her side by the garland, and pulled her into a standing position. Wade held her steady as she placed one foot on either side of Ryan's hips, then slowly she bent her knees, drifting down to impale herself on his erection. Every inch of his thick, hard cock spread her wider and wider as he slipped inside. He filled her like no man ever had.

Wade released her once she was situated on her knees again.

Ryan moved his hands to rest on her hips and assisted her to set a gradual pace. Every stroke rubbed the head of his cock deep within, igniting a fire that tightened her nipples. Hot shards of sensations filtered through her breasts and pussy, increasing the friction and moisture between her thighs.

"She's so wet, Wade." Ryan's hands slid up her side, until he held both breasts in his hands. "Hot and slick." He played with her nipples, pinching and squeezing, making her arch into his touch, begging for more. Breasts heavy with need, she rocked her hips against his.

Angie felt Wade's hand on her back pushing her forward. She stiffened. With her arms immobilized against her sides, she envisioned falling forward and bumping heads with Ryan. But he was there to catch and guide her down so they were chest to chest.

The position was a little disconcerting, because it left her butt in the air and Wade stood behind her. Not a pretty picture, she was sure.

Angie released a squeal when she felt something cool against her ass. Her buttocks clenched.

"Relax," Wade encouraged, as his finger spread a lubricant over the tight entrance. "Have you ever been fucked in this sweet spot?"

A slight pressure against the area made her silently cry, *Oh shit!* Probably not the best exclamation to make as Wade lubed her backdoor.

"No." She breathed the single word. There was no use in hiding the fact that she was apprehensive, but she wanted this. Wanted to know what it felt like to be fucked by two men—two cocks buried deep inside her.

An audible breath slipped from Wade's mouth. "You're beautiful." With both hands, he spread her cheeks and his palms caressed her gently. "So tight." He released her and more of the cool gel touched her skin.

Slowly, she felt herself stretch and open to his probing finger. Earlier experience with Wade was that he liked things rough, but he took care not to rush her. Before she could think too hard on what Wade was doing, Ryan kissed her. As usual, he demanded her full attention, stroking her mouth with his tongue.

When Wade's finger breached the first ring of muscle, she felt a burn and gasped against Ryan's mouth.

"Breathe, baby." Ryan thrust his hips and began working his cock in and out of her pussy. She was so slick and wet. He slid in and out of her easily. Still, she couldn't quite forget what was going on behind her. She'd been so consumed with what Wade had in mind, she hadn't realized that she'd stopped riding Ryan. As Wade's finger sank deeper, she exhaled and he passed the second ring without protest.

After a moment, Wade began to move his finger in and out of her ass, stopping only to add more lubricant to prepare her. When two fingers slipped into her, she groaned, long and low.

"Feels good, doesn't it, baby?" Ryan rimmed her ear with his tongue, his hips thrusting to an easy tempo.

"Yes," she hissed, silently wanting more—and that's just what she got.

Wade removed his fingers to position his cock at her entrance. He held her hips as he entered her an inch at a time. The burn was welcomed as he leaned closer, going deeper.

It was an incredible feeling. She had never felt so full—so complete—in her life. Two cocks inside her—the idea itself was mind blowing. The actuality was pure heaven. But when they began to move in unison, Angie knew she was going to die. It was almost too much. The pleasure/pain sent tentacles of sensation to every part of her body.

Air left her lungs in a rush, as her inner muscles clamped down on both men. "*Ahhh...*" she screamed. Spasms made her body jerk over and over again, as her orgasm ripped through her like she was being torn in two.

Wade and Ryan fucked her hard and fast, giving no purchase.

"Fuck," one of them said. Which one? Angie had no idea. She couldn't breathe—couldn't think beyond conscious feeling.

When both men's bodies slammed against hers to wedge her tightly between them, they groaned deep and long. She felt the moment their climaxes exploded because their cocks grew larger, jerking and pulsating, inside her. Silent strength held her in its grip. She had never felt anything so intense.

Country music mingled with their heavy breathing. Wade was the first to move. He extracted himself from her body and rose. The sudden emptiness was disconcerting. He was back in no time, a warm, wet wash cloth cleansing her tender area.

It was a thoughtful gesture, but the intimacy was a little shocking.

With a sudden twist of her body against his, she found herself beneath Ryan. "Do you have any idea how gorgeous you are when you come?" His blue eyes sparkled. "Next time I fuck you, it'll be in front of a mirror."

She felt her eyes widen. "Now?"

There was laughter in his voice, as he said, "No honey. I think it's time for bed."

Angie liked the sound of that—falling to sleep in Ryan's embrace.

# Chapter Five

Angie woke with a start. Male voices were yelling. From between the parted curtains, bright light flooded the room. For a moment she was disoriented. She glanced around her unfamiliar surroundings, moved her leg and the most delicious ache reminded her exactly where she was and what she'd done with Ryan and Wade way into the morning hours. The clock on the dresser announced that she had slept the day away. It was already past three in the afternoon. A satisfied grin surfaced and died quickly when the voices rose again.

Something crashed, without pause she slid her legs over the side of the bed and jerked to her feet. *Oh my God they're fighting. Damn men.* She knew there had been a little tension last night, but not to the point of fighting.

Stark naked, she ran from the room toward the sounds of chaos.

The marble was cold beneath her feet as she slid around the corner and into the living room to a dead stop. Ryan, Wade and two other men sat perched on the edge of their seats watching the Giants and Cowboys play football.

Blood drained from her face as four sets of male eyes turned to greet her.

*Oh shit!*

The game was completely forgotten in lieu of staring at the

naked maniac who suddenly turned and ran.

"Angie." Ryan called her name.

But she didn't stop until halfway down the hall.

*No fighting. A fucking football game.*

As she stood there clothed in embarrassment and catching her breath, she got angry. For two cents she would have knocked the shit-eating grin off Wade's face. He had sat there with a smirk a mile long and so did the other guys. Only Ryan looked like she felt—stunned.

"Be back." She heard Ryan say. The chuckles that rose behind sent another rush of heat across her face.

*Damn men.*

With quick steps she headed toward the bedroom. He caught up with her and snaked his arms around her. "Sorry about that. I forgot they were coming over to watch the game."

"Sorry? Or—" she attempted to wiggle out of his embrace, "—did you expect me to be the entertainment at half-time?" He had forgotten to tell her about Wade. Was there a pattern here?

His eyes gaped. His jaw dropped. "What? Angie—no."

She raised a brow in disbelief. It was time to dress and get out of here. Only problem was her dress lay on the table in the foyer. To retrieve it she would have to pass the living room and the men watching television. "My dress and purse are in the foyer. Get them for me and I'll be out of here."

A frown pulled at his mouth. He tightened his hold on her. "No way, honey. You said you'd spend Christmas with us."

She snorted. "You have guests—"

He stole her words away with a kiss hot enough to melt butter. She was a fool. It was hard to stay mad. The moment she softened against him she had lost the battle, and he knew it. A devilish smile touched his mouth. "You made quite an impression on them."

She gave him a little push against the chest. "Ha-ha. Let me go."

"Come on, Angie. Ignore them. It's not like they haven't seen a naked woman before. I'll drive you to your house. You can pick up a couple of things and we'll be back before dinner is delivered."

"You'll miss the game."

He nuzzled his nose against hers. "I'd rather spend time with you."

"I feel like a fool," she whined, burying her face against his chest.

He held her at arm's length. "Baby, you look great and those hound dogs are salivating because you're mine."

*Mine?* She liked the sound of that. If only it were true.

Ryan released her. "I'll get your dress."

While he retrieved her dress from the foyer, she went to the bedroom to grab her shoes and undergarments. She slipped on her bra, garter belt and heels. Her thong, or what was left of it, lay on the floor. Her now-tattered stockings were still draped around the bedposts.

The door swung open and Ryan entered carrying her dress. He slung it on the bed and went immediately to her side. "Damn. You're hot." His hand reached out to grab her, but she evaded his grasp. "Come here. I need a taste of your honey."

She ducked, dodging another lunge to catch her. "Down, boy. You have company."

His brows pulled together as he gave her the most boyish look. His dimples were simply adorable. "Come on, Angie. How about a quickie?"

"Not on your life." She wasn't touching that one with three

other men in the house.

"Then just a kiss?" His voice dropped, becoming low and sexy.

"Yeah. I'm not falling for that one either." Still she let him catch her this time. No way would she'd turn down one of his kisses.

There was something extremely arousing being almost completely naked and pressed to a fully clothed man. Ryan's cotton T-shirt rubbed softly against her silk-covered breasts. His jeans pressed to her hips and legs. The friction between their bodies made her nerve endings tingle. Add to that the wicked spell he was weaving with his kiss and she was a goner.

Angie didn't want to spend Christmas alone. She wanted to spend it with Ryan.


Ryan steered his Hummer into the parking lot of Angie's upscale condominium complex. Lush green landscape surrounded the stucco structure. She had been quiet during the drive, only giving directions when required. Before leaving they had fought. She insisted on driving herself and he refused, knowing there was a fifty-fifty chance she might not return— and that was unacceptable. For whatever reason, he wasn't done with this woman. There was so much more he wanted to explore with her.

"Right here. You can park next to that tree." He pulled the Hummer into the parking space she identified. After he exited, he went to the other side of the vehicle and opened her door. She stepped from the car and led the way, stopping before a door with a bright, cheery wreath hanging from it.

When she turned the key and pushed the door open, the light scent of pine greeted him. Further in the room he felt like he had walked into Wonderland. Her small living room was a tribute to Christmas. Above her mantle a nativity set was neatly arranged. Her Christmas tree was small, maybe five feet, but the care with which each strand of tinsel was draped and the symmetrical design of white and red bulbs made it look like a candy cane.

It appeared she took great pride in every aspect of her life. He liked that quality. His mom was like that.

She hung her purse on a coat rack just inside the door. "Give me a minute. The bar is over there." He followed the path of her finger to a quaint little makeshift bar decorated with garland and fairy lights that twinkled softly.

The wine cooler door creaked as he opened it and retrieved a beer. With a twist of his hand, the bottle cap came loose and a hiss followed. He tipped the bottle to his mouth. The amber liquid was cold, chasing the dryness in his throat away as he swallowed.

Casually, he walked about the room. Pictures of her family hung on the wall. One picture caught his attention. Angie was held in a bear hug by two young men. A tinge of jealousy surfaced. When the same men appeared in what looked like a family picture, he realized they must be her brothers.

Ryan chuckled at his illogical behavior. Still he couldn't help but admire how happy they all seemed, especially the one where she was laughing, wrestling on the ground with her brothers.

Obviously, family was important to her. He liked that quality, too. In fact, like him he bet it was hard spending Christmas without family around.

He heard Angie's footsteps before he saw her. Her makeup had been refreshed. She wore a tight pair of blue jeans, a spaghetti-strapped white T-shirt that showed off her bellybutton and a pair of tennis shoes. She was dragging a sweatshirt jacket over her arms when he approached her. Cupping her face, he pressed his lips to hers.

It thrilled him to feel her reaction each time he touched her. She was putty in his hands as her body folded into his. Slowly, he began to push her jacket from her shoulders. It fell to the floor and he inched her shirt higher. When he didn't come in contact with a bra, he smiled.

Her eyes held a dreamy state, a sexy innocence. "Ryan." Her voice cracked as he bared her a little at a time.

He knelt so that he could caress her abdomen with his lips. As her shirt rose so did he, kissing a path until he sucked a firming nipple into his mouth. He flattened his tongue against the hard nub, intrigued with the rise of bumps surrounding the swollen flesh.

"What, baby?" He cradled the weight of her breast in his hand, kneading, as he flicked his tongue across her nipple. He pulled her shirt over her head and tossed it aside. Then he slipped his fingertips into the waistband of her jeans and jerked her to him. It wasn't an easy feat, but he squeezed his hand further down her pants until he cupped her pussy.

She gasped. "I need you."

She was soft beneath his touch as he rubbed his cheek against hers. Then he slipped a single finger inside her. "Need me?"

"Dammit, Ryan," she whined, reaching for the zipper of his jeans. "Shut up and fuck me."

"I thought you'd never ask."

Within minutes they were both naked and in each other's arms. She arched her neck as he bathed it with feather light kisses. He only paused when she breathed, "Condom. Bedroom. This way."

She led—he followed.

The small room was all woman—pink and lace. Sheers hung from the window, the carpet a rich mauve. The comforter on her queen-size bed was a patchwork quilt of different shades of pink. Her closet doors were large sliding mirrors.

As she pulled the bedding back, she said, "There's a condom in the top dresser drawer."

That wasn't the only thing in there Ryan discovered. From the drawer he extracted a vibrator with an attached clit stimulator that looked like little rabbit ears, and a flogger.

"Oh my God." A stream of nervous laughter erupted from her, as he held them before him. "Those were gag gifts from a Christmas party I attended the other day."

"Never tried them?" he asked, approaching. The thought of her lying upon her bed, her thighs spread wide, pleasuring herself made him rock-hard.

Color heated her face. "Well, maybe the vibrator."

"Maybe?" He grinned, snapping the flogger. Her eyes brightened, as she watched the thongs move through the air. "Don't lie or I'll punish you."

*Crack!* The sharp, sudden movement of the flogger next to her body made her jump.

"Okay." She yanked her heated gaze back to his. "Yes. I've used the vibrator."

Another step brought him nearer where she stood. But he didn't make contact, allowing the heat of their bodies to simmer. "Baby." His voice deepened as he let the straps of the whip dangle down her chest between them.

Gently, he placed his mouth near her ear. "Did you enjoy using it?"

There was no hesitation in her answer. "Yes."

With a nudge, he pressed the vibrator into her hand. "Pleasure yourself for me." He didn't touch her until his tongue slid along the shell of her ear. Their bodies met. His arms circled her.

"But—"

With a kiss Ryan silenced her objection.

Vibrator in one hand, Angie slid her free hand across his ass, loving the feel of muscle beneath her palm. His arousal was firm against her belly. The heat of desire burned across her body, drawing her nipples taut. When he finally broke the kiss, she was willing to do whatever he wanted.

In fact, if a show was what he wanted, she would push aside her inhibitions to please him. Her hand dropped from around him and she moved away from him, toward the bed.

Heart pounding, she placed the vibrator on the bed, before piling several pillows, one behind the other, against the headboard. The bed creaked as she slid atop it. With exaggerated movements, she stretched her body, slinking toward the heap of pillows to place her back to them. In a sitting position, she drew her knees to her chest, dropping them slowly to each side so that she revealed herself to him.

Her wanton display won her a quiet growl. In one hand he held the condom package and the flogger, the other one he wrapped around his erection. A vein in his neck twitched as he began to stroke himself.

The sight of his strong hand around his cock was so hot that moisture released between her thighs.

Retrieving the vibrator, she held it to her mouth, her tongue licking the length before she circled the crown.

"Fuck." His voice was low and coarse.

The rubber was cold against her slit as she eased it inward, until it was buried deep. The little horns of the clit stimulator fit tight against her bud. With a flick of her finger, the sex toy hummed to life and she was filled with a multitude of sensations. Her mouth parted on a sigh.

"That's it, baby. Fuck yourself." His hips moved to mirror the rhythm as she pushed the vibrator in and out of her cove. His eyes dilated. His hot stare was pinned to her center.

All she wanted was the real thing wedged between her legs—Ryan. The thought made her belly clench, first signs that her orgasm approached.

"Play with your breasts," he rumbled, making it sound more like an order than a request.

No stranger to touching herself, she rolled and pinched her sensitive nipple. The tingling set off a series of explosions deep within her womb as her orgasm struck. Her head lolled back, the pace increasing as her hips rose to meet each thrust. A sudden contraction bore down on her and she screamed.

"Don't stop fucking yourself, baby, or you'll be punished," he warned.

But she couldn't continue. The clit stimulator was driving her crazy—her body caught somewhere between pleasure and pain. The vibrator fell from her hands. She sucked in much needed breaths to calm her raging pulse. When she came down from her cloud, he stood beside the bed, cock sheathed and the flogger in his hand.

He hit the whip against the palm of his hand. "You've earned your first punishment."

# Chapter Six

Unbelievable. Watching Angie pleasure herself was beyond hot—it was explosive. The way her body trembled, the desperate cry from her lips as her climax rolled across her body made Ryan's cock swell, throb. Blood rushed his balls, slamming into them to cause a delightful ache.

Spread across the bed, naked and exposed, heat simmered in the depths of her eyes. Her legs were still splayed wide, a sated expression upon her softened face. Even when he threatened to punish her, the anxiety he expected was instead a sensual smile of anticipation.

*Damn.* This woman was special. His grip tightened on the flogger he held. She matched him in every way. Personal, business and sexual needs. The kind of woman he could see himself settling down with.

"You've been a bad little girl." He widened his stance. The cords of muscles in his thighs drew her attention. Her gaze began to slowly rise. His sheathed erection jerked beneath her scrutiny. "Stand up."

Like a cat, she crawled across the bed, sliding off the side to stand before him. She reached for him, but he moved away.

His arousal stirred as their images appeared in the mirror across the room. "I want to take you before the mirror." Without hesitating, she walked past him, throwing a heated glance over her shoulder that told him she'd do anything he wanted. When she faced the mirror, approximately three feet away, he said, "Spread your legs." She slipped them shoulder-length apart. "Wider." He loved how responsive she was when she quickly complied. "Lean forward, palms against the glass."

Wide-eyed, she paused for only a second before bending at the waist and placing her hands against the glass. Her mouth gaped as if in surprise at the picture before her.

Flames of fire shot across his skin. Not only was her sex completely exposed to him, the submissive position was to his advantage. She was his to do with what he wanted—and he wanted her more with each tick of the clock.

The illusion of power raged through his veins hot and wild. Primitive.

*Mine.* The single word whispered through his head.

He stood directly behind her. His gaze stroked her ass as his finger caressed her folds. He felt the release of moisture between her thighs and the tremor that shook her.

"Bad little girl," he murmured, hiding his smile.

The cool straps of the flogger slid across her ass, her back, as he smoothed the whip over her skin. His light touch made goose bumps prickle across her flesh.

"Ryan—"

"No talking." He continued his gentle exploration of her body, stopping to pay special attention to her breasts. He kneaded tenderly, the flogger dangling from his hand. "Do you know why you're being punished?"

Her tongue swiped across her lips. "Because I disobeyed you."

"That's right. For that you must be punished." His hands stilled. "Do you want me to punish you?" He wanted this to be pleasurable for both of them. Eager anticipation, not fear, is what he sought.

"Yes." Her response was quick, leaving no doubt in his mind she looked forward to their play. This time he allowed himself to smile.

Man, she looked sexy staring into the mirror at him. "Do you remember your safe words?"

"Red—stop. Yellow—ease up," she breathed, but before she completed the sentence he flicked his wrist and the flogger stung one ass cheek.

He knew she saw it coming, but still she flinched. Her mouth parted on a startled cry.

"You're so beautiful spread wide for my pleasure." He snapped the flogger a second time, making contact with her thigh as it wrapped around her leg, leaving faint pink lines. "And I will take my pleasure out on every inch of your body. One way or another," he promised, wickedly sliding a finger across her moist slit.

"Ryan?"

He thought of reminding her not to speak, but he loved the wild look in her eyes reflecting back to him from the mirror. He wanted to know what she was thinking—feeling.

"What, baby?" As he spoke, he cracked the whip through the air and watched it bite into her ass, color rising against her skin "Does being flogged turn you on?"

She groaned. The weighty sound made his balls draw closer to his body. The throb made him grit his teeth. He sucked in a much needed breath.

Her back arched. "Yes. Oh God, yes. But—"

As he released the flogger once again, her voice caught. It cracked and struck her tender skin. She was pretty in pink—his mark upon her ass and thighs. He couldn't resist touching her, feeling the heat rise against his hand.

"What, honey? Tell me what you need." She was so soft and warm.

Eyes misty, she whimpered, "You. I need you inside me. Now."

The passion in her voice broke his will. With a flick of his wrist, he tossed the flogger aside and moved directly behind her. Fingers wrapped around his cock, he positioned himself at her swollen folds and thrust.

Bombarded with sensations, he gripped her hips to steady himself. She was hot, tight and sexy as her beautiful lips formed an "o" and her eyelids fell, shuttering her eyes. He had never had a woman so pliable, so willing to please him.

Not to mention the scene reflecting back from the mirror set him barreling towards a meltdown. Her fingertips clawed the glass. As she strained, she pushed back against his hips, driving him deeper. Her breasts bounced each time they came together. But it was the carnal expression, raw and sensual, that tightened his hold on her.

"Harder," she gasped, throwing back her head and sending her blonde hair into waves around her shoulders. Her body clenched around him, squeezed and released, over and over. Quick, shallow breaths announced her approaching climax—a climax that shattered upon a cry.

Violently, his body gave into its need, releasing a firestorm down his shaft. The intensity of his orgasm rocked him against her so that her elbows bent with the impact, throwing them off-balance. As they fell, he twisted her above him to take the brunt of the impact against the carpeted floor.

Locked in his arms, Angie erupted into a stream of giggles.

"Oh my," she breathed through her laughter. "That was

indeed earth shattering." With her palm, she brushed back his hair from his face. "Thank you." Blue eyes sparkled with sincerity and innocence. It was refreshing—almost hypnotic. He felt the pull just before he captured her lips.

The titters that shook her body stilled as their breaths mingled. She folded into his arms, softening beneath his touch. Without being coerced, her mouth parted and he dipped inside to taste her.

Gently he rolled her beneath him. His cock hardened within the spent condom. Even as he pushed between her parted thighs, he knew it wouldn't last another go-round.

Gazing into her eyes, he pressed soft kisses around her mouth, nudged her nose with his and then he whispered, "What do you say we skip dinner at my house with the boys and stay here? Besides it's already six. The food could be gone by now." For some reason he couldn't bear the thought of sharing Angie with Wade again. He wanted the entire night alone with her, discovering her likes and dislikes, and getting to know the woman who had bewitched him.

A bright smile brightened her face. "Really?" After what looked like a moment's thought, her grin faded. "What about Wade?"

A tinge of jealousy pinched his chest. He was right. A weighty sigh expressed his disappointment. He moved from atop her and stood. What woman would want one man, when she could have two? "Okay. Let me clean up and we'll go."

"Wait!" She pushed into a sitting position, looking up at him with an air of apprehension. "I— Dammit." A blush tinted her cheeks. "Although the threesome was a fantasy come true—" The muscles in her throat tightened. "I—I would rather spend time with you—alone." Her troubled voice lowered along with her lashes. The cautious look on her face asked if he felt the same way.

He smiled. "Just me?" He extended his hand. When their fingers locked he jerked her into his arms. Their mouths were a breath away.

A twinkle flashed in her eyes. "Well, until Santa Claus arrives. You'll have to move over for him."

"Not on your life. I'm not sharing you with anyone tonight or any night."

Well fuck! Nothing like laying your cards on the table face up, he thought. Where did his suave business sense go?

To add to his anxiety, Angie's expression went blank.

Not a good sign.

Again, Angie was having problems with her hearing. Ryan did not insinuate that there was more to this relationship than just a one night stand, did he?

Excitement welled up inside her, but she fought to hide it. It was too much to hope for. From the moment she laid eyes on him she knew they were meant to be together. Call it intuition, karma or animal magnetism—she had been drawn to him from the beginning.

Now that they had touched, she had an uncontrollable desire to please him—to explore her sensuality, her darkest secrets with him—and only him.

*Stay cool, Angie. It was a comment made in the heat of a moment.* Still her heart sped. She couldn't stop desire and expectation from taking hold of her.

A rumbling sound made them both stare down at his stomach. The churning reminded her that neither of them had eaten today. "We missed dinner."

The back of his hand smoothed across her cheek. "Hungry?

Do you want to go back to my place?"

*Not on your life!*

Her pulse sped. With a little too much eagerness in her voice, she said, "I have everything for Christmas dinner here. In fact, most of it is already prepared. We'll just have Christmas dinner on Christmas Eve. Why don't you sit down and I'll get started."

He smoothed his palms down her arms and then released her. "Why don't I help you?" Stepping away from her, he removed his condom and disposed of it in a trash can next to the bed.

As he approached, she headed toward her dresser. "Great." She opened a drawer, extracting a shirt when he grasped her wrist.

"What are you doing?" he asked.

Her brows furrowed. "Getting dressed."

A devilish grin greeted her as he shook his head.

Angie chuckled, dropping her shirt back into the drawer and closing it. "I've never cooked in the nude."

"There's a first time for everything." He slapped her hard on the ass. She startled, then burst into laughter and dodged him. But when he opened his arms she went straight into them. He nibbled lightly on her earlobe. "Feed me, so we can get back to playing."

When Angie drifted out of his arms she knew she was lost. How could she go back to looking at Ryan as her boss, passing him in the hallways without stealing a kiss? A solemn mood washed over her.

As she headed out the door toward the kitchen, he headed toward the bathroom. "Need to wash up. I'll be there in a second."

While Angie whipped up the dressing for the turkey, Ryan made a quick call to Wade to let him know he and the boys know he wasn't coming home.

He mumbled something she couldn't hear into his cell phone, snapped it shut and laid it on the table, before he joined her. "What can I do to help?"

"Get the potatoes out of the microwave." She spooned the dressing into the pan around the small turkey breast. "There's butter, cheese and green onions in the refrigerator. Salt, pepper and garlic on the table."

When he pushed a button on the microwave, the door popped open and he retrieved the two potatoes inside. "Baked potatoes, not mashed?"

"Twice baked potatoes." She handed him a knife and spoon. "Cut them in half. Scoop the insides out in a bowl. Add the other ingredients and stuff it all back into the potato skins. Then we'll bake them again."

"Okay. I'm with you now." He bounced the hot potatoes from hand to hand, then tossed them quickly on the counter.

It was a small, but efficient kitchen. Angie didn't realize how confined the space was until she kept bumping into Ryan's naked body—a brush here, a touch there as he moved around retrieving a plate and bowl.

Angie could have sworn that as the heat in the oven rose, so did the temperature in her body.

A rush of hot air greeted her as she opened the oven and pushed the pre-cooked turkey breast inside. "It shouldn't take more than about thirty minutes to warm." As she started the asparagus, she asked, "So how come you're not spending Christmas with your family?"

"Too much to do here." He added a slice of butter to the bowl. "My parents aren't happy, but they understand." He released a heavy sigh of what sounded like disappointment. "I'll miss seeing my brand new nephew."

"A baby?" She couldn't help the longing sound in her voice. "So you have siblings?"

Ryan spooned the potato mixture back into their skins and sat them on a plate. "An older sister and brother. This was a special Christmas with the new arrival. Janie, my older sister, can't have children. It was up to Kelvin, my younger brother, to supply the grandchild." His expression grew thoughtful.

"Family means a lot to you?" she asked, adjusting the fire beneath the vegetable.

"What else is there? If I didn't have issues to handle in the office next week and Wade over, I'd be with them." He pushed away from the counter and held open his arms. "Come here."

She wiped her hands on a towel and stepped into his embrace. He didn't speak or try to kiss her, he simply held her close.

The serene moment was shattered when he released her. His expression had gone from gentle to almost stern. "Where are the dishes? I'll set the table."

🎁 🎁 🎁

The scent of turkey still mingled with pecan pie as Ryan shoved the last bite into his mouth. The pie was sweet and still warm, melting in his mouth. He chewed slowly, trying to chase away thoughts of Angie, his family, and how nice it would be if all of them were together for the holidays. Glasses clinked as she stuffed them in the dishwasher, while he stared into space wondering what was happening to him.

What had this woman done to him? They hardly knew each

other. Thoughts of warming his feet against her body every night was a little too much too soon.

Maybe it was because of the holidays or the fact he missed his family. It wasn't like he was lonely—not with Angie's naked ass parading before him as she wiped off the counter. And since he was being honest, he had to admit there wasn't anyplace he'd rather be than here—with Angie.

Towel in her hand, she turned around, gracing him with a smile. "What?" she asked.

"You're beautiful." She was more than beautiful. She was everything he wanted in a woman.

With a flick of her wrist she playfully threw the cloth at him. "Stop looking at me like that."

He caught the rag in one hand and set it on the table, then he pushed to his feet. "Looking at you like what?"

She took a step backward as he approached. "Like I'm the final course of tonight's meal."

He closed in on her. "But aren't you?" She squealed when her ass struck the cold counter behind her. He grasped her by the waist and heaved her on top of the counter. "I've made a decision." Slowly he parted her knees, baring her pink flesh before his eyes.

She leaned back on her palms, her head resting against the cabinet. "A decision?" Her nipples beaded into peaks. He bent forward and licked one and then the other. Whether it was conscious or not, she arched into him.

The knuckles of his hands smoothed up the insides of her thighs, until they met at her core. One finger slid across her wet folds. "I've decided to make you my Christmas present."

"Oh yeah?" She cocked a brow. Her chest rose and fell as her breathing elevated. "Are you the type of kid who opens one present only to toss it aside for a bigger and better one?"

No. He wasn't that way with presents or relationships, and a relationship is just what he sought with this woman. "Not me. When I find something I like I hold on to it." He didn't want whatever was between them to end—not now—maybe ever. Only time would determine their path.

A tremor shook her as she released a weighted breath. "What are we really talking about, Ryan?" Color drained from her fingers as she tensed against the counter.

"Angie, I don't know where this will lead us, but I want you." She swallowed hard and opened her mouth as if to speak, but he placed a finger against her lips. "Not just the weekend, but as far as we can take it."

When he removed his finger, her lips parted. "I—"

The ringing of his cell phone sitting on the table interrupted her.

Damn that phone.

Ryan frowned. "I really need to get this." It was almost ten o'clock. He knew a call this late on Christmas Eve couldn't be good.

Angie slid off the counter as he went to the table and retrieved his phone. He flipped up the cover, placed it to his ear and said, "Hello."

"Boss, we got it." Manny's voice rang with excitement. "Just received the email."

What the hell was his Senior Editor talking about? "What email?"

Manny laughed. "Sorry. The Bender account—they're signing with us. Been gone the whole day at the in-laws. I just signed onto the internet. Thought the news would make a great Christmas gift."

Ryan watched Angie put the pecan pie in the refrigerator. Her naked body, sleek and sexy, drove him to distraction. He stumbled for his thoughts. "What about the meetings next week?"

"Cancelled," Manny announced. "Old man Bender said he'd talk to you after the first of the year."

This changed everything. Excitement rushed through Ryan's veins. "Fantastic news. Thanks, Manny." If he could catch a flight tonight, he would be home before his mother put breakfast on the table. "Merry Christmas." He ended the call and then pressed the number to American Airlines.

When the person on the other line answered, he said, "When is your next flight to Manhattan?" From the corner of his eye, he saw Angie's eyes widen and something close to disappointment or anger hardened her expression. With a small rise to her chin, she squared her shoulders and walked from the room.

"Five a.m.," he repeated. "Great." After retrieving his wallet from his pants lying on the living room floor, he gave the attendant the necessary information and hung up. Angie was nowhere around, so he headed to the bedroom.

Water was running behind the closed bathroom door off the bedroom. When the door squeaked open Angie appeared dressed in a long, black nightgown. The minty scent of toothpaste and light perfume, sweet with a hint of citrus, followed her into the room.

Ryan's feet were already in motion, as he moved toward her. "Damn, baby, you're beautiful. Now come here and let me peel that gown off you."

Wariness dulled her usually bright eyes. "Don't you have to leave?"

"Not for a couple of hours." He wrapped his arms around

her unyielding body. Even when he placed several kisses against her neck, she didn't soften. "I want you to go with me." He gazed into her widening eyes.

"What?" The pitch in her voice rose.

"I want you to come home with me." Before she could argue he continued, "You don't have anything holding you here. Come home with me and meet my family."

She attempted to pull out of his embrace. "I—I can't impose. And what about Wade?" He tightened the arm he had around her waist.

With a brush of his free hand the strap of her nightgown fell off her shoulder. "Wade's gone." Ryan feathered his thumb across her silky skin.

A shiver shook her as she asked, "Gone?"

The other nightgown strap gave beneath his hand. "When I spoke to him he was getting ready to head back to Texas."

"Why?" Her voice caught as the gown slithered down her chest to barely cover her hardened nipples.

With a step backward, he released his hold on her and the soft material fell between them, past her breasts, pooling around her waist. He cupped a warm breast, his thumb smoothing across her erect peak.

"Jessie, a childhood friend of ours. He asked her to marry him. She turned him down. Guess he isn't taking no for an answer. And neither am I." He dipped forward and sucked her nipple into his mouth. His lips moved against her swollen flesh. "Come with me."

Angie was speechless, even as her mind filled with excitement. Her fingers threaded through his dark hair, holding him close as he suckled her peak.

"Please," he murmured before nipping her nipple.

She squealed, and then giggled. "Okay. Okay." His fingers rimmed her thong, pushing it down her hips, thighs and legs to remove it, as well as her gown.

Happiness bubbled up inside her. *He wants me to meet his family.*

With a sweep of his arm beneath her knees, she found herself cradled next to his warm body being carried to the bed. Together they fell into the downy covers. Pinned beneath his weight, he used his hips to spread her legs wide, his kiss to mesmerize.

He nestled his cock against her wet pussy, her palms smoothed across his taut ass. She raised her hips to receive him as he thrust. He buried deeply, filling her completely as he rocked gently.

It was heavenly.

His lips were soft against hers. "You're amazing." He bit her bottom lip pulling it into his mouth to suck. Then he kissed the corner of her mouth, before taking her lips in earnest. His tongue mimicked the slow, expert caresses of his cock moving in and out of her body.

"Mine," she thought she heard him say against her mouth. Just the thought made her body burn, her abdomen tighten as her arousal built.

Ryan's breathing sped. She felt him push her thighs wider, his pace quicken. He moved to a kneeling position, looping her legs through the bend of his arms. His eyes darkened as he watched the area where their bodies came together.

The hunger in his eyes made contractions quake in her womb. She reached down and circled the base of his erection with her index finger and thumb. He slid freely through her hold, drawing in a shaky breath.

"Fuck, baby." His voice was coarse, breathy.

The sounds of flesh slapping flesh made her body tense. Her fingers curled in the sheets as hot-white flames flared, igniting like firecrackers inside her.

He slammed into her, threw his head back and groaned. Together they tumbled into ecstasy, their bodies taking and giving.

When the aftermath cooled, she curled against him and listened to his soft breathing. Only then did it dawn on her he wasn't wearing a condom. There was a moment of dismay.

A child? With this man? They didn't even really know each other.

Still, a smile crept across her face. If it happened she would deal with the matter. For now, she only wanted to enjoy the man beside her.

It was getting late. Angie glanced at the neon clock on the dresser. Midnight. It was Christmas.

"Merry Christmas." He kissed her forehead. "I can't wait for my family to meet you." The promise of a future lingered in his words.

"Merry Christmas," she whispered, snuggling closer.

*And a Happy New Year*, she hummed beneath her breath.

# Bound by the Past

# Dedication

To Jess Bimberg, Patti Duplantis, Claudia McRay, Sharis Mayer and Kendra Egert. Five wonderful women whose friendship I treasure. Thank you.

# Chapter One

Damn this thing called love.

Wade Peterson stood beside his black four-wheel drive Dually, staring blindly at the auction house looming before him. There was a flurry of activity beyond the large barn-like structure judging by the hollers and whistles mingling with cattle mooing and a horse's whinny. The scents of too-ripe fertilizer heightened from last night's rain rose in the crisp morning air.

He licked his dry lips. Had he made a mistake returning? It was the twenty-seventh, two days after Christmas.

Fuck no. It was not a mistake to pursue what he wanted.

A moment of doubt resurfaced. Recently he wasn't as confident. Life seemed to have gotten complicated. He slipped his Stetson off and ran his fingers through his hair, before adjusting the hat atop his head once more. For the last week he had felt like Cupid shot him in the ass with a shit-load of arrows, leaving him confused and agitated.

Hell. He wasn't a one-woman man. He loved them all.

Literally.

Short. Tall. Thin to a full-figure. Women fascinated him. They were soft and pliable, bending to his will easily. Those that didn't made the game even more intriguing. He lived for the chase. He wasn't one to fall head over heels for a woman, especially only one.

So why now? Why Jessica Evans? A gal he had known since high school, and who, by the way, had abruptly refused his heartfelt proposal days before Christmas.

Yeah. That's right. He had proposed. Mr. Love 'Em and Leave 'Em had fallen right into the very trap he'd been avoiding.

Commitment.

Living life free and easy, he played hard—loved even harder. Well, until now.

Nothing in his life fit. From living at home and working the family ranch to waking up alone, there was something or someone missing. He rubbed his thumb and index finger from his close-cut mustache to his beard, anticipation of seeing her again needling him. How had he gotten to this point?

"You're burning daylight or avoiding the inevitable," he mumbled to himself.

Truth? Wade was scared to death to be returning to San Antonio—scared to death how a slip of a woman could force him to his knees. Still his mind was made up. He wasn't taking no for an answer. He was a man who got what he wanted—and he wanted Jessie with every fiber of his body.

Squaring his shoulders, he headed for the corrals where he knew the manager of Carmel Livestock Auction would probably be working. Jessie kept a sharp eye on every aspect of the business. Hell. She wasn't above herding cattle or cleaning stalls. The woman was amazing, even more so when the bedroom door shut and the lights went off. The stirring behind his zipper confirmed that. In fact, he had driven from Arizona back to Texas with a constant hard-on just thinking of what he would do once he had her back in his arms.

A rock popped from beneath his boot. With each step, his

confidence strengthened, as well as his erection. Jessie might not know it now, but she was his. Now all he had to do was convince her.

Rounding the building, his breath caught as she came into sight. Long black hair braided down her back. His gaze caressed her five-nine frame from head to toe, taking in every delectable curve. Hands propped against narrow jean-clad hips, she was raising hell with one of her workers as he headed for a young Paint pony in a corral of six horses.

Jessie shook her head and yelled, *"Alto Juan. Consiga el caballo marrón."* She jutted her index finger in the direction of the large sorrel horse she wanted him to cut from the herd. Juan released the halter of the pony and pointed to the sorrel. Jessie nodded. *"Si."*

On quiet footsteps, Wade approached. He knew she didn't hear him. That's just how he wanted her—off guard.

Moving quickly, he pressed his body against the back of the unsuspecting woman who haunted his dreams, trapping her against the steel railing of the corral. Her surprised gasp made him smile.

"Hello, darlin'." His voice sounded deep and hoarse even to him. But that's the effect Jessie had on him. She stripped him of control. Made him weak in the knees, but he would never let her know. The man inside him needed to dominate her. Prove to her that he could take her or leave her—even if it wasn't true.

To his surprise she remained silent, unmoving. A cool breeze whipped around them, threatening to steal her sensual scent away, a soft feminine perfume that even distance hadn't been able to erase.

"I'm back," he whispered against her ear, resisting the urge to nip the tender earlobe adorned with a single diamond stud. Wade wanted to do much more than to kiss and feel the earring pressed to his tongue, between his teeth.

God, she felt good against his body. He couldn't wait to remove her clothes so nothing lay between them.

Several tendrils had worked their way loose from her braid and danced around her neck in the breeze. He smoothed his lips along the exposed skin, and then he blew lightly.

"Back?" Her voice trembled, but she quickly repressed it as she gazed over the acres of corrals. "I didn't know you'd left," she stated calmly, even as she grasped the steel bar before her and the tendons in her throat grew taut.

*Well, that hurt.* But what had he expected?

To his disappointment and embarrassment, Jessie had rejected him. Well, she hadn't exactly said no. It'd been more like *hell no*, stating she wasn't the marrying type.

Like an idiot, he had run—hauled ass out of town, accepting an old school chum's invitation to join him for Christmas. When what he should have done was made love to her until she changed her mind.

She glanced smugly over her shoulder, hitting the rim of his Stetson with her forehead. "What do you want, Peterson?"

Okay, this wasn't a good start. Yet he was like a dog with a bone when his mind was made up. His mom called it stubborn. He called it determined.

With her still looking over her shoulder, Wade stared into her crystal blue eyes, never breaking their connection, and pressed his lips to her neck again. In slow, seductive swirls, he smoothed his tongue over her skin before nibbling on the area. She jerked her head forward and he felt the tremor that whispered through her, reviving his confidence that she felt something—anything.

That's what he loved most about Jessie. She came apart in

his arms, made him feel all man when they were together. She had to care. He couldn't help the triumphant grin that tugged at his mouth when she tried to pull away.

Sliding his arms around her waist, he pulled her closer. "Tonight," he breathed against her neck, watching her skin prickle.

Jessie's grasp tightened even more on the railing, knuckles turning white. Then her attention was stolen from him. "Poyo, not that gate—the next one," she yelled at the *vaquero*, a Mexican cowboy straddling a sorrel horse. "Plans." The clipped word was meant for Wade. She pointed toward three bay geldings and hollered, "Gilbert, move those three over to the next pen."

"Clancy's?" he asked, slipping several fingers beneath her white down vest and between the buttoned-space of her long sleeve shirt. Wade didn't quite understand Jessie and Clancy's relationship. They were close—intimate—but neither blinked an eye when Wade joined them to make a threesome. In fact, Jessie and Clancy gave him the impression there wasn't anything deeper to their relationship than sex.

When his fingers met skin, she inhaled sharply and he smiled. Jessie had the smoothest flesh and the greatest body he had ever held. Not to mention she was a wildcat in bed. Callused hands from hard work turned to silk during lovemaking. She knew what a man liked and she never held back her own desires.

She was made for him. He had known it the minute she allowed him to tie her up. Their tastes ran alike—uninhibited and wild, both into multiple partners and a little dominance and bondage. They were suited for each other. Why couldn't she see that?

There was a pregnant pause before she spoke. "Uh-huh,"

and then she stuttered, "No. No. No. Back the Paint out of there. I want the black filly next."

Wade continued to stroke her skin with his fingertips. "His house?"

The young colt evaded Poyo's grasp and headed the other direction. "Well sonofabitch. Catch her," Jessie yelled before turning her attention back to Wade. "Yeah. His house."

"I'll be there." Already the thought of stripping her naked, of tasting the sweetness between her thighs was making him harder. He shifted his legs before pressing firmly against her to show her exactly how much he was anticipating the evening.

Again she glanced over her shoulder, raising a brow. "I don't recall inviting you."

This time her voice was tight, strained, but he recognized the sexual hunger in her eyes that had him responding, "I don't recall you saying, 'No'."

Jessie opened her mouth and for a moment he thought she might protest. A wave of satisfaction swept over him when she pinched her lips together.

The black filly was becoming frustrated as Poyo tried to force her compliance to move along the fence toward the chute. Something spooked her and the young horse banged into the fence, causing Wade to step backward and allowing Jessie a chance to escape him.

She moved quickly out of his reach. For a moment Jessie stared at him as if struggling with what to say next. With a sense of unrest, she inhaled deeply. "I've got to get back to work."

Did he detect a hint of sadness in her tone?

"Poyo, move the buckskin over to the last pen. Later, Peterson." She passed him, heading toward the auction house without another word.

Wade couldn't keep his gaze off the sway of her sultry hips. Damn. That woman turned him on. Yet for some reason an uneasy feeling crept beneath his skin. Something didn't feel quite right or maybe it was that he knew getting her to agree to marry him wasn't going to be easy. Either way, tonight he would do whatever it took to persuade her back into his arms.

Hell. Why wait until tonight?

Without delay, he headed for the auction house. The heavy wood door creaked as he opened it and stepped inside. Shafts of late morning light and the cold December day seeped through fissures in the walls and the large gaps above the gates leading into and from the closed-in arena.

From the box high above the arena the auctioneer's voice pitched, "*Eight!*" Butch Randall pointed to a young man bidding on a gray mare, as he rattled on. "Do I hear nine? Nine. Nine. Nine. Who'll give me nine? *Nine!*" His chanting continued driving up the bid as a war began against the stranger and the Mendez family, cattle ranchers out of Leon Valley.

Wade made his way down the aisle between two sets of bleachers filled with neighbors and business associates, speaking to some as he scanned the area for Jessie. She was on the stairs leading to the auction box. When she disappeared from his sight, he turned, catching the eye of Clancy and his cousin, Trevor, a cocky young man who had moved to Texas from California.

Clancy gave Wade an upward nod.

It would appear unusual if Wade didn't join his friend, so he proceeded to climb the bleachers and take a seat next to him. They shook hands, shared hellos, and watched as one of Clancy's ponies moved into the arena.

"You okay with tonight?" Clancy asked, watching the

crowd. Satisfaction touched his mouth as the bid began to rise.

A series of alarms went off inside Wade. He hadn't spoken to his friend about joining them this evening, nor had she had the time. They weren't apart for longer than a couple of minutes. "Okay with what?"

Clancy turned his attention to Wade. "Jessie. Me. Trevor."

A Cheshire cat was plastered across his cousin's face.

"Trevor?" Wade choked unable to hide his surprise. "But—I—" He scanned the auctioneer's booth, locating Jessie again. Anger whipped through him like a twister. Heat swarmed up his neck. Tendons grew taut across his shoulders.

What that hell was she up to?

"She's fuckin' hot." Trevor sucked in a breath of excitement as his hungry stare devoured her.

She spoke nonchalantly to the auctioneer's secretary, seemingly unaware of the storm brewing in the stands. The damn cowboy next to Clancy didn't even realize he was seconds away from becoming a dead man.

Wade's fingers curled into fists. "Touch her...and I'll kill you." His quiet words drained the color from the young man's face. He shot a glance to his cousin and then back to Wade. By a thread, he held onto his composure. "Who arranged this?"

Clancy looked apprehensive as he admitted, "I did. Man, you just disappeared. Left. No explanation—nothing. Jessie has been as uptight as a long-tailed cat in a room full of rocking chairs. She refused to spend Christmas with me or come over. I thought it would calm her. Make her happy."

*Happy? Fucking someone else?*

Every nerve wound tighter than a spring. "Who made you responsible for her happiness?" Wade barely held himself from releasing all his frustration and anger on Clancy. At least his cousin wasn't grinning anymore. His color had yet to resurface.

"I just thought—"

"I'm back." Wade cut Clancy off. His trip to Arizona to visit his friend Ryan had been a revelation. Ryan's little filly had willingly taken both of them to her bed, but it hadn't felt right. Wade couldn't get Jessie out of his mind. He speared his fingers through his hair. The fact was he didn't want another woman— he wanted Jessie.

"But—"

Wade's hot glare bore into Trevor.

He appeared to second-guess his decision to defy Wade when Clancy laid a hand on his arm and shook his head in warning.

"Whatever Jessie wants," Clancy stated. "Does she know you're coming over?"

"Hell, yes," Wade snapped.

Had that been Jessie's plan, to take on three men tonight? Just the thought set his insides on fire, burning like an inferno. Well, she would just have to settle with two, and if he had it his way only one.

Dammit. His gut tightened. After tonight he'd make sure she'd never think of being with another man.

Standing in the auction booth, Jessie skimmed over the crowd. Her gaze froze when Wade came into view.

Crap.

The cowboy who made her body sing was frowning big time. His furrowed brows, wrinkled forehead and rigid posture spoke loudly, he was angry. Yet it was the lightning flashing in his eyes as he spoke with Clancy that gave her pause and caused every nerve ending to draw taut. He must have found out that their *ménage a trois* tonight would include Trevor.

Before she could tear her gaze from him, Wade turned to pin his glare on her. Her breathing stuttered. The simmering heat in his eyes could singe the hair off her arms.

Well, good.

Two was company, three a party, but surely he would find four a crowd, which had been her plan. It might not be right to use Trevor in such a way, but if it put an end to Wade's attraction for her, it would be worth it. Then again, she should have had the *cojones* to tell him no—cut the strings completely. The thought made a wave of sadness swell and roll over her.

Why did the idea of wiping him out of her life make her stomach churn? Why did she feel like crying, when she never cried?

Who was she fooling? She didn't want him out of her life. What he represented scared the shit out of her. Rejecting his marriage proposal had been the right thing. Difficult, but the right thing.

Wade Peterson was dangerous.

A sudden chill made her tug the ends of her vest together and zip it closed. Flannel instead of the long-sleeve cotton shirt she wore would have been a better choice. The heater humming loudly had never worked well. Then again, she doubted it was the weather making her feel exposed and cold.

"Sold." Butch's yell jerked her out of her stupor. She forced a smile as the livestock secretary looked up from the stack of papers she was thumbing through.

Jessie bent low and whispered, "Do you two need anything?"

The short blonde shook her head. "Not a thing, boss." Carrie gazed into the crowd. "I didn't expect so many people two days after Christmas."

"It's unbelievable," Jessie agreed.

The holidays sucked. It was the loneliest time of year for a person without family. Well it wasn't that she was completely without family. She had a mother in Las Vegas with her... What was it now? Fourth or fifth husband? Jessie had lost count of Marie Evans's turbulent marriages after her third husband had almost raped Jessie.

A feisty bay slammed against the chute, making Jessie jump, but it didn't erase the memory of her lousy childhood.

Carrie's gaze hardened on her. "You okay?"

"I'm fine." Jessie tried to reassure her friend.

Carrie shook her head. She gave her one more long look, before she turned back to the papers lying in front of her and went back to work.

*Yep.* Marriage was not for Jessie. Her parents had taught her that lesson. With an internal shrug, she pushed the thought away, catching Wade's eye once again. It might be silly, but the heat radiating from him was a turn-on. She pulled at the collar of her shirt. Too many clothes.

Releasing a deep sigh, she closed her eyes. Wrong thing to do as the image of a pair of strong hands caressing her naked body materialized. *Dammit.* This was not where her mind should be going. Even still, the thought of seductive lips against hers made slivers of desire tingle through her breasts.

The sudden slamming of the gate below the auction booth forced her eyes open. Larry, one of the ring men, carried a box of leather and several pieces of tack into the arena and sat the stuff on the dirt floor.

"Who'll start this bid off?" Butch's singsong voice continued. "Who'll give me thirty? Do I hear thirty?"

Wade placed his finger to the rim of his Stetson and dipped his head.

"Thirty!" The auctioneer yelled as his finger jutted in Wade's direction. "Now, boys, there's a lot you can do with strips of leather. Who'll give me forty?"

Oh yeah. Butch didn't have any idea how right he was. There were a lot of things a person could do with leather, especially Wade Peterson.

As he exchanged lead with one of the Mendez brothers, all Jessie could think of was the six-lash, flat-braid whip Wade had made. It was a work of art. His touch had been tender one minute and then firmer the next as he broke it in upon her flesh. The sting had been deliciously wicked. The sex that had followed had been earth shattering. Moisture dampened her panties. Her nipples drew taut to a delightful sting of arousal.

She'd lay a bet few people, including his family, knew that he hosted not one, but two internet sites. One site specialized in a variety of livestock tack including halters, bridles, reins, whips and riding crops. His business cards could be found around the city in feed stores and even the auction bulletin board. His other site wasn't as openly marketed.

Leather and Lace revealed the darker side of Wade few knew about. His virtual store offered whips, single tails and bullwhips, soft slappers, paddles and other sex toys. Her favorite were the bondage gauntlets or forearm bands he had made specifically for her. She swallowed hard, her body heating. The cowboy had a thing for rope. The multiple D-rings on the handcrafted gauntlets allowed him to slip rope, or at times silk ribbon, through them to tie her up.

The thought of the cool satin rope slithering across her

naked skin sent a shiver up her spine. That session had been a particularly intense one. For over two hours Wade and Clancy had worshipped her body. Brought her to the brink of fulfillment, eased her back down, and then started all over again.

The memory made her heart leap into her throat. Her clothes felt stifling as the silk bra she wore rasped against her nipples, now tender and raw. Carrie said something she couldn't hear.

Dammit. She had to stop thinking about Wade.

When she moved closer to the secretary, the ache between Jessie's thighs built with each step. She swallowed hard and leaned into the administrator.

"Will you take these papers to the office?"

"Sure." Jessie took the papers.

"Sold!" She nearly jumped out of her skin at Butch's loud and abrupt inflection. Jessie wasn't surprised when he announced that Wade had won the bid.

Slowly, he got to his feet, slipping a hand in his front pocket. The subtle move drew Jessie's eyes to the bulge behind his zipper. The cowboy was hard and he took no means to hide it.

She inhaled a shuddering breath. Had he been thinking of that night?

He descended the bleachers. Each slow and seductive step brought him closer and messed with her head. *Dangerous,* her subconscious whispered. She ignored the warning. Instead she slid her gaze up his muscular frame until their eyes met. Beneath his Stetson, eyelids half-shuttered, he trapped her in his seductive web.

He wanted her.

It was in the depths of his eyes and the predatory way his body moved promising a night filled with passion.

Jessie's heart stuttered, and then took off like it had entered a horse race. Her breasts were heavy, ripe with need. The moisture between her thighs intensified.

One of the ring men pushed the container through the railings and handed it to Wade. He nodded, accepting the box before pinning her once again with his heated stare. For a moment he didn't move, only stood there looking up at her.

When the devil winked, he set off a hundred butterfly wings in her chest to flutter. Without a word, he turned and headed back up the bleachers to sit beside Clancy. He set the box alongside his feet and withdrew several pieces of leather.

Powerless to look away, she was mesmerized at the deftness of his fingers as leather strands slipped through them. In seconds he had a red and black braided strap, snapping through the air. With each crack, her skin prickled.

He was taunting her and it was working. She couldn't think clearly, her body out of control. The ache developing low in her belly drew tighter. She sucked in a breath and it quivered through her. God, she needed release and she needed it now before she made a fool of herself and came for an audience.

"Carrie, I'll be in my office if anyone needs me." Her voice sounded shaky.

"Sure, hon. You sure everything is okay?"

Jessie managed a quick nod as she headed for the stairs. Her clothes felt too tight, especially her jeans, the seam finding its way into the V of her thighs, rubbing and caressing. She licked her parched lips, ducking her head as she strode along the bleachers, past Clancy and Wade, narrowing her sight on the door leading to her office.

"Boss—"

The lanky teenage boy she had hired as her assistant stopped when she said, "Not now, Dean."

"You okay?" He tossed back his shoulder-length hair, stood and moved from around his desk.

*Fuck.* Could everyone tell she was off-center today?

"Yeah. Fine. I don't want to be disturbed." The door of her office slammed shut behind her. She twisted the lock, barring the outside world from entering.

A heavy sigh released as she unzipped her vest. *Clothes too many—too tight.* She wiggled out of the vest and threw it aside to land on a chair as she made her way to the desk in the small room. It wasn't much, but she had never needed much. Right now what she needed was relief. Her body was burning up and one wicked cowboy was responsible.

Her hands shook as she released the button of her jeans. The zipper was next, hissing as she tugged it down. There was no hesitation in her movements as she pushed her pants and panties down around her knees. As she sat, the cold leather of her chair struck her ass. Goose bumps rose across her skin. Her pulse sped. She resisted the urge to squirm. Instead, she reached for her purse. On second thought, she veered her hand away and switched on the radio. The low baritone voice of Josh Turner singing "Your Man" filled her office. Even when she wasn't aroused, the singer's seductive voice made her hot.

Retrieving a small velvet pouch from her purse, she unveiled the contents, a small two-inch vibrator hooked to a wire leading to a small, black control box. The Bullet was great in situations like this.

She didn't think twice, spreading her thighs as wide as her jeans allowed before lifting her hips and slipping the vibrator deep inside her moist core. Her inner muscles immediately clamped down, relishing the coolness and invasion. A push of a button and the sex toy began to vibrate. The rapid rhythmic movement shot through her pussy, fogging her mind to anything but the pleasure.

"Oh God," she breathed, pushing her hands beneath her shirt, shoving her bra up to expose and cup her breasts. She cradled them for a moment and then lightly rubbed her thumbs over her nipples. "Good. So good." A little pressure exerted between her thumb and forefinger and sensation splintered in all directions, making her thrust out her chest and squeeze harder.

"Wade," she whispered his name, imagining it was his hands plucking at her nubs—him driving her out of her mind. Slowly she smoothed a palm down her abdomen. Fingers threaded through her curls covering her mons. She stroked the length of her slit, circling her clit when a knock sounded on her door.

"Jessie?" She nearly died when she heard Wade try the doorknob.

A gush of air left her lungs. "No. This can't be happening." Her swollen clit throbbed beneath her fingertips. She couldn't stop pressing firmly and then rubbing it several times. Rays of fire shot from her touch.

"Do you think she's all right?"

*Crap.* Clancy was with him.

Well, wasn't this just great? Perhaps she should open the door and invite them in. Jessie muffled the moan that caught in her throat. Hell. They could have a party. A particularly strong contraction bore down on her and she gasped. She was so close.

Honestly? There was something friggin' hot about the position she found herself in behind locked doors, perched on an orgasm while two gorgeous men stood outside her office. The thought made her inner muscles shorten and thicken, squeezing and driving her nearer to fulfillment.

"Jessie?" Wade's insistent knocking grew louder this time. "If she doesn't answer, I'm breaking down this fucking door."

Her eyes widened. *Shit. Shit. Shit.* She couldn't let that happen. "Yes?" Her voice sounded small even though she tried to raise it above the radio.

"Let me in," he demanded.

She stood at the threshold of climaxing. Every muscle in her body tensed. Fingers of sensation crawled along her nerve endings. All she needed was few more seconds.

"Hold your horses. I'm coming." She pushed another button on the control, increasing the movement and hum of the vibrator. That's all she needed to carry her over the top. A sudden pinch in her abdomen robbed her of air. "Oh God." She threw back her head, releasing a muffled moan as one after another waves of pleasure swept through her.

"Now, Jessie."

Her silence met Wade's threat. She couldn't move or speak. Her body had become one big pulse of sensation.

"Jessie!" Wade barked.

As she slumped back against her chair, every muscle inside her relaxed. This would be laughable if it wasn't so serious. She couldn't be caught in this position at work.

Her body still hummed as she tried to pull herself together. Sitting up to dislodge the vibrator, she pushed it and the bag into the top drawer of her desk. Her hands were shaking as she jerked her jeans up and tucked in her shirt before she fastened them. At the same time, she moved to the door, unlocking it before she pulled it wide.

"What the hell is wrong?" She attempted to sound

indignant, but even to her she heard the guilty tone. Not to mention, her knees felt like rubber barely holding her up.

Wade looked past her as Clancy moved beside him and Dean got up from his desk to approach.

"What? Is the barn on fire?" She jerked her palms to her hips to hide the tremor in her hands. "I don't smell smoke."

Wade fixed his eyes on her, and then a grin raised the corner of his mouth. "Hold my horses. You're *coming?*" He emphasized the last word.

Five shades of embarrassment flooded across her face.

He knew.

If the grin Clancy tried to hide behind a cough was any indication, he knew too.

Of course, the musky scent of sex didn't help. Thank God Dean was clueless as he stared at her and then each of the men, confusion pulling at his brows.

"Whad'ya want?" she snapped, anger now taking control.

"Just to know you're okay." She didn't miss the concern in Wade's voice as his smile faded. He reached for her, but she eluded his grasp. She felt shaky inside, still embraced in the aftereffects of her orgasm. Having him near, the scent of his sandalwood cologne, made her weak.

"I'm fine." Turning away from Wade, she focused on Clancy. "Really." Her fingers closed around the doorknob. "Now if you don't mind. I've got work to do." She tried to shut the door, but Wade caught it and held it wide.

Heat had returned to his eyes. "We need to talk..." He paused before continuing, "...about tonight."

Jessie watched Dean stroll back to his desk before she forced a tight smile. "Can't wait." She tossed her head and her long braid swung over her shoulder as she took a quick peek to ensure her assistant wasn't within hearing. "Always wondered what it would be like with three men."

It was a lie. Her dreams weren't filled with the company of three men, but one—always one and it scared her to death.

Wade reached out, catching her arm as she turned away. Anger flickered in his eyes. Apparently, he wasn't amused. "Not gonna happen, darlin'." A growl rose in his deep voice.

"The hell you say. Remember I make the rules," she reminded him.

A vein bulged in his forehead. He stood rigidly, almost as if he were made of cold stone. She felt the tremor that assailed him before his hand dropped, releasing her. He glared at her a moment longer, and then without a word, he turned his back to her. His boots clicked hard and fast across the floor as he departed.

"Jessie?" Clancy startled her. She sucked in the breath she hadn't known she held and turned toward him. "That man is crazy about you."

She shrugged. "Shit happens. You know how I feel about getting involved with one man."

A finger beneath her chin, he raised her gaze to meet his. "You're crazy about him too."

She jerked away from him. "You're friggin' nuts. You know me. Besides he wants me to marry him. You and I both know that would be disastrous."

Surprise brightened Clancy's blue eyes. "Marry?" Evidently Wade hadn't shared his plans or feelings with their friend. "No wonder—" He looked away. "Uh, best be getting back out there. Don't want to miss my stock." As he turned, he glanced over his shoulder. "Tonight?"

*Tonight?* She dropped the "M" bomb and he had nothing

more to say? Mentally she shook her head. When they were younger, after one of Clancy's parents' fights, he and Jessie had made a pact never to marry. That's when their friendship had blossomed. Later on, they became friends with benefits. It worked for them.

Yet she had expected a little more from him than a moment of surprise and then a quick dismissal.

Oh well. Whatever.

"Yeah. Tonight." At least now she didn't have to worry about Wade showing up, not if the speed at which he left meant what she figured it meant. He was mad. Perhaps he had finally realized that this was her life. She enjoyed multiple partners. The door didn't make a sound as she pulled it shut. "The more the merrier," she said.

But if that were true, why did she feel like something the dog dragged home? Shouldn't she be elated that she had finally pushed him away?

Jessie plopped down in her chair. Gripping the desk, she slid her chair beneath it before retrieving this morning's records. That's when an unexpected emptiness swept over her.

Wade was gone for good.

# Chapter Two

"Hold up," Clancy yelled as he quickened his steps.

Wade reached for the door handle of his Ford Dually. His fingers closed around the steel, grip tightening as he jerked the door open.

His friend stopped several feet before him. "Wade. Hear me out."

Slowly Wade turned around. Dark clouds were moving in from the north as quickly as his mood was heading south. He didn't cotton to talking at the moment, least of all with the guy who had arranged another man to take his place in Jessie's bed—and she was looking forward to it. Just the knowledge she would welcome a stranger made him as cantankerous as a grizzly bear.

Well it wasn't fuckin' going happen. He'd kill Trevor if he laid one finger on her body.

For longer than was comfortable Clancy stared at him. The rumble of a truck and trailer pulling out and several neighs from the horses within washed over the strained silence. Clancy's expression was unreadable, but if he thought of singing his cousin's praises, no amount of song or dance would change Wade's mind. If he even thought—

"You push too hard...you'll lose her." Clancy's serious tone and rigid stance drew Wade up short.

"What?" Had Jessie told Clancy he'd proposed? He pushed a breath from his lungs. Of course she would.

There was something strange about Jessie and Clancy's friendship—a closeness he had never understood. It hadn't bothered him in the past. Of course, he hadn't expected to fall for Jessie. He had just been out for a good time, but things had changed. He wanted her to look to him when she was happy, sad or needing something—not Clancy.

His friend pulled off his hat and pushed his fingers through his black hair. "Man, she'd murder me if she knew I was talking to you."

Wade didn't doubt that, but why *was* Clancy helping him?

Something in his friend's expression, the anguish in his eyes was confusing, as he continued. "You need to keep things low-key, status quo. Slip in beneath her radar. If you push too hard, she'll erect a wall around herself so high and thick you'll never penetrate it. Then we'll both lose her."

Both lose her? What the hell was he talking about? Wade moved out from between his truck and the door. "Care to tell me what that means?"

Silence lingered as Clancy thought hard about his next words. "There's things about her you don't know." The intensity in his stare made Wade uneasy.

Pain? Anger? Love? What the hell was going on here? White-hot jealousy took hold of him but he held onto it, barely.

"It's not my place to share her history. Let's just say I'm her friend—your friend. I want to see her settled, happy. But—" Clancy's stare hardened even more. "Hurt her and I'll have your hide pinned above my fireplace." The firmness in his voice made every word believable. Clearly he loved Jessie, but not like a man looking for forever—a wife—not like Wade.

He hadn't expected this streak of luck. Clancy was willing

to help him. "So what do you propose?"

The man squared his hat back on his head. "I'll make the excuse why Trevor isn't joining us. Then, buddy, it's in your hands. We'll play this one by your rules. But let me warn you, the minute you exclude me—she'll bolt. I'm her safety net if you haven't noticed. Until she trusts you implicitly, she needs me. Hell. What am I saying? I need her." There was something haunting—lonely in his words. "I only wish I was in your boots." As if he realized the melancholy he'd slipped into, a grin tugged at his mouth, the smile not reaching his eyes. "Besides I enjoy the ride. There isn't anyone like our Jessie."

Wade knew Clancy's new façade was to hide something. He just didn't know what.

&#8451;

Gravel popped beneath Wade's boots. Each step filled him with uncertainty as he slipped his keys into his jean pocket. Jessie hadn't been happy to see him earlier today. Not exactly a good sign. An even worse one to know she was looking forward to a foursome tonight which he'd put a kink into.

Something had snapped inside him when she had said, "Always wondered what it would be like with three men," and then she reminded him that she called the shots. He had to get out of there before he said something he would regret. There was no way he could share her with Trevor—no way would he allow another man other than Clancy to touch her. Just the thought made him sick to his stomach, creating so much turmoil inside him he couldn't think. He crammed his hands into his leather jacket and took a calming breath.

Clancy was right. Jessie wasn't the type of woman to be manipulated or forced. She knew what she wanted. Maybe that was why Wade loved her. She was strong, independent. Not to mention a hell-cat in bed.

A smile raised the corner of his lips. Damn woman turned him every which way but loose. She consumed his mind—his body.

The memory of her face flushed with fulfillment when she had jerked open her office door made his groin tighten. The scent of sex, her feminine musk, had given her away. Just the thought of her pleasuring herself, touching and stroking her pussy, had made him hard, like now. His thighs brushed his testicles, causing a mild throb as he stepped on the sidewalk.

Gray moonlight and a dusting of stars peeking through rain clouds lit his way to the front door of Clancy's Spanish manor. The house sat on two-thousand acres of prime land. A slight breeze feathered across the back of his neck, teasing the tendrils showing from beneath his Stetson. Some people would die for a place like this, but Clancy and his mother, Theresa, had paid dearly.

Larry Wiseman had been a sonofabitch.

Wade had been young, more involved with being a boy while Clancy had been focused on saving his mother and his own life. On more than one occasion he had seen bluish-black fingerprints around Clancy's neck and the bruises covering his body when they had changed for gym. Another time he had heard his mother speaking to his dad about Clancy's mother. She was in the hospital again, beaten and bruised. The next thing he knew Mrs. Wiseman had disappeared. The scuttlebutt was that a women's group had helped her escape.

The thought of the man striking his wife and child made Wade's skin crawl. His own father had never raised a hand to his mother. It was just the opposite. His father idolized her. Wade had no doubt he would treat his wife—Jessie—the same.

Yet there was no denying his tastes ran a little kinky. He was into rough sex, a little bondage and domination, as long as his partner was willing. He enjoyed the game of give and take—enjoyed the illusion of power and force. Yet respect and safety was always present in his scenes. Inflicting pain for the sake of cruelty was unthinkable.

Wade stomped his feet, shaking off the mud that rimmed his boots, before he reached for the door he knew would be unlocked and opened it. The scent of pine burning in the huge stone fireplace caressed his nose. His gaze slid over the elegant residence bathed in shadows. Leather and dark wood furnishings marked the home a male's dwelling. Western art and sculptures reeked of money, the same money that had saved Larry Wiseman from jail, time after time.

A day after Clancy's mother left, his father, in a drunken rage, had hopped up on a Brahma. It was Larry's last ride and Clancy's salvation. He was fourteen, parentless, when an uncle stepped in and finished raising him.

Walking down the familiar hallway, Wade thought of how Clancy's childhood had been so different from his. He had a loving mother and father, two older brothers and a younger sister. The ties between them as a family were strong. There wasn't anything he wouldn't do for either of them. Perhaps that's why they worked the ranch so successfully together. It made building a place of his own and moving out even harder, but all he could think of was being alone with Jessie.

Wade stood before Clancy's bedroom door, realizing he knew very little about Jessie's childhood. It didn't really surprise him. She had always been a private person—Clancy her only confidant.

Wade curled his fingers into fists and then spread them wide before shaking them. Damn. He was nervous. Wrapping his fingers around the doorknob, he twisted and pushed. The air in his lungs caught at the sight before him.

He hadn't known what to expect or how Jessie would receive him. This was more than he could have dreamed of. In the middle of the room, she was bound and blindfolded. Her wrists circled with rope that hung from D-rings in the ceiling. The sexiest fur-lined domino hid her eyes. But it was the black leather corset with red stitching that made his hungry gaze skim down her lithe body to the fur-lined thong that matched her mask. Long legs met his eyes as he breathed in the sight of the three-inch stilettos she wore.

An ache pulsed in his groin. The tightening welcome as he started to speak, but was stopped when Clancy placed his finger to his lips, shaking his head. He mouthed, "*Shhh...*"

So this was how they were going to play. By the gleam of Clancy's eyes and his insistence that Wade remain quiet, he knew Jessie was expecting Trevor, not him.


As the door creaked open and the click of boots sounded upon the wooden floor, Jessie's senses jumped into high alert mode. In the darkness that surrounded her, she strained to use her sense of hearing and smell to detect the subtle differences in the room. She inhaled deeply, catching the scent of sandalwood, the same cologne that Wade wore, mixing with a hint of citrus aftershave that Clancy had used this evening.

That's all she needed, one more thing to remind her of Wade, the man she really wanted to touch and caress her body. A shiver of disappointment raked through her.

To the left Clancy shuffled his bare feet. Earlier, when he'd secured her wrists, he had been wearing a pair of black satin pajama bottoms. He had kissed her softly before slipping the mask over her eyes, but she had caught a glimpse of his mischievous grin. If she didn't know better, Jessie would say he was up to something. She knew he was worried about her. This entire session was his way of pulling her out of the depression she had fallen into. With a little luck his cousin would be just what the doctor ordered.

The moan of the heater kicking on and the brush of warm air caught her attention for a second, reminding her of the chill that filled the room. Of course, it was probably the way she was dressed or perhaps it was the fact she was bound and blindfolded in the middle of Clancy's bedroom awaiting a stranger's touch. Like always, it had been her choice. She set the rules, defined the boundaries, before handing over control to her partners.

Jessie wielded her sensuality like a weapon, enjoying the dominance she held. Although she was the one tied up, she called the shots. Yet recently she had discovered that control was a figment of her imagination. She had Wade to thank for that revelation. With just a touch, he could melt her body into a pool of sensations. He carried her to places she hadn't dared traverse—made her want more.

*Dammit. Forget about him.*

Who was she kidding? All this was a mind game—an illusion. The blindfold might hide the truth that she was hesitant about this new arrangement, but it wouldn't turn Trevor into Wade.

Feeling a little weak-kneed, she wedged her legs apart to steady herself. The corset she had purchased with Wade in mind hugged her ribcage like a second skin. The red lacing meant to show off her curves and small waist. She had arranged her hair atop her head, allowing ringlets to curl down her neck. She loved the sexy slide of fur against her skin. She just wished Wade could have seen the outfit.

When Clancy and Trevor's steps grew nearer, anxiety slithered up her spine. She resisted the urge to wet her lips, her mouth suddenly dry. Instead, she gripped the silk rope and held on, trying to relax, but it was a worthless attempt. When all movement in the bedroom paused the breath in her lungs froze.

What was wrong with her? A night of unbridled passion should have excited her. It offered her a release from the tension she'd felt this past week. Yet she couldn't quite put her finger on it—something wasn't right.

Fact was she didn't have the energy to pretend to enjoy Trevor's caress when there was only one cowboy she wanted.

A wave of anger engulfed her. Damn Wade Peterson for confusing her—making her want him. She tried to push him from her mind. When that didn't work, she focused on the silence which only served to irritate her more.

Forget him.

With a lack of patience, she opened her mouth ready to say, "Let's get this show on the road," when a finger pressed against her lips.

"Not a word or you'll be punished," Clancy murmured in her ear as his palm smoothed down her arm. It was out of character for him to play-threaten her. He was always so gentle with her. That's why when he slapped her ass hard she let out a squeal of surprise. "Tsk, tsk. What a shame," he teased. "Do you want to do the honors?"

Trevor didn't speak, but she heard him move away and soon she heard the crack of a whip. Apprehension skittered over her skin. Not everyone could handle a whip. There was an art to making it sing through the air and sting, but not cut. A wild flick too close to the kidneys—

A shudder quaked through her. "Clancy, I—"

"Hush, babe. You trust me?"

She didn't hesitate. "Yes. But—"

"He knows what he's doing. Relax."

Easy for him to say. She didn't know much about Trevor. He seemed a little young, a little cocky—

*Crack!* When the first butterfly kiss touched the cheek of her ass, all thoughts of his inexperience dissolved. Not many people could wield the whip with such control. Of course, it could have been a lucky hit. The following feather-light caress to her other cheek made her release a sigh of relief. He knew what he was doing. In fact, she knew only one other person as skilled.

But it wasn't until the tip of the whip teased the sweet-spot where her thigh and butt met that she let herself enjoy the sting. She loved when Wade stroked that area with his whip. He called it her love spot because it did wicked things to her body, like sending chills of delight through her, making her nipples tighten and rays of sensation fill her breasts. She couldn't help the moan that spilled from her mouth as he nipped the area once more.

"Do you like that, baby?" Clancy asked as she felt a tug on the lacings of her corset. Cool air drew her nipples into taut nubs.

"Yes," she breathed. It was silly, but she prayed Trevor wouldn't speak, wouldn't break the spell falling over her. With her eyes blindfolded, the experienced way he handled the whip, she could almost believe it was Wade. The thought should have upset her, but instead she found herself wanting more— wanting Wade.

Moisture dampened her thighs. A pinch developed low in her belly.

Little by little the lashes grew in strength. Each sting

lingering longer before the next one fell. When one particularly strong one wrapped around her thigh, she arched, her breasts spilling out into Clancy's waiting palms as the corset slipped to the floor. She leaned into his caress.

"You're gorgeous." Clancy kneaded her breasts, his fingers plucking at her nipples. "Come take a look."

Jessie heard the whip fall, striking the floor with a thud as the pad of booted feet approached. Her anxiety soared, but she had to admit there was something wicked about being blindfolded, held in Clancy's hands, while another man stared at her exposed breasts. A quiver raced through her when a warm, wet tongue slid across her sensitive nipple. Cool air danced around the moist flesh as that same tongue flicked several times across it, teasingly. The rim of a cowboy hat pressed into her chest—this was Trevor. He had the same close-cut beard and mustache that Wade had, while Clancy was clean shaven. Jessie pulled in a sharp breath when he dipped his head and began to suck, pulling gently at first and then firmly.

When Clancy circled his tongue around a nipple and then began to suck, Jessie yanked against her bindings. She needed to touch them, to hold them close and feel her fingers slide through their hair.

Trevor nipped her sensitive nub, causing her to cry out at the pleasure-pain. Wade had teased her in such a way while Clancy did just the opposite, his touch gentle and cherishing—but not tonight. Her pussy clenched, excitement taking hold of her as Trevor scraped his teeth, tugging on her nipple.

Jessie loved her breasts to be fondled. The stimulation sent shards of heat to explode between her thighs. She tightened her inner muscles. Arched into their caresses and begged they would never release her, but all too soon they did just that, leaving her unfilled.

116

The silence that followed raised her anxiety and anticipation.

When cold sharp steel touched her skin, Jessie startled. The prickles of a spur began a path from the swell of her breast trailing to the tip of her nipple, goose bumps rising in the wake of the spur.

Clancy had coached Trevor well.

This was exactly how Wade would have pleasured her. Clancy knew she loved the jingle and feel of Wade's Mexican spurs against her flesh. The way the long metal spikes bit into her skin made every nerve ending come alive.

Within seconds, both spurs were moving across her flesh, tossing her into a maelstrom of emotions. Alternating light and then harder, they kept her guessing where on her body the spurs would appear next. Every touch of the cold steel built her arousal. Pleasure tipped with pain cascaded through her bound body as her mind followed the prickly sensation down her midriff to her mound. She held her breath waiting for the spikes to trail over the pulsing flesh between her thighs when firm lips brushed hers and then kissed her earnestly.

She purred and leaned in for a taste. This had to be Trevor, Clancy never demanded, never took without asking. Only Wade demanded taking what he wanted. Trevor forced his tongue between her lips to devour her mouth. God... He and Wade shared the same taste, down to the hint of whiskey on his breath. If she didn't know better she would swear it was Wade, but it couldn't be. It was just her imagination—her need to lose herself in his arms.

When he threaded his fingers through her hair, grasped the nape of her neck, tipping her head back to take control and forcing her to take him deeper, Jessie knew who held her in his arms.

# Chapter Three

Blindfolded, with her wrists bound by a rope hanging from the ceiling, Jessie stood before Wade. He captured her moan as he deepened their kiss. Did she have any idea what she did to him? His stomach felt like a stampede had passed through it. His heart pounded. His cock was hard as rock, waiting for the moment to part her tender folds. The shot of whiskey he'd had an hour earlier did nothing to calm him. He wanted this woman with a passion that went beyond normal. But normal was exactly what he wanted. He wanted her as his wife. He wanted her working beside him, maybe even heavy with his child—a little girl that looked like her or a boy that would shine in his image.

He silently cursed her for making him lose his self-restraint. He was weak when it came to her. His fingers clenched, grasping her hair and pulling her head back farther to ravish her mouth with his.

She feverishly returned his kiss, nipping his bottom lip before delving her tongue within. She pressed into his body, her sweet powdery scent wrapping around him like arms. Her ardor was both arousing and maddening. For all she knew he was Trevor. A fact that had him abruptly releasing her and staggering backwards.

Wade pulled in a strangled breath and fought to gain

control of his emotions, jealousy at the top of the list. Damn the fur-lined domino that hid the truth of his identity from her. He wanted her kiss to be for him and him alone.

Jessie looked downright sinful in nothing but stilettos and a thong, while he was fully dressed. Hell. He still had his hat on. Her firm breasts rose and fell rapidly. She was aroused, which only served to piss him off more.

Was it his touch or the fact that a she thought someone else kissed her?

Her tongue slid sensually along her bottom lip, tasting and teasing. "More," she purred.

He wanted to give her more, but not until he could control the situation. Right now he wasn't sure that was possible.

He silently cursed her once again.

Clancy stepped forward and took over where he had left off, pressing his mouth against hers. To Wade's relief, she didn't kiss Clancy with the fervency she had him, or maybe he was fooling himself. Seeing what he wanted to see. It didn't matter. Tonight he would make love to her until she wanted no other man.

With haste he began to undress, boots first. He unfastened the cuffs of his long-sleeve western shirt, before fumbling with the buttons down his chest. It was killing him to watch Clancy and Jessie as he gave his shirt a fling across the thick bedposts of the knotty pine bed. As he jerked down his jeans and skivvies the fire burning low in the flagstone fireplace was warm on his skin.

Much to Wade's surprise, on top of one of the nightstands by the bed lay a variety of items: condoms, lubricant, a small bottle of lotion, nipple clamps, a flogger, a bucket of ice and a heating pad. His friend had done well setting the scene. Wade knew exactly what to do with the heating pad as he buried his hands into it. When Clancy joined him he plunged his hands into the ice and grinned.

Temperature just right they extracted their hands. Together they strolled over to Jessie, both of them kneeling before her. Wade mouthed, "One, two." On three they each reached out and placed their palms on each of her breasts.

She sucked in a breath. "OhmyGod, that's amazing." Immediately her skin prickled. A tremor assailed her. "Touch me—all over."

That's what he loved about her. She knew what she wanted. There was no pretense behind closed doors. The woman loved sex, the kinkier, the better. Without delay, they did just what she asked.

Clancy took her left side, Wade her right. They started at her neck, smoothing over her shoulders and down each arm and back up before paying special attention to her breasts again. Moisture glistened everywhere Clancy touched, wet and cold, while Wade heated her skin to a rosy pink. She leaned into their palms. Her lips slightly parted as she savored the hot and cold sensations.

They left her for only a moment to sink their hands back into the ice and heating pad.

"More," she moaned, encouraging them to explore her body.

Wade and Clancy approached. Each of her inhales was breathy. Her sexy body called to them. She gasped as four hands, two cold—two hot, caressed down her ribcage toward her back.

Clancy slipped a finger beneath the elastic of her thong and Wade did the same on the other side. They slid the material down her slender legs, past her stilettos. Wade tossed the thong aside before he settled his palms on the taut globes of her ass.

"Yes," she hissed, squirming when Clancy joined him.

"Touch me more."

Wade knew what she wanted as he ran a finger between the crease of her ass and between her thighs. Wet and slick. Just how he liked her. He cupped her pussy, allowing the heat of his hands to warm her, removing his hands only to allow Clancy to cool her off. It wasn't long before the temperature faded again and they were left to their own devices.

As Clancy made his way back to the table, Wade knelt before her. Raising one of her legs, he placed it over his shoulder, and then he leaned forward to sample her nectar.

The second his tongue smoothed across her tender folds she released a whimper. The soft cry nearly undid him as he lapped at her juices, savoring her feminine musk. He blew on her moist folds and she inhaled sharply. Several times he flicked her clit with his tongue and relished the way her body jerked.

Fuck. His cock was so hard that his balls ached. Yet he wouldn't take her now. Instead he wrapped his tongue around her swollen nub and sucked.

"God. Yes," she groaned, grinding her sex against his face.

He shook his head rapidly as he devoured her. Her sweet scent all over him was provocative and damn right hot. With his hands, he cupped her ass, held her immobile as he lapped at her folds, stabbing his tongue inside her again and again.

A sharp hiss squeezed through her teeth. He glanced up to see Clancy circling her nipples with ice cubes, alternating from cold to hot when he applied his mouth to each taut peak.

She bucked against his face. Her clit throbbed against his tongue, anointing him with her juices. She tensed, her inner muscles squeezing, preparing her body to orgasm. But it wasn't time—not yet.

Wade moved up her lithe frame while Clancy stepped aside,

allowing him to kiss a path up her abdomen, the valley of her breasts, her neck, before he captured her lips. Not gently, but with a need that bordered on hunger.

She moaned against his mouth. He nipped her bottom lip and she cried out. They were both breathing hard as he slanted his head and deepened the caress.

She tasted so good.

Over and over, he plunged his tongue between her lips. His fingers fisted her hair, tightened in his frenzy.

Damn. He needed to fuck her. Prove to her that she belonged to him.

Positioning his hips, he thrust, nestling his raging hard-on between her thighs. With the right angle he could be cradled in her warmth, but the fact he didn't wear a condom stopped him.

When they parted on a breath, Jessie murmured, "Fuck me." She inhaled sharply. "I need your cocks in me, now." Her body was trembling as she gripped the rope like it was a lifeline. Evidently, she needed them badly because her next words came out on a growl. "Dammit, Wade. Don't tease me any longer."

He and Clancy shared a startled glance. She knew all along it was him, not Trevor. Tender emotion tightened Wade's chest.

"Condom," he muttered, making haste toward the table. His hands were shaking as he rolled the latex on his pulsing shaft.

Her kisses had been for him. Whether the woman wanted to admit it or not, she had feelings for him.

In seconds he stood before Jessie, while Clancy took her back. Her lips parted on a sigh as he prepared her rear entrance to accept him. Her breasts were full, nipples tight and erect, and her lips were kiss-swollen. Wade licked the tender area of her throat where her pulse beat wildly.

"I've missed you," he whispered against her skin. The words

had slipped out. He hadn't truly realized how much he had missed her until this moment. This was the woman he whose arms he wanted to wake up in each morning.

With a bend of his knees, he looped his arms behind her knees and raised her so that she locked her legs around his waist. A slight angle of his hips and his cock breached the opening of her body, sliding into warmth—heaven.

She gasped.

"So fuckin' good," he murmured.

Hot and wet and welcoming, she sheathed him completely.

Securing her with one hand, he used the other to remove the mask from her face. "Look at me." He needed her to know exactly who was taking her body and hopefully stealing her heart.

Jessie squinted against the light in the room. She was finding it difficult to clear her vision when her head felt so foggy. The flames of desire continued to dance across her skin. Her heart raced erratically. She needed her hands free to embrace Wade, hold him close.

No.

She needed to come. That was all it was. But she knew differently when her gaze met his.

The man had no right to be so devastatingly handsome. She needed something to help her resist the lust simmering in his dark eyes. With each minute that passed, she felt herself losing control.

"Clancy," she managed to say before adding, "Now."

Sweet pain exploded at her rear entrance. It burned, making her catch her breath on a cry. Inch by inch, he stretched her wider, carefully pushing deeper. She closed her eyes, breaking the connection with Wade, choosing instead to experience the physical rather than the emotional.

When Clancy was seated inside her, both men began to move. Strong hands gripped her. Skin against skin, their bodies, slick from perspiration, moved in unison. This is what she needed—craved—as the muscles in her belly clenched.

"Tight," Clancy growled against her ear. "Damn, Wade. She's so tight."

Wade buried his head against her shoulder. She could feel a tremor shake him. He acted as if he was on the brink of climaxing. Something was wrong. He always outlasted both her and Clancy.

"Jessie." Her name was a cry upon his lips as his fingers dug into her waist. He slammed his hips into her hard, striking a sensitive chord that sent shudders through her. Before she could recover, Clancy ground his hips forward.

It was too much.

Stars burst behind her eyelids as she relished the sensation of two cocks pumping in and out of her.

She couldn't breathe, didn't try.

The tingle inside her pussy grew into contractions, squeezing harder and harder until her body splintered. She laid back her head and screamed as she came apart in their arms.

Fingers of electricity raced in all directions throughout her. Her heart felt as if it might jump from her chest. Wade's name was on the tip of her tongue, but she held back releasing it, managing a muffled sob instead.

Clancy's balls slapped against her ass, once, twice, before he buried his cock deep inside her so there wasn't a lick of space between them. A resonating moan accompanied his orgasm. Wade followed on their heels, throwing back his head, releasing a low growl as he went rigid. Their cocks jerked several times and then stilled.

Jessie leaned back into Clancy, resting her head on his shoulder, needing the safety he offered. With him she didn't have to worry about losing herself.

He kissed her softly on the cheek. "Damn, baby, you were good tonight."

She chuckled. "You weren't too bad yourself."

"Did you forget about me?" Wade's whiskey-smooth voice slid over her like silk across glass. He had yet to release her, her legs still locked around his waist. His now semi-hard cock still buried inside her.

Her eyelids slid open to meet the intensity in his. "Never." It was too late to retract it, especially since it was the truth. She could never forget him and that was the problem.

When she had determined it was Wade who kissed her and not Trevor, she should have called a stop to the night, but couldn't. She should also leave now before it went any further. She raised her head from Clancy's shoulder and opened her mouth to speak, but was interrupted when Wade pressed his lips to hers.

There was something different this time. A tenderness he had never touched within her. He moved his mouth across hers, gliding his tongue along the seam of her lips, tempting her to open to his caress.

Jessie was helpless to deny him.

When her lips parted, he dipped inside to taste her. He held her almost as if she were fragile and feared she would crumble in his arms with any pressure. So enraptured in the kiss she barely noticed Clancy extract himself from her. In seconds her wrists were free, arms wrapped around Wade.

He continued to kiss her as he moved toward the bed. She felt the mattress's softness beneath her, then his weight pushing her farther into its depths. Between her legs she felt his cock stir, hardening and lengthening. Slowly he began to thrust.

The moment was poignant as he released her lips and stared into her eyes. They were pools of heartfelt emotion. She wanted to look away—needed to break the spell he was casting over her, but she couldn't. He touched his nose to hers, rubbing it softly against her skin. Lightly, he drew his lips over hers, never releasing her from his enchantment.

Her breasts were swollen, heavy. Her sensitive nipples scraped back and forth against his chest as he moved. Small spasms ignited low in her belly. The unexpected orgasm struck without warning or mercy. Fire lanced through her pussy, tearing her back off the bed.

"Keep your eyes open." His voice was gravelly, strained.

The expression on his face was so profound it captivated her—trapped her completely within his gaze. Unable to hold back, a cry of pure ecstasy ripped from her very soul. She held onto him as if her very existence demanded it.

As her body milked his cock, a vein in his forehead bulged. His jaw clenched. A rumbling began deep in his throat. He thrust one more time, holding his body tight to her cradle. Pain and pleasure filtered across his face, and then he groaned low and deep with his release.

They panted in time with each other, their heartbeats melting into one. When he carefully rolled over to his side, he carried her with him. He snuggled into her, making her feel vulnerable and on the verge of tears.

What?

She didn't cry—she never cried.

Without a word, she pushed out of his arms. Her gaze quickly scanned the room looking for Clancy, her anchor in this trio. The one man she trusted to keep this arrangement from getting too intimate, but he was nowhere to be found. A tight whimper pushed from her mouth as she scrambled to her feet.

"Jessie?"

*Breathe. Just take a breath.* When she felt strong enough, she turned around to face Wade. He had moved to the edge of the bed, removed and disposed of his spent condom in a wastebasket next to the bed, and then he rose.

Jessie forced an uneasy chuckle. "Looks like we lost our threesome." She shrugged. "Sorry about that."

"I'm not," he said, walking toward her.

*Please. Please don't come any closer.*

She was holding on by a thread. The wrong move or word and she'd lose it. It took all the strength she had not to run to the door as she turned to leave. A hand around her arm stopped her. His touch made a knot form in her throat.

"Jessie?" He turned her around, cupped her face in his palms, and forced her to look into his eyes. She didn't like the raw emotion she saw or the silence that lingered between them.

Jessie shot a glance toward the clock on the mantel that said it was eleven o'clock. "Damn it's late." She placed her palm on his chest. Muscle rippled beneath her touch as she gave him a push, placing distance between them. If he tried to talk, to kiss her, she didn't know what she'd do. "I have a crapload of things I need to do tomorrow." She leaned in and gave him a friendly peck on the cheek. "See ya around."

This time when she pulled away, he let her go.

Her heart was pounding in her ears as she pulled open the door and walked through it. How she made it down the hall and to the bedroom where she had undressed, she didn't know. Her clothes were lying across the bed where she'd left them. She didn't waste any time getting dressed. Her hands were shaking so badly she was barely able to button her shirt. The jeans went on a little more smoothly, but she didn't even attempt slipping her boots on. Instead, she gathered them in her arms along with her purse and headed for the door.

Midway down the hall she ran into Clancy. "You sonofabitch." She pushed past him without another word.

"Jessie?" He chased after her, moving in front of her so that she was forced to stop. "He loves you."

Her eyebrows shot up as an indelicate snort slipped from her mouth. "Love? What the fuck do you know about love?" She was trembling. Jessie hated losing control like this, but who the hell did he think he was?

Clancy ran his palms up her arms. She ignored the sadness in his eyes. "I just want you to be happy."

"Who died and left you the fairy of happiness? Besides, I don't see you running to the altar. It's just the opposite. Any woman gets too close and you're down the road. *God*," Jessie huffed. "You're such a hypocrite."

His hands dropped away. His backbone went straight. "We're not the same."

"You're wrong," she snapped. "We're exactly the same. Now get the hell out of my way." He stepped aside, and she stomped down the hall.

By the time she made it to her truck, she was a mass of emotions. Anger. Resentment. And strangely she felt grief. Tears stung her eyes, but not one fell. She felt as dry as a desert inside.

Clancy had betrayed her—she should have known it was only a matter of time.

# Chapter Four

"Looks like I screwed the pooch on that one," Clancy grumbled as Wade stepped into the hallway fully dressed, holding his Stetson in his hand. His friend was barefooted, sporting his satin pajama bottoms.

"What happened to make her so leery of commitment?" For that matter, what was up with Clancy? Wade had heard Jessie's outburst. Knew she regretted spending time alone with him. It hurt, but at the same time he would have sworn the moment had meant as much to her as it had him.

"Every man that she's ever known has betrayed her, including me." Sorrow glistened in Clancy's eyes as he pinched his nose. "I should have known better. She wasn't ready." He released an uneasy spurt of laughter. "Here I warned you off from pushing too hard and I shoved her over the edge." He threaded his fingers through his hair. "Now I've lost her too."

Wade didn't want to hear the answer, but he had to ask the question. "Do you love her?"

"Love? Well, in that matter she's right. I don't know if I'm capable of loving someone. But I care deeply for her." He hesitated, and then continued, "Yeah. Maybe I do love her, but not in the way you do. She's been my rock—my friend." Wade heard the same sadness in Clancy's voice as when they spoke outside of the auction house. "Hell. Maybe I should go after her.

Talk to her."

Fuck. What a mess. It should be Wade going after her, not Clancy. Yet, Wade was the reason she had stormed out of there. All because he wanted to love her—take care of her.

Whoa.

He needed to get that thought out of his head. He'd lose her in a heartbeat if he tried to strip her independence from her. No. If he wanted to win her heart, he had to be smart. He had to push aside the primitive need to protect and own her.

Wade set his hat upon his head and slid his fingers along the rim. "Wait until morning," he suggested. "Maybe she'll be more receptive to your call." He doubted it, but stranger things had happened.

"I could use a drink. How about you?" Clancy asked. His sallow expression began to gain strength. "On second thought, why don't we haul ass to Buffalo Bill's and get shit-faced?"

That sounded like as good a plan as any to Wade. Besides his mind was working overtime, he needed a diversion. "You're on."

Two and a half hours and a bottle of whiskey later both Clancy and Wade were stumbling out of his truck. Wade took one step and tripped over the curb to land hard upon Jessie's lawn. It was damp from the earlier rain, now seeping through his jeans and shirt. As he lay there trying to get his bearings, he had enough sense to wonder if visiting her so late at night was a smart idea.

Clancy staggered over to him and extended him a hand. "Need a hand?" But when he bent over, he lost his balance, barely missing Wade as he joined him sprawled upon the ground. He lay there motionless. "Fuck. I'm wasted. How about you?" he slurred.

Wade rolled over to his back, staring into the cloudy sky. "Yep." He patted the ground, looking for his hat that was nowhere to be found. It wouldn't be the first time he lost the sonofabitch. As he attempted to sit up, the world spun around him. He closed his eyes, willing the ride he was on to stop.

"*Jessie!*" Clancy yelled, just before he turned over and spilled his guts all over the grass.

The sour stench reached Wade's nose, making him queasy as he made it to his knees. He wasn't ready to attempt standing, so he crawled a few feet, hesitated and crawled some more. The cold settling into his now muddy and wet knees and palms seemed to sober him up some.

"Shit," Clancy groaned. "That woman is going to be the death of me." He hiccupped. "*Jessie!* Get your ass out here."

A dog barked as light spilled across the lawn. Jessie's door sprang open and there she was—an angel haloed in porch light. She looked so heavenly even with her palms plastered on her hips as her golden lab bounded past her.

Damn. Wade loved that woman. He was going to show her just how much. Unsteadily, he got to his feet. Apparently standing wasn't in the cards as he tripped over a hose, landing face first in a puddle of mud. Breathing restricted, sight nearly gone, he swiped blindly at his eyes as a long wet tongue bathed his face. He swung out at the dog, but missed, ending right back in the muck.

"Oh my God." In seconds Jessie was by his side. "Shoo, Jax." The dog jumped back and sat.

"*Jessie!*" Clancy hollered.

"Shut the hell up and get over here and help me." She tugged at Wade's arm, assisting him into a sitting position. He sputtered, trying to clear the gritty taste of mud from his mouth. Sweet laughter filled his ears.

"Look at you." A smile danced in her eyes. "Clancy, get over here and help me," she repeated over a shoulder, wiping Wade's face with the sleeve of her pajamas. Her touch was so gentle and caring. He thought for a moment of just lying there in her arms.

"What about me?" Clancy asked moving to his knees. "Sure. Run to him. Leave me here all alone." As he climbed to his feet, he rattled on, "Fine friend you are. Jessie, I don't feel well." He dropped to his knees, keeling over on his side.

"Crap. Clancy? Are you okay?" she asked Wade. Her gaze went toward Clancy, concern pulled her brows together.

Wade wanted to say no, but instead he said, "Yes." He liked having her attention. But Clancy wasn't moving, while his head was beginning to clear—well, maybe not clear. He was in better condition than their friend.

Jessie stood and moved quickly to Clancy's side. "You big baby." She knelt, giving him a shake. He moaned. "Come on." It didn't appear to be an easy feat, but she helped him to his feet, wrapping an arm around his waist.

"Are you still mad at me?" His rubbery legs almost took both of them back to the ground, but Jessie held on, counterbalancing his weight. "Please don't be mad."

She shook her head. "What am I going to do with you?" There was a hint of amusement in her voice.

"Take me inside and fuck me."

Funny, but Wade had the same idea. Though he doubted either he or Clancy was in any condition to perform.

"Forget it. You smell like a distillery." She covered her nose with a palm. "Worse. Whad'ya do puke all over yourself?"

"Baby." There was a whine in Clancy's voice as he pulled them to a stop.

"Don't baby me. I ought to let you rot out here."

"But you won't."

"No. I won't. But it's tempting." Clancy leaned on her and she made a straining sound. "Wade, I'll be back for you."

As Wade fought to find his footing, he watched Jessie and Clancy disappear into the house. He had almost made it to his feet when the world began to spin again. Falling was the last thing he remembered before the lights went out.

Sprawled upon Jessie's lawn, Wade was out cold. What the hell happened to the two men after she left?

Duh.

It was obvious. They drank themselves into oblivion. The stench of whiskey was now all over her as she tugged on Wade's arm, trying to pull him into a sitting position. He was dead weight. There was no way she was moving him without help. In a last ditch effort, she gave him a shake. "Wake up, big guy. I need a little help here."

He stirred, mumbling something unintelligible, before throwing an arm around her to pull her close. She landed hard against his chest. The pajama top she wore hiked up, giving anyone in the vicinity a clear shot at her brand new thong, which meant her ass was glowing in the moonlight. Not to mention, the man was wet, muddy and cold which meant she was too.

"Wade." No response. She raised her voice. "*Wake up.*"

Heavy eyelids flickered open as a grin rose across his handsome but dirty face. "Hey you." He pulled her closer, rubbing his face against hers, smearing the gritty stuff all over her.

Jessie should have felt anger or at the very least put out with two drunken cowboys waking her up in the middle of the night. Instead, something squeezed her heart. "Hey," she said, coming to grips with the fact that when it came to this man she was a pushover.

A shiver raked her spine, the cold finally getting to her. Her teeth chattered and she snuggled closer to him.

Wade frowned. "Darlin', you're freezing." His gaze slid down her body, eyes widening when he saw her exposed bottom. "Where's your clothes?"

"Inside with my bed."

Perplexed he looked around taking in where they were. "Shit." He released her, embarrassment or frustration furrowing his brows. "Jessie, I'm sorry."

She crawled to her feet, pulling down her pajama top to cover herself. "Do you think you can get up if I help you?"

"Shit," he muttered, already attempting to stand. "Yeah."

With her help, he made it to his feet. He was unsteady, swayed into her a few times. Yet he seemed to be wide awake as they headed toward the house.

Propping him against the wall, Jessie opened the door and then helped him in. Clancy lay on the couch where he'd collapsed. She had tried to get him to the spare room, but didn't make it.

"Let's get you into the shower."

"Naw. I've imposed enough. Just show me to my truck." He tried to pull away, but she held on tightly.

She couldn't let him leave. "Get real. There's no way you can drive." What if he passed out or fell asleep at the wheel? Just the thought of him in an accident turned her stomach.

"Let's get you cleaned up and then you can leave in the morning." Slowly they made it to the bathroom. "Do you need help?"

*Please say no.*

He lowered his head. "I'll be fine." But as he crashed into the wall, she knew he wouldn't be. Even now she could picture him falling through the glass shower in her small bathroom. Besides, she was dirty too. It wasn't like they hadn't seen each other nude.

Wade refused to look at her as she helped him undress, pulling off his boots, smoothing her hands over firm muscle as she slipped his shirt over broad shoulders to reveal his chest.

Damn. The man was gorgeous.

He tried to help her remove his pants, but his instability nearly took both of them to the floor.

Jessie worked overtime not to let his nakedness affect her, but it did. She hungered for his touch—his kiss.

What was she thinking? God, it was true. The forbidden was exciting, drawing her like a magnet.

Easing him down onto the commode, she pulled her pajama top over her head, tossing it aside before she stepped out of her thong. The linoleum was cold beneath her numb feet as she reached into the shower and turned the water on.

"Jessie, I can do this myself." He used the counter to pull himself up, swaying with his first step.

She moved quickly to his side, snaking an arm around his waist, before she looked up at him. "You think I'm gonna let you use all the hot water? Not on your life, buddy. Now watch your step."

The floor of the shower was slippery from her earlier shower. To ensure he didn't fall she propped him against the wall. Using the backside of her body to keep him stationary, she leaned over and adjusted the water. Surprise filtered through her when she felt his cock stir, hardening. A perfect fit between her thighs.

The man was amazing. This intoxicated he shouldn't even be able to function, much less be up for a roll in the hay. She glanced back and caught him looking at her ass. He flashed a sheepish grin.

Jessie couldn't help the laughter that spilled forth. "Come on, cowboy."

Lord. The warm water beating on her skin felt good while it lasted. All too soon he moved between her and the spray.

"Close your eyes," she said.

He tilted his head, allowing the flow to rinse off the remaining mud from his face, while she grabbed a bar of soap. As he scrubbed his face, she soaped his backside, enjoying every minute. No one looked as good as he did in a pair of tight jeans or naked for that matter.

It wasn't any surprise that her nipples were hard peaks or that an ache had developed between her thighs. She moved in closer, running her palms beneath his arms and over his firm pecs. Slick. Strong. And all male.

He trapped her arms to his chest, pulling her closer. "Jessie."

She tried to jerk away. What was she thinking?

Without letting her go, he turned in her arms. "Honey, I'll never ask for more than you can give." He stared at her through bloodshot eyes. "Just don't lock me out of your life."

She swallowed the lump in her throat. If only it was true. "It's getting too complicated."

"It doesn't have to be. We have Clancy."

Clancy? The damn man had set her up—fed her to the lion. "I—"

"Don't make a decision tonight." He released her, caressing the back of his hand over her cheek. "Sleep on it. Things will look different in the morning. Now let me soap you down."

Jessie should have refused him. But when he took the bar from her, his hand smoothing suds down her arm, she closed her eyes. She had never showered with him and craved to know how it would feel.

*You're playing with fire, girl.*

But she didn't care. The odds were that he wouldn't remember anything in morning anyway.

His large palms cupped her neck, massaged her shoulders before soaping her hair. Instantly, she felt her muscles begin to relax. A gasp escaped her mouth when he stroked his hands down to her breasts and kneaded. Sharp, penetrating rays shot through her globes. She opened her eyes just to see him descending upon her lips.

He nibbled lightly, whispering against her mouth. "Fuck me."

"Wade—"

He kissed her silent. When they parted, he growled, "Now," gliding a finger down the crest of her ass. His touch clouded her senses, her resistance fleeting.

Yet she had the good sense to say, "Let me rinse the soap out of my hair. Go dry off. I'll be there in a minute."

As he stepped from the shower Jessie smiled a little giddily. But her happiness faded almost as it appeared.

So much for taking control of the situation.

"Fuck it. What's one night?" She quickly rinsed her hair and hurried from the shower. Pulling a towel from the rack, she dried off and then ran the towel over her hair several times.

As she left the bathroom, she thought of Clancy and padded across the floor to check on him. He was snoring softly, stretched out on the couch. She went to the linen closet and took out a blanket and pillow.

Standing before him, she leaned over and stuffed the pillow beneath his head and kissed his cheek. "Brat," she whispered before dragging the blanket over him. There was so much she adored about this man. Other than tonight, he had been a good friend. Hell, everyone screwed up. He was entitled to one.

Jessie looked toward her bedroom and her body heated with the thought of Wade in her bed. No man had slept there, not even Clancy. Her home was her sanctuary. The thought she was about to break one of her rules was suddenly frightening. She slid her bottom lip between her teeth.

*Coward*, her conscience taunted.

Yet she wasn't a coward. She took one step and then another, before long she stood before her bedroom door. Taking a breath of courage, she entered.

Her jaw dropped.

Wade was spread out on her bed sound asleep.

Relief and disappointment slammed into her all at once. He was a vision of heaven. Just as she had imagined him night after night, except he was awake and had that drop-dead gorgeous smile upon his face. Not once had she envisioned him passed out and snoring.

A heavy sigh pushed from her lungs as she walked to the bed. It wasn't meant to be. She pulled the comforter over him. How long she stared down at him, she didn't know, before she finally turned and walked out of the room toward the spare bedroom.

As Jessie slipped between the sheets, she never realized how a bed could feel so empty or lonely. She punched the pillow several times, then picked it up and threw it across the room.

# Chapter Five

The mother of all headaches had taken root just above Wade's eyebrows. Each step increased the pounding as he wrapped a silky white sheet around his hips and strolled out of the bedroom—Jessie's bedroom. Not a bad place to be since it had been his plan all along. The only dilemma was he couldn't remember what happened after the shower.

Did they make love or had he passed out? Now that would be embarrassing as hell.

He brushed a palm over his sleepy eyes before he looked around for his clothes. Like Jessie, her room revealed nothing. The typical things you would expect to find in a woman's room were absent, except for a brush, comb, and a bottle of perfume on her dresser. No family pictures hung on the walls painted a soft green. No evidence of a whimsical obsession like fairies, cats or dogs were present. That included his missing clothes.

The rich smell of coffee made him tip his nose to the air. The enticing aroma led him out of the bedroom, down the hall, through the small house and to the kitchen. He licked his lips. His mouth felt nasty, cottony. He could sure use a cup of java to wake him up.

When he stepped inside the small kitchen, Clancy and Jessie sat at the round, wooden table with cups in their hands. She blew the steam off her cup and took a sip, her eyes meeting his briefly. Over in the corner by the stove, her golden lab was fast asleep.

"Morning." Clancy grinned over his coffee.

"Morning," Wade said, trying to gauge Jessie's mood as she set her cup down on the table and rose.

As she passed by him, her feminine scent made him ache to reach out and take her into his arms. Had he let the opportunity of a lifetime slip through his fingers?

"Coffee?" She opened the cupboard and took a mug out.

"Sure." He glanced at the cat clock on the wall, watching the tail move back and forth as its eyes opened and shut. Eight o'clock. That meant he'd had all of what? Five hours of sleep. He had a full day at the ranch. There were fences to mend, cattle to brand, and a number of other things that needed his attention.

"Aspirin?" She already had the cap off the bottle, spilling two pills into her palm.

"Please." He met her halfway, taking both the coffee and relief she offered. She had yet to give him any hint of whether she was angry. He cleared his throat. "Jessie?"

On a heel, she spun around, moving back to the table to take a seat. "No need to apologize. Clancy has done enough for both of you. Just don't let it happen again."

Wade popped the aspirin in his mouth and took a drink. The hot liquid felt good against his throat. "My clothes?"

"Tumbling. I washed them this morning." Now that she mentioned it he could hear the thud and whirl of a dryer behind a door off the kitchen.

Clancy set his cup down. "You didn't wash my clothes."

"You passed out in yours," she countered.

"You could have stripped me naked." Clancy took another

141

sip of his coffee before he added, "I wouldn't have minded."

Jessie shook her head. "I bet you wouldn't have." But Wade saw the amusement in her eyes.

A knock on the door had the three of them turning their heads toward the entry to the front room. Jax stirred from where he lay.

She frowned. "Who could that be?"

As she rose, so did Clancy and Wade. Jax stood, wagging his tail as he followed on her heels. Wade tightened the sheet around his hips, leaning against the door jamb as she answered the door.

Jessie's backbone stiffened. Her hand dropped from the doorknob as she took a step backward. "What are you doing here?" Bitterness rang in her words.

"What? Can't a father visit his daughter?"

Father? Wade glanced down at the sheet riding low on his hips. Not exactly how he had anticipated meeting Jessie's old man.

"No," she said sharply, attempting to close the door, but thick fingers slipped into view holding the door open. "You're not welcome here." Jax growled and Jessie set her hand on his head.

"Ahhh... Jessica." Daniel Evans moved through the door, keeping an eye on the dog as he kept a safe distance between. "Don't be that way. We need to talk." He reached for her.

Jessie stumbled backward, almost falling to avoid his touch. "There's nothing to talk about."

Her father was a large man. As he took his Stetson off, Wade could see the resemblance between him and Jessie. Ebony hair, but his had gray threaded through. High cheekbones that denoted the Cherokee blood Wade remembered

Clancy mentioning. Wade couldn't remember ever meeting her father before, but by the looks of things, Evans had lived a rough life. Weathered skin, his face held a ruddiness that announced he hit the bottle more frequently than was healthy. Not to mention there appeared to be bad blood between father and daughter.

Evans tried once again to reach for her, but she dodged his touch. It was then that he noticed Clancy and Wade. "So the apple doesn't fall far from the tree."

"What are you insinuating?" she barked, hands flying to her hips. Jax moved closer to her. Protecting his owner, he snarled a warning.

The sonofabitch. Wade stepped forward to stand next to Jessie. "I'd thank you to have more respect for your daughter."

Clancy took her other side. "Or leave," he added. His face had turned stone-cold. There must have been some history between the two of them, because Clancy's hands were fisted, and there was a scowl on his face that announced he wanted a piece of the man.

Evans paused as if re-evaluating his position. "I didn't come here to fight. I need a place to stay for a couple of days."

An uneasy huff squeezed between Jessie's lips. "And you think you're welcome here?" Her tone rose in pitch. "You can get back on the horse you rode into town on and leave."

"Sweetheart—"

She jutted her flattened palm out to him. "Don't."

"Okay. Truth? I don't have any money. I can't hardly expect your sister to sleep in the truck."

Jessie's expression went blank. She turned sheet-white. "Sister?"

"Yeah." Evans smiled as if he were a proud papa. "She's six.

143

A pretty little thing." He shot Jessie a tender expression that Wade doubted was sincere. "Looks a lot like you."

"Sister?" she repeated. Suddenly her knees buckled. Thank God Wade was next to her. He wrapped an arm around her waist to steady her. She didn't refuse his assistance. In fact she leaned into him.

"I'll pay for a hotel," Clancy snarled, glaring at Evans. Wade had never seen his friend like this. Both Jessie and Clancy were acting out of character. The air was thick with hostility and animosity.

She stared at Clancy. For a moment she looked bewildered, speechless. As if her confidence and strength returned, she stepped out of Wade's embrace and leveled her gaze on Evans. It took her moment to find her voice. "No. Daniel Evans is my problem—not yours." She squared her shoulders. "Where is she?"

Evans attempted to hide his triumphant smile, but Wade saw a glimpse of it, so did Jessie. Lightning flashed in her eyes changing abruptly when he added, "She's outside."

"Outside?" Her voice strained. "In this weather?"

Through a part in the curtains Wade could see it was raining again. It was nothing like the storm that was brewing between these walls.

Jessie released a tight breath. "You haven't changed a lick." She paused only a second before she demanded, "Get her in here."

Evans moved to the door, opened it and hollered, "Shelby."

A dark-haired girl with big blue eyes just like Jessie's shuffled into the room. Her nose was red. Her hands pushed deep into a worn coat too big for her. Mud caked her dirty tennis shoes. She wiped the rain off her face with the back of one hand and eyed Jessie taking her measure. "This her?"

Jessie's gaze was pinned on the child.

"You'll mind your manners," Evans snapped.

Shelby turned toward him. "Sure, Dan."

"I told you not to call me that."

"Fine." There was a pregnant pause before she added, "Dan."

Evans's face turned red. He took a step toward the child, who raised her chin defiantly.

If the situation wasn't so serious, Wade would have chuckled. He could see the same stubborn streak in Shelby that was in her older sister.

Wade couldn't read Jessie's emotionless expression as she watched the interplay between her father and newfound sister. Until a breath shuddered through her and she blinked.

"Work. I gotta go. There's food in the fridge." Jessie shot another glance toward Shelby. She swallowed hard and put her feet in motion. Jerking her purse off the end table against the wall, she headed for the door like her jeans were on fire.

Wade started to follow when the sheet he was wearing began to slip. Shelby giggled as he grappled with the cloth. Frustrated he couldn't go after Jessie, he said, "Clancy?" His friend was already on it, the door slamming behind him.

"You live here?" There was an inquisitive look in Shelby's eyes well past the age of six. Evans leaned closer, curiosity shining on his face as he awaited Wade's answer.

When he stated, "No," Evans looked relieved.

"You stayed the night." Shelby's brows rose as if she dared him to challenge her observation.

No need to deny the obvious. "Yep. It was late."

She hummed, "Hmmm...Where'd you sleep?"

Okay. It was time to put an end to this line of questioning. "Well, shortcake, I need to get dressed and go to work myself." He moved toward the kitchen.

Shelby perked up taking a step toward him. "Can I go?"

He slowly turned around. Why on earth would a child ask to go with a stranger? The question bothered Wade more then he wanted to admit. From Jessie's reaction to seeing her father, Wade wondered if Shelby would be better off with him than her own father. "Can you ride a horse?"

Her shoulders drooped. "No."

"If your father doesn't mind, I guess there's no time like the present to learn."

A bright smile surfaced as she joined him in looking toward Evans for approval. He nodded. Wade didn't miss the expression of relief on the man's face.

"Give me a minute to get dressed." Wade remembered hearing the dryer off the kitchen so he headed in that direction. As he disappeared into the kitchen, he heard the front door open and close. He had just opened the door to the washroom when he heard Clancy enter the kitchen. Wade reached into the dryer before he looked askew at his friend. His expression was grim.

"How is she?" Wade extracted his shirt, skivvies and jeans.

"Moving like a bat out of hell. The sonofabitch," Clancy grumbled. "She wouldn't talk to me."

Wade's clothes were warm against his chest. "So what's going on here?" He stepped behind the laundry door to slip on his underwear before dragging his pants over his legs and hips.

Clancy immediately caught a case of lock-jaw. Nothing different from the many other times Wade had asked questions about Jessie. In the past he had let it go, but something wasn't right here. "I'll find out sooner or later."

"Not from me," Clancy said, moving toward the door. "Can I hitch a ride home?"

Frustrated, Wade crammed his arms into the sleeves of his shirt. "Yeah." The fresh scent of flowers met his nose. Great. He smelled like a fuckin' daisy. "Just so you know, Jessie's sister will be going with us. She is spending the day with me."

Clancy stopped in the doorway and pivoted. "Why?"

"She asked."

"No need to get chummy with her. They won't be staying long." Clancy's coldness was a little disconcerting. Yet no more words were exchanged between them as Wade walked past him to retrieve his boots and belt.

After locating them and putting them on, Wade, Clancy and Shelby strolled out to his truck. The vehicle had a six-inch lift, making the girl look small in comparison. Wade opened the door. She made an attempt to crawl up using the running boards.

When he scooped her into his arms to help her, she squealed, "I can do it." But he knew she couldn't. Ignoring her objection, he placed her on the front seat before releasing her.

Without being told, she scooted over to the center to make room for Clancy, flinching when Wade reached across her for the seat belt. As he dragged it across her lap, she silently watched him buckle her in.

Had she thought he was going to hit her?

Damn. He didn't want to scare the child. Moving quickly around the truck, he opened the door and crawled in behind the steering wheel as Clancy slipped inside.

As Wade turned the key and started the engine, Shelby asked, "Are you her boyfriend?" The child must be as curious about her sister as Jessie probably was of her.

"We're friends—all of us." Wade steered the truck out of the driveway. "Have been since high school." His words sounded a little awkward to him. Friends shared their thoughts with each other. Jessie shared nothing but her body.

Staring at the taillights ahead of him, he wondered at what moment his casual feelings toward her had changed. It didn't matter. What mattered was where they went from here. He wanted to know everything about her. The brief glimpse into her past he got today only made him curious to know more.

Clancy cleared his throat, obviously uncomfortable with the situation. "Where's your momma, Shelby?"

"Dead."

Wade jerked his attention off the road onto the child sitting beside him. She glanced up at him and there were no tears, no emotion—nothing. He had seen that look on Jessie's face when he had asked recently about her family and she'd responded, "I don't have any." He knew it wasn't true, but he hadn't wanted to pry.

"How?" Clancy asked.

She turned her head, staring blindly out the window before her. "Drugs."

Clancy's gaze jerked to Wade's. The chill he had worn seemed to melt as his grimace disappeared. He seemed to understand that the child's silence meant she didn't want to talk about her mother or anything.

Damn these so called parents who brought children into this world unwanted. A child, especially one so young, shouldn't know anything about drugs. When he had children his would be loved and protected. He'd fight the devil himself to ensure their safety.

As they pulled up in front of Clancy's house, Wade couldn't help wondering what kind of life the child next to him had lived. Was it her mother's death that thrust her into the arms of Evans?

Shelby's eyes widened, her small frame stretching to get a better look as Wade pulled the truck to a stop. "Is this your home?"

Clancy opened the door and stepped out. "Yep." He extended his hand to her and she shook it. "It was a pleasure meeting you. Thanks, Wade." He gave a push and the door shut tight.

A bounce was in Shelby's voice when she asked, "Is your house this big?"

Wade laughed, releasing his foot from the gas. "No. Not this big."

"How many horses do you have?" Apparently, she had found her voice and a topic that intrigued her.

"Last count over a hundred."

A multitude of questions followed one after the other. She was an endless well of curiosity. *Guess that's where the resemblance between her and her sister ended.* Wade remembered Jessie as more of a quiet girl. Reserved.

As he pulled in front of his parent's house, his mother waved from the porch. A breeze feathered back her short brown hair. Unlike many of her co-workers, she dressed casually. Today it was slacks, a baggy sweater and loafers. She always said the most important thing was to make people comfortable. If she wasn't comfortable, how could her clients be? His mother was a trauma counselor.

He cut the engine, got out of the truck, and moved around to assist Shelby. By the time her feet hit the ground, his mother was by their side perched on her toes and offering him her

149

cheek. He kissed her softly before gathering her up in his arms for a big bear hug.

When he released her, she dropped her gaze. "So who is this charming young lady?"

"This is Shelby, Jessica Evans's sister." Shelby didn't notice the slight lift of his mother's brow, but he did. "Shortcake, this is my mom, Madeline."

She tipped her chin up. "Hello."

His mother drifted to her knees, coming eye to eye with the child. "Well, hello to you." She glanced up at Wade. "Your girlfriends are getting a little young."

Shelby pinched her lips, frowning. "I'm not his girlfriend."

Madeline chuckled. "I know, sweetheart. You're too cute for this son of mine." She pushed to her feet. "You're just in time for breakfast. Are you hungry?"

Shelby eagerly wagged her head.

"Well then, why don't you come with me?" His mother offered the child her hand. Shelby looked at his mother's hand appraisingly.

What was going on in the girl's mind?

Madeline didn't force the issue, she waited quietly and patiently. That was his mother's style. She had a way with people, especially children. Before long Shelby reached out and took her hand.

"So where are you from, Miss Shelby?" his mother asked as they headed up the stairs.

"Tombstone."

"Arizona?"

Shelby nodded.

"Oh my. A place filled with history. Do you know who Wyatt

Earp was?"

Shelby shook her head.

His mother never ceased to amaze him. She was the calm in the storm. Always knowing the right things to say, making everyone relax and feel welcome. Plus her timing was impeccable. This was the chance he needed to call Jessie.

Jessie felt like her head was stuffed with cotton. She couldn't think clearly not to mention she hadn't realized her telephone was ringing until Dean ducked his head into her office and said, "You going to get that?"

She reached for the telephone misjudging its position and knocking it off the cradle. Fumbling with the receiver, she finally got a hold of it and pressed it to her ear. "Carmel Livestock Auction, Jessie."

"Hey, honey." The sound of Wade's deep voice wrapped around her like a coat. "You okay?"

"Sure." Her voice cracked, giving her away. "Of course," she said with a little more confidence she didn't feel.

Jessie knew she hadn't fool him when he asked, "Anything I can do?"

"Naw. I'm up to my knees and elbows in alligators here." She laughed, but there was no amusement in her tone. "Just busy."

"Tonight?" he asked.

"Maybe." For some reason moisture filled her eyes. She swallowed hard, jumping to her feet. "I gotta go." She slammed the telephone into its cradle without saying good-bye, choking back tears she refused to release as she headed for the door. Where this emotion was coming from Jessie couldn't fathom.

She didn't care about her father.

So what if he had another child?

Even as she tried to convince herself that she wasn't curious about Shelby or her mother, she couldn't help wondering how any woman in her right mind could hand over a child to Daniel Evans.

Had he hit Shelby? It didn't happen frequently with Jessie, but when her father was in a drunken rage and she got into his way—

Her hands began to tremble. She shook them rapidly, and then crammed them into her jean pockets.

What Dan Evans was best at was abandonment—never being there when a father/daughter event occurred or when she was scared. There was no one to protect her from her mother's boyfriends or husbands. The knot in Jessie's stomach tightened, acid burning her throat. No child should go through what she had.

For a moment she gazed around her office and then out the open door into the main office. Dean had returned to work. The sound of paper shuffling and the hum of the heater pulled her back to the problem at hand.

Why had she agreed to let her father stay at her home? *Dammit.* Why hadn't she slammed the door—sent the bastard on his way? But even as the thought entered her mind, she saw Shelby's big blue eyes—sad eyes Jessie had seen reflected in a mirror.

"Those days are gone," she stated firmly.

Dean jerked his head up, looking through strands of hair that covered his face. "What?"

She brushed him off with a swipe of her hand through the air. "Nothing." Her father couldn't hurt her. None of her mother's free-loaders could hurt her. No man would ever hurt her again, which included Wade.

A single tear bloomed and rolled down her cheek. She pulled a hand out of her jeans and swatted at the emotion, angry at her father, but more so with herself. Jessie couldn't believe she had allowed her father to reduce her into feeling like a child again.

"I'm in control," she said aloud.

Dean looked up again. "I know, boss."

"I— Uh... Forget it." She pulled other her hand out of her pocket and reached for the doorknob, slamming the door to the office.

The passage of time was like a ticking bomb to Jessie. She had never seen the hands on the clock move so quickly or perhaps the fact that an out-of-town rancher had showed up with his cattle two days early was to blame. Add the complication of two dead sheep leaving her dealing with an irate owner and the local veterinarian. By three o'clock she was climbing walls. She would have to go home, but not now.

Picking up the telephone, she hesitated. She wanted to call Wade, hear his voice, but she didn't. Instead, she punched in Clancy's telephone number. She offered no pleasantries. "I need you," was all she said, hating the desperation in her voice.

"Come on over, baby."

She dropped the telephone back into its cradle, grabbed her purse, and headed out the door.

# Chapter Six

The front door of Clancy's house sprang wide and Jessie walked in. Clancy started to speak, but she held her hand up. Wade could feel the tension that surrounded her in every rigid step, arms tight by her side. Her face was pale and drawn. Her eyes so intense there was a wildness about them.

Without a word, she walked over to Wade and placed her hands upon his chest. Jaws clenched, she sucked in a shaky breath as her fingers curled, gripping his shirt. Suddenly, she jerked in opposite directions. Material ripped and buttons flew pinging off the wooden floor. In less than a heartbeat, she was all over him, wrapping her arms around his neck, forcing his lips to hers.

Both Jessie and he liked sex rough, but there was something in her caress—something urgent and disconcerting.

Teeth clashed. Tongues met. She tugged desperately at his clothing, fingernails biting into his skin. When she encountered resistance from his buttoned cuffs, she released a strangled whimper that almost broke his heart. Jessie was hurting and there wasn't a thing he could do to ease her pain, except hold her. Even that was impossible now that he was tangled in his shirt.

"Jessie. Honey." He tried to break her hold, put distance between them. "Let's talk." But she wouldn't hear of it. "This

154

won't make things better."

"Fuck me. Hard," she choked, blinking her eyes as if she fought tears that weren't there.

Clancy came up behind her, wrapping his arms around her waist. "It's okay, baby."

She spun around, pushing Clancy so that both of them stumbled backward colliding with the wall. "Do it now. Please, Clancy." Her plea broke on a strangled breath as she trembled.

There was a brief moment when Clancy and Jessie's eyes met and something unspoken exchanged between them—an understanding that left Wade feeling like the third-wheel. Jealousy raised its ugly head when a growl rumbled in Clancy's throat. He jerked Jessie against him, moving his mouth hungrily over hers.

*You won't shut me out.*

Wade shrugged out of his shirt, moving to sandwich her between them. The second he laid his hands on her waist, she gasped, breaking their kiss and looking back so that their gazes met.

*Mine*, the thought whispered through Wade's mind. But there was more than just a possessiveness streaming through him. He needed her to want him. She was hurting and he wanted to be the man who comforted her, made her woes disappear.

Dammit. He loved her.

The thought took control of him as he smoothed his hands forward, pushing between Clancy and Jessie so that he could begin to unfasten her shirt. With each button that released, he bared her further, scenting the heat of her skin, soft and feminine. She cried out when he glided his palm over a breast, teasing a nipple through her satin bra. It thrilled him that his touch affected her in such a way. She truly was his woman.

155

Now if she would only realize it.

Leaning into him, she wiggled her ass against his growing erection, teasing him into action. With a tweak of his fingers her bra came loose.

As Clancy stepped away, Wade spun her around, pushing her against the wall. Her eyes were glassy, filled with lust and, sadly, pain as he continued to work on her shirt and bra. Clancy knelt between them to remove her boots. The wisp of her zipper sounded. In seconds they had her stripped.

"I need you naked," she moaned as Wade slid down her body and took a taut nipple into his mouth. He flattened his tongue against the hardened peak, flicking it several times before he began to suck. Clancy was beside him in a heartbeat giving her other breast the same attention. Jessie lolled her head back against the wall. Her eyelids closed as she weaved her fingers through their hair, cradling their heads to draw them against her.

"Touch me." An air of desperation rang in her tone. It was a plea that made something in Wade's chest knot. He knew no amount of lovin' would ease her suffering. Yet he would try anything just to see her anguish vanish.

Her thighs parted as his fingertips slid down her abdomen. When he encountered the small patch of hair at the juncture of her thighs, he gave the short-hairs a pull, forcing a moan from her lips. She flinched as he stroked her sensitive clit before he slipped his fingers between her swollen folds.

Jessie went wild. The slow pace he had begun wasn't what she wanted or needed. She thrust her hips back and forth violently against his hand—rode him hard and fast.

Blood slammed into his groin, filling his balls with a pressure bordering on pain. For a second he forgot to breathe. The sting of her fingernails across his back made him inhale sharply. Her urgency was driving as a catalyst. He needed to be inside her. Feel her warm sheath surround him.

When he removed his fingers, reaching for the button and zipper of his jeans, she mewled. Clancy pushed his hand between her thighs, taking over where Wade left off. He didn't even bother with his boots, pushing his jeans to his ankles.

Clancy was moving out of the way when Wade pulled Jessie to him. Their teeth clashed, tongues dueling as he kissed her roughly. When they parted, both were breathing heavily. With a twist, he turned her to face the wall so that she stood about two and a half feet away.

"Palms against the wall," he demanded. Wade knew what she wanted and he wanted it too.

The position forced her to bend at the waist, stretching her frame to give him a bird's eye view of her firm ass. She enjoyed a good spanking from time to time. He loved the way her ass grew hot and pink beneath his hand. He popped the cheek of her ass with his palm and she jumped, releasing a yelp. She was so damn sexy, her dark hair cascading over her shoulder as she turned and stared at him. Her eyes glistened beneath eyelids drawn half-mast. He pulled his attention back to her ass, watching the imprint of his hand rise against her ivory skin.

Another flick of his wrist, she moaned, turning her sight toward the wall. "Yes," she hissed, resting her head against one arm.

Clancy dropped to his knees and buried his face between her succulent breasts. He was a titty-man, through and through. Yet Wade knew Clancy couldn't deny there wasn't anything as delectable as the taste of Jessie's pussy, that's where Wade would be if he was on his knees before her. Oh yeah. He would be sucking on that little buddle of nerves, driving Jessie out of her friggin' mind.

Clancy must have been thinking the same thing as he began to move south. The minute his friend wrapped his mouth around her clit, she threw back her head. Her ass flexed and so did the taut skin of her anus. Now that was an appealing thought. It had been a while since Wade had taken her there.

He worked his hand between her legs, smoothing her juices across the puckered flesh, over and over. His slick finger probed to prepare her. He took his time. He didn't want to hurt her, but he could tell by the way she moved against his hand she wasn't satisfied. When he delved a finger inside and met the taut ring of muscle, Jessie groaned. "Now, Wade. I need you now."

"Honey, you're not ready." He wasn't a small man by any means, both in length and girth. Add to that his control was beginning to slip. His cock was rock-hard. His heart raced. He needed to be inside her sweet, tight body. "I'll hurt you."

"No," she panted. "Now. Need you."

God. He wished that were true. But it was her body's need, not her heart. "Clancy, back off a minute."

"No," she whimpered.

Cock in hand, he slid his hard erection along her folds, lathering it with her juices. One thrust drove him inside her pussy. She was so hot—wet.

Jessie moaned.

He pumped his hips several times, hissing as he eased out, barely holding on as fire shot down his shaft. The air in his lungs froze. He allowed the tingle to subside before he positioned himself at her anus.

Jessie sucked in a short, tight breath. "Now." She pushed against him, driving him forward.

Slowly, Wade began to stretch her wide. He knew it was

burning, probably hurt like a sonofabitch. When he tried to ease back, she did just the opposite, inching him deeper and stripping whatever control he had left.

Dammit. He was shaking as his hands went to her hips, fingers pressing into her skin. When he heard her inhale, felt her bear down, he thrust, ripping past all resistance.

"Fuck," she screamed, trembling as her knees buckled. Wade wrapped an arm around her, holding her to keep her from falling. He'd hurt her.

"I'm sorry, honey."

"No. More." Her words were as shaky as her body beneath his grasp.

"Jessie—"

"Fuck me. Now."

Wade's jaw clenched. He closed his eyes, savoring the feel of her body tight around him. Now this was heaven—hell. He was hurting her and she wanted—no needed, more.

Jessie's breathing was short, quick pants. For a moment, he thought she was crying. Then he heard Clancy's muffled growl and realized that he was feasting between her legs, sucking her tender flesh into his mouth. The juicy sounds he made said he was enjoying himself.

The temperature in Wade's body rose both with jealousy and lust. He tried to go slow, be gentle, but his hips had a mind of their own and picked up the pace. He was a goner as he slammed into her again and again.

She was so tight—so hot.

Jessie's arms quivered. "Harder." Her fingers were turning white with the pressure she exerted against the wall. Her request did not go unanswered.

While Clancy ate her pussy, Wade fucked her ass, hard and

fast. His sensitive balls slapped against her ass, making them throb and sting unmercifully as they drew close to his thighs. When his climax flowed to the surface, threatened to release, he tightened his grip on her hips and inhaled. He wouldn't lose it, not before Jessie reached hers.

Wade began to tremble. Fuck. He was going to come.

Jessie jerked once, twice. She screamed. Not of pain or agony, but a shout of unadulterated ecstasy. Her body shook as Clancy continued to feast between her thighs.

Wade couldn't wait any longer. He released the hold he had on his control. Red-hot fire shot down his cock, curling his toes and ripping a cry from his mouth.

Both Jessie and Wade were riding high in the middle of their climaxes when Clancy pushed from his knees to wedge himself between the wall and Jessie. "It's my turn. On your knees, baby."

Clancy didn't give Jessie time to catch her breath before he placed his palms on her shoulders and drove her down to her knees. It was a good thing because she didn't have the energy to stand. Her skin felt alive as if it hummed with electricity, while her body felt empty without Wade as he slipped from her ass. From her kneeling position, she heard the fall of Clancy's zipper. She stared up at him. His eyes were heated with lust. He speared her hair with his fingers, guiding her to his jutting erection.

"Fuck me with that precious mouth." When she blew a warm breath across his cock, it jerked. He hissed, nudging her closer. "Don't tease me, baby." His voice was coarse, strained. "Now." Jessie heard the tension in her friend's voice. She could have sworn Clancy needed this as badly as she did.

Her fingers closed around Clancy's shaft. Desire raged in

his eyes as he stared down at her, waiting and watching. She glided her hand up and down, once, twice.

His nostrils flared. "Mouth."

With her free palm, she cupped his balls, fondling them gently, while she continued the slow stroke of her other hand. Pre-come glistened from the small slit in his crown.

"Now," he growled impatiently.

Oh yeah. Clancy needed this. She leaned forward, opened her mouth and slipped her lips over the head of his cock.

A shiver raced through him. "Fuck." He thrust his hips, pushing farther between her lips, so deep that she gagged and pulled back.

Clancy tasted of salt and raw masculinity and the heat of anger. Anger for what her father had put her through and what his own father had done to him. Clancy and Jessie were two of a kind. They understood each other.

Jessie eased back, swirling her tongue over the sensitive head of his cock before taking him deeper and sucking hard as Wade watched. She couldn't read his expression and didn't try. All she could think about right now was pleasuring Clancy, releasing the demons inside him.

She loved the strangled sounds that squeezed from his mouth. His fingers clenched in her hair, sweet pain exploded at her roots. Several more glides of her mouth and he started to tremble. His cock extended and then exploded. Warmth bathed the back of her throat, choking her. She swallowed, over and over, the pressure on his organ forcing another moan from him.

Collapsing against the wall, he loosened his hold on her. His eyes were closed. He still trembled. "Damn. Baby."

Jessie fell back on her haunches, but strong arms brought her to her feet. She was standing only a second before Wade scooped her up, cradling her against his chest. He padded across the room to the sofa and sat with Jessie on his jean-covered lap. Unlike previous times he had attempted to hold her after sex, she embraced him, holding onto the strength and comfort he offered.

He nuzzled her ear. "Talk to me, Jessie."

The moment was shattered. Her backbone straightened. She attempted to stand, but he didn't allow her. "There's nothing to say."

He brushed the hair away from her eyes, stroking her tresses. "You're unhappy. I want to help."

"Help?" A burst of laughter followed the single word.

Damn him for making the situation rise to slap her right in the face again. All she had wanted was a moment to forget, but forgetting wasn't in the cards.

"Can you erase memories or the past?" She couldn't help the sarcasm that crept into her tone. How could anyone change years of neglect and abuse? What did it matter anyway?

"No. But I can listen. Sometimes it helps to talk these things out." He slid his palm along her cheek. "I care about you."

She jerked out of his arms, getting to her feet. "Thank you. But I'm a big girl. I don't need your help."

He stared at her. "What happened to you, Jessie? What did he do to you? Why won't you let me get close to you?"

She turned away from him. "Leave it alone, Wade." He would never understand—not the way Clancy did. The fact that she didn't feel the same way about Clancy as she did Wade was the problem. Wade made her want the impossible—a home, a family—and it scared the shit out of her.

Dan Evans's return was enough to remind her that men

couldn't be trusted, even Clancy had betrayed her. The one man she had trusted.

Wade got to his feet and caught her before she could dodge his grasp. Holding her at arm's length, he shook her. Not hard, but enough to let her know he was agitated. "I'm not your father." There was a bite in his tone. "I'll never hurt you. I want to love you. Be with you." He sounded so sincere.

She wanted to believe him, needed to believe in something—anything other than that this world was filled with insensitive bastards.

The knot in her throat tightened. "That's what you say now. I've heard all the lies a man can promise, seen them firsthand." Hell. She had lived them. From her father to each man who passed through her mother's life. Abuse and neglect had shaped Jessie to the woman she was today. Bitter and resentful.

Anger—or was it frustration?—furrowed his forehead. "We're not all alike." Wade gave her another little shake. "Dammit, Jessie. Give me a chance."

"I don't know if I can." The words spilled out before she could stop them. But it was true. She didn't know how to trust—how to love. She didn't even know if she was capable of the emotions.

He smiled so softly. "I'll help you. We'll do this together." His arms felt so right folding around her. For a moment neither spoke.

"You two hungry?" Clancy asked.

Jessie squeezed her eyes close. "Hungry?" She'd forgotten that Clancy was in the room. Had he heard everything that transpired between her and Wade? If he did, he gave no indication when their gazes met.

"I better get going," she said, stepping out of Wade's

163

embrace.

Clancy placed a palm on her arm. "You don't have to go."

"Yeah. I do." No matter how she wanted to avoid her father, it was time to face him. Besides she had a sister. Jessie didn't quite know what that meant, but she did know that the little girl would need someone.

Wade started gathering her clothes. "Do you want one of us to go with you?" He held out her shirt so she could slip her arms into the sleeves. Her bra was nowhere in sight.

Jessie forced a smile. "No. I'll be fine." After putting her panties on, she wiggled into her jeans. Bending down to retrieve her socks and boots, she saw her bra peeking out from beneath the couch. Clancy must have spied it too because he strolled over and retrieved it.

"Will you call one of us later?" Clancy handed her the bra.

She leaned in and kissed him on the cheek. "Yeah." He looked so concerned that she repeated, "I'll be just fine." But she didn't know if it was the truth. Right now she didn't know about anything.

# Chapter Seven

Chair legs screeched across the linoleum as Jessie stood in the doorway of her kitchen, holding two sacks in her arms. Emotion tightened her throat as she watched Shelby drag a heavy wooden chair across the floor to the counter while she struggled to hold onto a frozen burrito she must have found in the freezcr. The child placed a corner of the cellophane wrapper in her mouth as she climbed up on the chair, making the cutest sounds of distress. With a single finger, she popped the microwave open, placed the package inside, and proceeded to dial in two minutes.

Moisture misted Jessie's eyes. How many times had she seen this image? Yet the little girl in her mind was herself. Waking up alone, going to bed alone, growing up alone and surviving on her own.

"Shelby," she choked on the child's name, swallowing down the lump in her throat. "What are you doing?"

The girl pushed back her mop of black hair, frowning. Jessie half expected her to say, "Duh." Instead she said, "Eatin'. Want one?"

"I thought maybe I'd make us some spaghetti." Jessie had stopped at the grocery and picked up a few things. It had been just another excuse to delay the inevitable. She moved farther into the kitchen. "Do you like spaghetti?"

"Spaghetti-O's?" Shelby's eyes brightened.

God. Jessie had almost forgotten about Spaghetti-O's. It had been her main diet for months when her mother started working, leaving her a latch-key kid. "No, the real thing." Well, as real as the jar of sauce she held.

The shrill scream of the microwave buzzer drew a frown back on Shelby's face. Her shoulders dropped with a sigh. "Dan says never waste food."

Anger swelled inside Jessie. *The sonofabitch.* She held onto her temper, barely. "Well, you shouldn't. I think Jax looks a little hungry, don't you?" The old dog raised his head from where he slept in front of the pantry. His tail thumped the floor several times.

Shelby stood straighter. "You think?" A smile found her again. "Yep. He looks real hungry. Think he likes burritos?"

"I bet he does." Jessie set the groceries on the table, walked over and slipped her hands beneath Shelby's arms, lifting her off the chair. "Would you like to help?"

"Really?"

Jessie nodded. She looked around the kitchen. "Where's Dad?" God. That sounded weird. Kneeling, she pulled a frying pan and a five-quart pan used to boil pasta from the cabinet.

Shelby started unpacking the sacks laying the contents on the table. "Looking for a job."

Job? That meant he would be hanging around or— "When did he leave?"

"'Bout five minutes ago."

When their father worked, he usually picked up the occasional construction job. It was seven o'clock at night. Kind of late to visit construction sites that usually close shop around three or four.

Something wasn't right, but Jessie didn't let on as she set the skillet on the stove and started to fill the other pan up with water from the faucet.

How many times had her dad stepped out for the evening never to return? Her gut clenched.

*No. He wouldn't.* She paused, looking at her sister as she finished unpacking the groceries. *Would he?*

"What are these?" Shelby held up the three DVDs Jessie picked up from the store. She didn't have a thing to entertain a child at her house.

"I thought maybe you'd like to watch a movie later."

"Yeah." Eagerness brightened Shelby's eyes—eyes that looked so much like her own. "What can I do?"

"While we wait for the water to boil, you can cook the meat." The chair that sat before the microwave Jessie retrieved, setting it in front of the stove. "Bring the hamburger over here." She opened a drawer and took out a spatula.

Shelby handed her the meat and then climbed upon the chair. She took the spatula Jessie offered her and waited patiently for her to open the package and dump it into the pan. The smell of raw meat made Jessie's stomach flip-flop.

An uneasy feeling stole over her as she scrutinized the child who apparently was her sister. If Jessie had wanted to rebuff her father's claim, she would be hard pressed in doing so. The resemblance was uncanny.

"Hold onto the pan's handle and chop the meat well, while I cut up an onion." There was something about Shelby that made her tear up and it wasn't the strong scent of the onion she began to peel. She swallowed hard, pushing away the unexpected emotion that rushed to the surface. Yet it didn't stop her from going back to the same question.

167

Just what was her dad up to?

Without money it was difficult to go honky-tonking. Of course, that had never stopped him before. Sometimes, when she was younger, there wasn't enough money for food, but there always seemed to be for beer and a night out on the town.

*Dammit.* She hated reliving her memories over and over. Grease popped and the scent of frying meat that filled the kitchen drew her attention to Shelby. The dark-haired girl glanced over her shoulder.

"I like Wade and Madeline." Her comment came out of leftfield throwing Jessie off-kilter.

Wade? Madeline? His mother?

Jessie remembered Madeline as being a kind woman, easy to talk to. She hadn't seen the trauma counselor in years, not since that night.

A shudder raked Jessie's spine. The court had forced her into counseling after she had accused her stepfather of attempted rape. Madeline had held her until all the tears were gone, but when the tears dried up, Jessie had made her mind up. She was alone in this world. She hadn't cried since and she refused to see Madeline again. Talking only made it worse, broke down her defenses.

"I think he should be your boyfriend."

Jessie jerked her attention to Shelby, who was hacking away at the meat. "What?"

"Wade. I like him. He's nice to me. So is his mom."

Jessie gathered up the salt, pepper, garlic and Italian herbs she always added to the meat. "When did you meet his mom?"

"Today." She stopped chopping the meat. "You left so fast." She turned her gaze to Jessie. "Don't you like me?"

The child's question made the air in Jessie's lungs catch.

"What? Me? No." She shook her head. "I mean, yes. It's not that. I— Well— It was a shock finding out I have a sister." Her words weren't coming out exactly the right way. "By the way, where did you see Madeline?"

"Her house." Shelby went back to grinding the meat in fine pieces. "Yeah. Me too. Dan said you might not let us stay." She switched directions as easily as Jessie had.

God. She hated that man. Not to mention this was beginning to feel a little awkward, because tossing them out was just what she had on her mind. She stumbled over the thought as another one intruded.

What did Shelby say about Madeline? "You were at her house?"

"Yeah." The girl gave her a big Popsicle grin. "I rode a horse. Pulled vegables from the garden and had chicken for lunch. It wasn't even a special occasion."

*Vegables?* The way Shelby pronounced vegetables almost made her chuckle, but Jessie was more interested in what occurred while she was at work.

"Who took you to Madeline's house?" She continued to pry as she used checking the water as an excuse to get closer to Shelby.

"Wade."

Why? Jessie asked herself. Why would a man spend the day with a child he didn't know?

Shelby slid her gaze askew. "I think he likes you. Do you like him?"

There was no hesitation in Jessie's answer. "Yes." More than she should. She moved away, picked up a can of stewed tomatoes and wedged it under the electrical can opener. She gave the lever a press and the can began to spin as the machine gnawed, grinding. Picking up the mushrooms and sauce, she carried them over to the stove.

Jessie was twisting the cap on the spaghetti sauce when Shelby said, "Is he sleeping over tonight?" The child cocked a single brow.

"No. Of course not." Jessie had forgotten how inquisitive children were, this one in particular. Maybe it was time for her to ask some questions. "Shelby, where's your mom?"

The girl stared into the simmering hamburger. Grease made a popping sound, when she said, "Dead."

"Oh, honey, I'm so sorry." So that's how she ended up with their father. Well, Jessie would give him credit for not leaving Shelby to foster care. Maybe he wasn't a total loser after all. Could it be that the man had changed?

*Naw.* No chance in hell. A leopard doesn't change its spots.

Shelby shrugged one shoulder as if it was nothing, but Jessie knew the truth. Even a bad parent was better than no parent in a child's eyes. God. Did she just admit that?

Yet she could see that Shelby had already erected a protective shell around herself to keep out the ugliness of the world. One thing she knew from past experience was if Shelby was anything like her, she'd just as soon not talk about those things that caused her pain until she was ready. Shelby's silence said she wasn't ready and Jessie would certainly respect her wishes.

She was just about to pour the strands of spaghetti into the boiling water when the telephone began to ring. "Shelby, can you get that?"

"Sure." The child bounded off the chair with one leap that nearly made Jessie's heart stop. Gone for only a second or two, she came bouncing back into the kitchen a Cheshire cat grin on her face.

"Who was it?" Jessie asked, stirring the pasta.

"It's Wade. Can he come over? Eat with us?" She looked up at Jessie and whined, "Puh-leeze."

How could she refuse her? Not to mention, she was curious to ask him about his visit with Shelby and discover his motives behind it. "Okay."

Shelby dashed out of the room again.


The door swung wide and Wade was welcomed with a great big smile. Hopefully Jessie would feel the same way as her sister. He had only called to check on her when Shelby had invited him over. Without delay, the child gathered his hand into hers, leading him farther into the house.

"How's Digger?" She spoke of one of Tori's horses, a big gray gelding as gentle as they come. His sister used Digger for riding lessons. Like all children, Shelby had fallen immediately in love with him. "Does he miss me? When can I go riding again?"

Something smelled good. The strong scent of garlic mingled with—he inhaled deeply—something Italian. He loved Italian food. Hell. He loved to cook. He even dabbled into the gourmet, watching cooking shows within the privacy of his bedroom. It was something his brothers had teased him about when they were younger, until they had tasted some of his cuisine. But lately working the ranch left him little time to pursue his passion. He couldn't wait to cook for Jessie. Oh, the things he could do with food and her naked. His stomach growled and Shelby giggled.

Wade ruffled her hair and she ducked away. "Digger's fine. Probably missing you as much as you do him." She had been a natural on the horse. Surprisingly, she had listened to Tori and followed directions. It was no time before she was riding alongside of Wade, taking care of a few chores he had.

The picture of Jessie at the kitchen stove stopped him in his tracks. She cooked? Taking a glance around her kitchen, he noticed she was neat. Not a crumb on the floor or counter. Everything had a place from the spices aligned against the window looking out into her back yard to the tin breadbox. Organized, just like her life. Just like how he had imagined her.

The primitive male within him was pleased to see that she had a domestic side. But there was so much more. Not only did her body make him hot all over, he could imagine her with several children around her feet as they prepared breakfast together. She would appreciate the kitchen he was designing for their new home.

Jessie glanced over her shoulder and something electrifying zinged between them. Their gazes lingered on one another.

Did she feel it too?

Wade had it bad for her. She was perfection in his eyes. Everything he had ever wanted. The woman did things to his mind and body that should be illegal. They were a perfect match. A tingle splintered across his groin, but a tug on his hand reminded him they weren't alone.

When he caught Shelby looking between them with a smile on her face, he cleared his throat. "What can I do to help?"

Jessie blinked as if coming out of a trance. She glanced at the bulge behind his zipper and jerked her gaze up quickly. Pink flashed across her cheeks. He fought the grin niggling at his mouth as he recalled the blush across her face after catching her masturbating in her office yesterday. He couldn't wait to see her touch herself, come for him beneath her own fingers.

"Help? Uh...table. You can set the table. The plates are in

that cabinet." She pointed to the left of her, while she reached over and dragged a drawer open. "Silverware is here. Shelby, get some napkins from the pantry."

As the child skipped off to do Jessie's bidding, Wade extracted three plates. On an afterthought, he picked up another one remembering Evans. Before Wade closed the cabinet, Jessie said, "Three."

"Three?"

"He's not here." Wade detected a note of frustration in Jessie's voice as he returned one plate to the cabinet. "Went looking for a job."

In his surprise, he released the cabinet door and it slammed shut. "A job? At this time of night?"

Jessie's eyes widened, gaze darting to Shelby pulling the pantry door closed, before she returned to him. Her subtle hint for him to keep his mouth shut didn't go unnoticed. Instead he busied himself with gathering the silverware.

After Wade had the table set, he moved up behind her, careful to keep an appropriate distance between them as Shelby continued to watch them intently from where she kneeled, petting the dog.

"Smells good." He knew Jessie thought he referred to the sauce boiling in front of her, but it was only a façade. He was using dinner as an excuse to get closer and inhale her light powdery scent. Both smelled good enough to eat.

She faced him, drawing them even closer. "Thanks."

Wade had the urge to close the distance between them and kiss her. His eyes were narrowed on her plump lips when Shelby broke his concentration.

"I helped."

He crossed the room. "I bet you did." When he picked her

up in his arms, she giggled, wrapping her arms around his neck. "How 'bout you and me wash our hands?"

When they returned, Jessie had set the spaghetti, a loaf of golden brown garlic bread, two glasses of wine and a cup of milk on the table. His stomach growled again and both Jessie and Shelby looked at him and began to laugh.

"What can I say? I'm hungry."

Dinner consisted of good food, a mass of questions from Shelby about the ranch, and stolen glances between him and Jessie. What he wouldn't give to be alone with her, strip her naked and have his way with her.

"Can we watch the movie now?" Shelby asked.

"Not until we clean up," Jessie said, placing aluminum foil around the remaining bread.

"Shortcake, you can wash the table." Wade tossed her a damp dishrag. Shelby caught the cloth, grumbling, but she did as she was told, stretching across the table to wipe it down. In turn, he helped rinse the dishes.

After loading the dishwasher, Jessie switched it on and folded the dish towel, setting it on the counter. "Now we can watch the movie."

Shelby ran out of the kitchen, leaving Jessie and Wade alone. He took the opportunity to take her into his arms. Spearing his hand behind her head, he dragged her to his lips. Even beneath the garlic, he tasted her sweetness and her hunger as she took the initiative and deepened the caress.

The heat in her kiss made his loins tighten. "I want to make love to you."

She opened her mouth—

"Are you guys coming?" Shelby yelled from the other room.

Jessie released a weighted sigh. "I guess we'd better get in there."

He didn't miss the note of disappointment and yearning. She wanted him too. This was good—real good.

# Chapter Eight

Shelby sat smack-dab in the middle of the couch holding a DVD. Her little legs swung up and down as she waited patiently. When Jessie reached for the movie, she noticed that the child had chosen *Beauty and the Beast*, a Disney cartoon. Wade was going to love this.

Jessie was a little surprised when he took a seat beside Shelby instead of making an excuse to leave or selecting a different seat. Jessie inserted the movie, using the remote control to skip the coming attractions and arrive at the main attraction. Setting the controller on the TV, she turned to find Shelby snuggled beneath his arm lying along the back of the couch. Something squeezed her chest, but she pushed the emotion away and headed for the big stuffed chair on the other side of the end table.

Her sister caught her eye and patted the empty space next to her. "Sit here."

Jessie had to admit that it felt a little strange as she sat and Shelby took her hand. Like many girls during their teenage years, Jessie had babysat, but she didn't relate well to children. Perhaps it was because she could never see herself having any kids. She certainly never expected to have a sibling.

The movie started as strong fingertips smoothed over Jessie's shoulder, burying into her hair. She glanced at Wade and he gave her a devilish wink before he tugged her hair.

Now how was she to pay attention to the movie with him continuing to stir the fire he started in the kitchen? The man was wicked.

She wanted him. Even the thought of making love to him alone—without Clancy—intrigued her. Time after time, she fought the desire to venture out on that limb.

The quiet child sitting between them watching the movie was unaware of their stolen glances. Shelby didn't stir when Jessie leaned into Wade's touch as he stroked her hair and caressed her neck. Even her elevated breathing had gone unnoticed.

What was he doing to her?

She had never desired a man like she did him. He made her want to believe in fairytales like the one playing before them. She dropped her gaze to the girl between them. Had her sister escaped through movies like she had at one time? Did Shelby dream of a family where love and patience existed? What lay in store for her? She was so young—so innocent, but even that could be taken from a child in less than a heartbeat.

Jessie tensed and sat forward. Why did her father have to return drudging up old memories? She glanced at the clock on the wall; it was nine-thirty.

"You okay?" Wade asked softly.

"Fine." She pushed to her feet. "Anyone need a drink?" Of course, she doubted her excuse to get out of the room would go unnoticed.

Shelby never took her eyes off the television. She gave a quick shake of her head, not making a sound even when Wade propped her against a sofa pillow and stood. "I'll help you."

Not exactly what Jessie expected, but it was a little difficult to refuse his assistance. He followed her into the kitchen pulling her immediately into his arms. "Now tell me what's wrong."

God. The man was insightful.

"He isn't coming back." Jessie knew it as well as she knew her name. Daniel Evans had skipped town, leaving Shelby behind.

"You don't know that." Wade smoothed his palms up and down her arms, but it didn't chase away the chill that seeped into her bones.

Jessie snorted. The indelicate sound made his eyes widen. "Oh but I do know him." She stepped away from him. "Any time things got sticky around the house he left. Mom and Dad would argue—he'd leave. Money got tight—he'd leave. Bottom line, he never wanted me—Shelby." She heard the lost girl in her voice. "He won't want to be saddled with her." She bit down on her bottom lip, clenching her fingers. "How am I going to tell her? Where will she go?"

"She's your sister." He said it like the mere knowledge that they shared the same father solved everything.

But what did that mean? They were strangers. Besides she didn't know how to raise a child. Look at her lifestyle—two men in her bed.

Wade gripped her forearms. "When the time comes you'll know what to do and say." How could he be so sure?

"Dammit. It's not fair." Not for Shelby—not for her.

"Life never is. It isn't easy either, Jessie. You have to take chances. Sometimes they work out—sometimes they don't." He tried to pull her closer, but she resisted.

Why did she get the feeling he was talking about more than the situation with Shelby?

"Jessie?" Wade released her as she spun around on her

toes to face Shelby. "I'm thirsty too."

How much had she heard? Jessie wasn't prepared to face the child's pain of being abandoned by yet another of her parents.

Wade came to her rescue. "Come here." He raised Shelby into his arms. "Why don't you and I go back and watch the movie while your sister fixes us something?"

Sister? Would Jessie ever get use to the fact that she had a sister? She stood rooted to the floor as he carried Shelby back to the front room.

What the hell was Jessie going to do with a child? Just the thought scared the crap out of her. When she could finally gather her wits, she went to the refrigerator, discovering she didn't have a thing to drink except milk. Her salvation was a bowl of lemons. Lemonade would have to do.

After squeezing the lemons and adding water and sugar, Jessie held three glasses of lemonade in her hands as she entered the empty living room. Ice clinked against the glasses, cold to her touch. Neither Wade nor Shelby was in sight. The movie had been paused, a picture of the Beast with birds sitting on his head and shoulders while Beauty laughed was plastered on the television screen. She set the glasses down on the coffee table and was preparing to search the house when Wade appeared from the hallway.

"She fell asleep waiting for you." He moved to her side, retrieving a glass of lemonade from the table. "I put her in your bed." He took a sip, puckering his lips. "I figured Evans was staying in the spare bedroom."

"Thank you." The moment was a little awkward for her as they stood there staring at each other, but not speaking. You could have knocked her over with a feather when he finally spoke.

"Jessie, you'd make a great mother."

She responded with a burst of uneasy laughter. "You've got to be kidding. Me? Remember who I am, Wade. The girl next door I'm not. Men don't take women like me home to meet their mothers. Can you imagine me at a PTA meeting?"

Wade set his glass down. "As a matter of fact, I can imagine you at a PTA meeting." He closed the distance between them, but didn't reach for her. "Why can't you see what I do standing before me?" He slid his finger beneath her chin. "A man would kill for a woman like you. Strong. Independent." His voice deepened. "I don't want the girl next door, Jessie. I want you." He lowered his head, capturing her lips.

His kiss was overpowering, seductive, drawing her closer until their bodies touched, hips to hips, chest to chest. She snaked her arms around his neck, held on tight. His mouth moved across hers hungrily. He smoothed one hand into the small of her back to hold her nearer. His other hand caressed her back gently. Aroused, his hardness pressed into her belly, igniting rays of sensation through her now heavy breasts.

As a wave of desire built and released between her thighs, Jessie was lost in his arms. Every stroke of his lips, his hands, pulled her further beneath his spell.

"Jessie," he murmured against her lips. "I need to be inside you."

God. The man was sexy, sliding his firm body across hers to send liquid heat simmering through her veins. She wanted nothing more than to feel him part her thighs and fill her completely. When he kissed a path down her neck, she arched, wanting and needing more.

A terrified scream ripped Jessie from the lust-induced haze her mind had become. She stumbled out of his arms.

Her feet reacted even as her mind tried to clear. "*Shelby.*"

She ran out of the room, down the hall and threw open her bedroom door. In the middle of her king-sized bed, Shelby was curled into a ball still asleep even though tears dampened her cheeks.

"Momma." She whimpered the most mournful cry.

Jessie's chest tightened. The air in her lungs froze. For a second, she saw herself lying there scared and all alone. Her eyes blurred. When she blinked to clear them, the image disappeared and Shelby lay before her.

The little girl cried out again, this time waking herself up. Wide-eyed, she shot into a sitting position, desperately looking around the room as tears raced down her cheeks.

Sucking in a much needed breath, Jessie crawled upon the bed and drew Shelby into her arms. She trembled, choking back muffled sobs.

"Shhh..." Jesse rocked her back and forth, trying to soothe her. "Everything is going to be okay."

What the hell was she talking about?

She knew from experience that everything wouldn't be okay. Still her words seemed to calm the child. She had stopped crying, but continued to hold tightly to Jessie. From the corner of her eye, Jessie saw Wade watching them intently. She was surprised when he climbed upon the bed and hugged up to them both. The moment made her throat thicken, but she leaned into him, gathering the strength he offered.

Her emotions felt raw and barely contained. Damn. She hated this feeling of uncertainty.

"Jessie?" Shelby's voice sounded so small, frightened.

Jessie pushed Shelby's hair out of her face, using her hand to dry her lingering tears. "Yes."

"Don't leave me."

Wade felt Jessie tense, her silence disturbing. Even more moving was Shelby's pensive expression as she stared at her sister, awaiting a response.

*Answer her.* The words lay on the tip of his tongue. *Give the child the reassurance she longs for.*

Shelby had lost her mother. For all he knew her father had skipped town too. Wade had no right to judge Jessie, but what about her sister? Where did the child have to go—foster care?

Even though Jessie didn't know Shelby, didn't owe her anything, he couldn't imagine her allowing her own sibling to go into the system—a system that had proven over and over to be flawed and detrimental to a child. Jessie had to care. A heartbeat slipped by before he gave her a little squeeze.

She sucked in a shuddering breath. The forced smile that fell across her face was hard to miss. "Sure. I'll stay with you tonight."

Okay. Maybe he had read too much into the scene playing out before him. His moment of doubt was dashed when Shelby said, "Not tonight—forever. Can I stay with you?"

Jessie closed her eyes and swallowed hard. "Shelby—" Her voice cracked as her eyelids rose. "I won't make a promise I can't keep. But we'll see." Her jaw clenched as if she struggled inwardly to control her emotions. "Okay?"

She did care.

Damn. Wade loved this woman.

Inhaling deeply, she slowly blew out the air from her lungs before pulling Shelby closer to her. "Let's talk to Dad and see what his plans are."

"Is he coming back?" It saddened Wade to know that she would even suspect that her father had skipped town.

Jessie's eyes grew misty, but no tears fell. Instead anger sparked in their depths. "He's left you before, hasn't he?"

Shelby lowered her head, nodding.

Jessie grinded her teeth before she asked, "Has he ever hit you?"

Her question was all Wade needed to hear to know what her childhood had been like. Red-hot fury made his heart race. He'd kill the sonofabitch if he ever laid another hand on either of these two.

"No," Shelby answered.

"No lies between us." Jessie dipped a finger beneath the girl's chin, forcing her gaze to meet hers. "Okay?"

Shelby nodded again. "I hide when he smells yucky. He can't find me. I'm a good hider."

Jessie chuckled as she pressed her lips to Shelby's forehead. "You're a smart kid. I never thought to do that."

Shelby yawned, her eyelids drooping. Jessie gazed up at Wade. "We better let her get back to bed." He moved off the bed as she tucked Shelby beneath the sheets. "I'll be in the living room if you need me."

Shelby turned on her side, cuddling up to a pillow. She closed her eyes before releasing another drawn out yawn.

Moving off the bed to stand next to it, Jessie gazed down at her sister. As Wade moved beside Jessie, she peered up at him, looking as if she held the weight of the world on her shoulders. Without a word, she turned and headed for the door.

He followed her into the living room. She paced the length of the room, stopping before the window to pull back the curtain and stared into the night. "What do I know about raising a child?"

He kept his distance, trying to gauge her mood. "No more

than any new parent."

An unfeminine snort squeezed from her lips. "What a joke. Me? A parent?"

"She needs you," he stated the obvious.

"I know." There was a moment of silence before she said, "God. I hate that man."

"Talk to me, Jessie. What happened?" Wade needed her to confide in him. He wanted to be part of her life if only she would allow him.

She continued to gaze out into the dark. Headlights flashed, disappearing around the corner. "Alcohol. Fights. Abuse. Neglect. My story isn't much different from Clancy's, sometimes worse—sometimes not."

Wade had no idea she'd suffered as Clancy had. He closed the distance between them, slipping his arms around her waist. Her cold hands touched his forearms. "Your father was gone a lot. Clancy said he was in the army."

"Lie," she said with an uncanny ease. "I learned early in life to tell people what they wanted to hear. I even went out for the soccer team to explain away any bruises. But some things can't be hidden like the senior trip."

He recalled that Jessie had missed the trip to Disneyland in California. Clancy had told him that her father was home and that he'd taken her to Hawaii. "No Hawaii?"

"No Hawaii. No father. It was a stepfather." For the first time since they entered the living room, she turned in his arms to face him. "He tried to rape me."

Wade knew she wanted to see his reaction, which he held concealed beneath a blanket of anger that rose.

"After my stepfather's attack, the judge ordered counseling. Your mother was assigned to my case."

Wade's jaw dropped.

*Rape?*

Jessie wet her lips nervously. "I take it your mother never told you?"

Damn. This just kept getting better.

His stomach knotted with shame. Had he lived his childhood submerged in his own interests, unaware of the rest of the world spinning around him? After the initial shock, he discovered his voice. "Mom's work is private. You confide in her, it's as good as telling a priest. There's no prying it out of her."

Relief or something like it filtered across Jessie's face.

"Jessie, I'm so sorry."

As he drew her tighter into his embrace, she laid her cheek against his chest, her arms circling his waist. "It's over for me, but not for Shelby." He heard the sorrow in her voice. "Wade, she's lost her mother. Dead. I don't know how, but—"

"Drug overdose."

She raised her head and their eyes met. "How do you know?"

"She told me her mom died of an overdose. I had Dieter check into it." Dieter was a local cop who owed him a favor. "The police reports noted her death as accidental, too much booze—too many illegal sedatives. Evidently your father found her. They were married, so Shelby was released to him without question."

"What a mess." Jessie looked toward the clock on the wall. The hands were inching toward eleven o'clock. "He isn't coming back."

"What are you going to do?"

"I guess I'll see a lawyer. Dad will abandon her for now, but he'll be back when he has no place else to go or needs money. If he can use her to hurt me, he will. I have to protect her. I have to protect myself."

"I won't let him hurt either of you."

Broken laughter met his promise. "This isn't your problem."

"Anything that affects you is of interest to me. I love you." The words slipped out, but he didn't regret them. Unlike the first time he had expressed his love, she didn't jerk out of his embrace, brushing his heartfelt emotions aside. Instead she held on tight.

# Chapter Nine

Jessie woke to the unfamiliar sensation of a warm body pressed against hers. Small and delicate, Shelby's leg was thrown over hers. Her arm wrapped around Jessie's waist, holding on as if she was afraid to let go. A flurry of emotions struck at the same time.

Sadness. She had lost so much.

Anger. Their father was such a loser.

Fear. That he wouldn't return—or worse—would return.

And, yes, there was happiness. Jessie had a sister, someone who needed her. Not to mention a man who loved her.

She held back the burst of laughter that tickled her throat. What a fool she was. The first sign of adversity and she had dropped her guard. Not only had she leaned on him, accepting the strength and support he offered, she had allowed him a glimpse into her past, a past she had wanted nothing more than to forgot. To make things worse, after he had expressed his love for the second time, she had finally admitted to herself that she cared for him. But what did that mean?

A tingle in her arm lying beneath her began to sting. She was dying to move, but afraid that it might wake the child.

All these foreign feelings and sentiments were confusing. Maybe it had been Shelby's innocence or how much the young girl reminded Jessie of herself that made her vulnerable. Maybe it was the fact that no one had reached out to save her, but she knew she could save her sister from a life of hell or at least one of abuse.

Who was she kidding?

A soft groan drew her attention. A halo of black hair surrounded Shelby's angelic face. A tender smile found its way to Jessie's lips.

*Dammit.* She could do this. She had to.

So where was their worthless, good-for-nothing father? She had secured the locks after Wade left last night. Unless her dad had broken in, she knew he wasn't lying in the room next door. Were they free of him or would he be back on her doorstep some rainy day?

Sleepy-eyed, Shelby gazed up at her. "Hi." Jessie didn't miss the trace of uncertainty in her voice.

Jessie smiled. "Morning. Did you sleep well?" She took the opportunity to move her arm. Pain exploded as blood rushed through the numb appendage. Add the cool morning air raising goose bumps across her skin and she shifted to find a more comfortable position which meant farther beneath the covers.

Shelby withdrew her arm and leg from around Jessie as if she mistook her movement as a sign of rejection. Jessie knew that feeling so she suffered the pang in her arm, wrapping it around to draw the child into her embrace and beneath the blankets. "I think you did because you snored."

"Nah-uh. Did not." Amusement filled her objection as she snuggled closer.

That silly grin she wore earlier found Jessie again. "Okay. Maybe it was me snoring. Hungry?"

Shelby shrugged a shoulder.

Jessie glanced at the alarm clock, eight o'clock. She had to be to work at ten. "Well, shortcake, we need to get dressed. You're going to work with me today."

"Hey." She sat up. "That's what Wade calls me."

True. Jessie wasn't into nicknames, so why had she done it? The answer came to her as she propped a palm beneath her head. "That's because you're short and look good enough to eat." She reached out and tickled her sister's side.

Giggling, she wiggled away from Jessie, a bright smile plastered on her face. "I like you."

Jessie smoothed a piece of hair out of Shelby's face. "I like you too. We'd better get crackin' if you want breakfast." Throwing back the covers, she crawled out of bed.

Shelby sprang to her feet. "Yay." She bounced several times upon the bed and then lunged off, making Jessie's stomach fall. With a thud, Shelby hit the floor running. It was a moment before Jessie could breathe again.

Lord. She wasn't sure she was ready for this.

ॐ

"Wade, you've got to be kidding. Jessica Evans? What are you thinking?" Wade's eighteen-year-old sister, Tori, leaned past him, retrieving a biscuit, and proceeded to slather it with strawberry jam. "Yeah. I know you've been seeing her." She paused before adding, "Clancy too." She gave him a knowing look, raising a blond brow that matched the long mass falling down her back. With a mouthful of bread, she said "She isn't the type of woman you bring home to meet your mother. She wouldn't fit into this family."

Red-hot anger flashed across his face as his steely glare

traveled from his sunny side up eggs to his sister. All he had asked her to do was to give Shelby a couple more riding lessons, maybe spend some time with her so that he could work things out with Jessie.

Before he could ream his sister for her outburst, his usually quiet father interceded. "Tori." There was no scolding tone to his voice as he addressed her.

Their father, Clint Senior, was a quiet and studious man. Even-tempered, he ran the ranch with his wits not emotion. Mom said they balanced each other perfectly.

That's what Wade wanted, a woman who excelled in his shortcomings and helped him ride roughshod over the family ranch. He knew Jessie was that woman even if his stubborn sister couldn't see it.

Their father weaved his fingers before him. At sixty-two, gray was overtaking his brown hair which he always wore short and neat. But to Wade he would always be young, the image of strength and reason. "Do you recall what I said about Sassy when you asked to keep that scrungy cat?"

Indignant, Tori muttered, "Dad, I don't see what this subject has to do with Sassy." His sister had a way with animals and children. She could tame the wildest of beasts or the most stubborn child. Their mother said it was a gift. A magical touch, but occasionally she had a sharp tongue, like now.

Their father gave her that look which meant he would get to the point in due time. Wade had seen that same expression on more occasions than he wanted to admit. "I told you you'd never tame that animal. Do you remember what you said?"

Wade knew there was a lesson here, a connection between Jessie and the cat. Yet by the confusion carving a frown on Tori's face, the meaning was escaping her as well as him. What the hell could that cat have in common with Jessie?

Their mother stepped up behind their father and placed her hands on his shoulders. "Hmmm... Let's see." Madeline Peterson had a memory like an elephant. She never forgot a word or a promise. "Tori said that with the right amount of love she could tame Sassy. If I recall you told us the cat had been abused, mistreated. Patience and compassion was the answer then." She moved next to Tori and bent to place a kiss on her cheek before she whispered in her ear, "Maybe it's the answer now."

Their mother stepped around the table, squeezing Wade's shoulder before she took her seat beside him. Quietly she picked up her coffee cup and looked over it. "Remember we don't know what life Jessie has experienced that has shaped her into the adult she has become. Even still, we mustn't pass judgment. Everyone deserves a second chance in life."

Color dotted Tori's face cheeks. "Shit. She's right."

"Missy!" Tori cringed beneath their mother's reprimand.

Regret filled her eyes as she turned to face him. "I'm sorry. Are you really serious about her? Like in death do us part and all that crap or is this just a lustful phase?"

"Tori!" The pitch in their mother's voice rose even higher.

Before he could respond, the back door slammed and his older siblings stomped into the large spacious kitchen—the heart of their home. Clint, the eldest of them, took his cowboy hat off and placed it on the hat rack sitting next to the large picture window looking over their land. As he headed for the sink to wash his hands, Ty took a seat between their father and Tori.

Ty picked up a piece of bacon and crammed it into his mouth. "What?" Chewing, he glanced from one family member to the other sitting around the table. "What'd we miss?"

Wade recalled that many issues had been resolved in a sitting just like this one. They were close-knit family and discussed everything—well, almost everything. Everyone had their little secrets, including Wade. He prayed his mom and dad hadn't gotten wind of the triangle between him, Clancy and Jessie. Although he wanted his family's approval, he didn't require it. In time they would learn to love Jessie, even Tori.

A mischievous grin and a gleam in her eyes, Tori said, "Wade's in *love*." Her voice dropped as she dragged the last note of the word out.

Another piece of bacon disappeared in Ty's mouth. "You don't say."

Clint quietly took a seat next to their mother and father. He picked up his coffee and took a drink. "So what does that mean?"

"It means your brother is going to ask Jessie and her sister over for dinner tonight," their mother explained. "Ty, I expect you to be on your best behavior."

"Me?" Ty's wounded expression was quickly replaced by a roughish grin. "Jessie has a sister?"

Wade knew exactly where his brother's mind was headed and so did their mother. "You can stop that train of thought from going down the wrong track. Shelby is six."

"Six?" Ty's disappointment was obvious, but it did nothing to curb his appetite as he reached for another slice of bacon.

After a trip to the local department store for something suitable for Shelby to wear, Jessie pulled into Wade's parent's driveway. As her sister gazed eagerly out the window of the truck, anxiety skittered beneath Jessie's skin. Wade and she were a world apart. He had the storybook life of loving parents and siblings. They worked the ranch together, even lived together. It was a pretty little picture that she didn't fit into. So why had she accepted Madeline's invitation to dinner?

Wade. The rat had extended the invitation in front of Shelby. Jessie didn't have the heart to shatter the girl's happiness. She had chatted about seeing Digger again all day long.

"Look." Shelby jutted a finger toward a pasture where a dozen or more horses grazed. "The big one is Digger."

It was a beautiful panorama. Beneath a caramel sunset, the powerful animals fed leisurely. Winter grass caressed their ankles as the wind teased the thick blades. In the distance were green rolling hills as far as the eye could see.

Shelby broke the calm, fumbling with her seatbelt and drawing Jessie's attention. When the restraint snapped open, she climbed to her knees, nose pressed against the glass. "I wish I had a horse."

Maybe someday she could get Shelby a pony. For now they just needed to take one day at a time. There hadn't been a peep from their father all day.

A small whirlwind entered the field, the narrow dust column heading straight for the horses. Shelby squealed with delight as the animals spooked, kicking up their heels and galloping across the field. "Isn't he pretty?" She sighed with longing.

"He sure is." Jessie grabbed her purse and opened the door. As she walked around the truck, she thought of what she'd accomplished today.

While Carrie had kept an eye on Shelby, Jessie had conducted a search on the internet. What she learned is that

Texas was the first state to enact abandonment legislation in September 1999. The bill provided for an affirmative defense or immunity from criminal prosecution against parents who leave their children safely in the hands of designated caregivers.

Go figure. If she was reading the law correctly, all the sonofabitch had to do was tell them she agreed to care for Shelby and he could get her back whenever he wanted to. But Jessie wasn't giving up. She would spend every penny she had to fight him. Maybe Wade knew a lawyer who could help her.

The front door of the house opened and Wade walked out to greet them. Shelby bounded from the truck with one leap, making Jessie's breath catch. She pressed her palm to her chest, heart beating madly beneath. The girl was going to be the death of her.

As Jessie exited the truck, Wade picked Shelby up in his arms but his eyes were on her. The man was so friggin' hot standing there in tight blue jeans, boots and a T-shirt that hugged every muscle. A gentle breeze feathered his hair across his eyes, making him look sexier than ever, with a gaze that made her feel as if he slowly undressed her one garment at a time. Her heart picked up the pace.

*Breathe, girl.*

She inhaled deeply, catching the sweet-smelling plum-like scent of the potted camellias on each side of the large oak door. The bushes were in full bloom donning red lacy flowers with a bright yellow center. But it was Wade's shower-clean aroma splashed with a hint of sandalwood that made her body yearn to get closer.

Whoa! Jessie needed to remember where she was. This was not the time or place. Smoothing her palms down her jacket and khaki pants, she closed the distance between them. She had a horrible time trying to determine what to wear tonight. A dress would say she was trying too hard. Jeans would have sent the just the opposite message. An Angora sweater and slacks was the best she could do.

Shelby looked absolutely adorable in the tights and dress she wore beneath the new wool coat Jessie had purchased. The shiny black shoes had clicked across the floor as Shelby had spun in circles to show off the full skirt at home earlier this evening.

"Hi," he said, leaning forward giving Jessie a soft kiss.

*Mmmm...*

"Hi," Jessie returned. Then the moment became awkward as Madeline came up behind him. Dressed in comfortable tennis shoes, jeans, and a loose sweater, she gave Jessie a hug that threw her off-kilter even more. She wasn't a touchy-feely type of person. Hugging was usually reserved for the bedroom.

"I'm so happy you're joining us." Madeline released her and turned to Shelby. "And who is this lovely lady?"

"It's me. Shelby."

"Shelby?" Madeline winked at Jessie. "So it is. I didn't recognize you all dolled up. You look so pretty."

"Thank you." Shelby had a grin a mile wide across her face.

Pride rose in Jessie's chest when Shelby answered politely. Gently, Wade placed her on her feet. Madeline scooped up her hand and both turned toward the door.

Jessie felt the heat of Wade's palm resting in the small of her back beneath her jacket. Strength and possession were in his touch as he guided her forward over the threshold and into the large ranch home. She shrugged out of her jacket, handing it as well as her purse to Madeline as the smell of bread baking rose. Casually, Jessie took in her surroundings.

The Petersons' home was one of those pictures out of a

magazine, homey but elegant. The big sectional leather couch had a patchwork quilt thrown over the back. A fire flickered in the huge stone fireplace. Several La-Z-Boys were positioned throughout. Western art adorned the walls with family pictures scattered about.

"You remember my sister Tori?" Wade said as a petite blonde entered the room. The young woman smiled, but beneath the polite façade, Jessie could feel his sister's blue eyes sizing her up.

She knew little about Tori Peterson, except that she taught riding lessons and apparently was involved with several charitable organizations. Which would make her pretty much a goody-two-shoes compared to her. Wade's beautiful sister looked as innocent as the driven snow.

Jessie needed to change her ways and fast if she was to set the appropriate example for Shelby. Yet she wasn't a fool. She knew the past had a way of raising its evil head. Oh well. She'd just have to deal with the fallout when the time came.

Tori and Jessie exchanged hellos, each keeping their distance.

It wasn't the same greeting from Ty, who entered and immediately embraced her. "Damn, Wade. Where have you been keeping this woman?" Like Wade he wore a short-cropped mustache and beard. She felt the bristles against her skin and could have sworn that he kissed her neck.

Wade pulled her out of his brother's arms. "Away from you." It was a possessive move that made Jessie smile inwardly.

Ty chuckled, dropping to his knees before Shelby. "And who is this little filly?"

Shelby's palms went to her hips. "I'm not silly." She scrunched her lips.

Ty drew back. "Spirited. I like that. A filly is a young female colt." He gave one of Shelby's braids a tug as he rose.

She huffed, moving against Jessie's leg, mumbling, "I'm not a colt. I'm a girl."

Wade's eldest brother and father walked in together. Amazingly, they looked alike except for their hair. Where they were tall and slender sculptured like athletes, Ty's and Wade's muscles were bulkier and more defined from hard work. There was a ruggedness that surrounded them, while quiet sophistication was what the other two were about. Clint Senior had a warmth about him as he took Jessie's hand, while Clint Junior's expression bespoke a man who had something burdensome on his mind. Even as he smiled, welcoming her, Jessie saw sadness in his eyes.

Shelby was immediately drawn to Tori. They both disappeared up the stairs. When Madeline headed for the kitchen Jessie attempted to follow, offering to help.

"Absolutely not." Madeline stopped in the doorway of the kitchen. "Wade, show our guest around the ranch. It'll be about an hour before we eat."

"Sure, Mom." He took Jessie by the hand and started to lead her out of the room when Ty said, "Maybe I'll join you." The mischievous grin on his face was probably the reason Wade's grip on her tightened.

"Son." It was Clint Senior who interceded. "I've been meaning to speak to you about the last herd of cattle you sold."

Ty stopped in his tracks. "Now, Dad?"

"Now." There was a tone in his voice that said end of discussion.

Wade and Jessie took the opportunity to make their exit, grabbing their jackets and donning them before heading outside. The minute the door closed behind them, she found herself in his arms, his warm, inviting mouth against hers. She

197

tasted his hunger as his tongue pushed between her lips. His hand slipped behind her head, held her stationary as he plunged deeply, devouring her. She was breathless when he released her.

Without giving her time to gather her thoughts, Wade grabbed her hand and took off down the driveway. "I want to show you something." His pace was swift as he led her to a Jeep and opened the passenger side door.

"Where are we going?" she asked climbing in.

"You'll see."

"But Shelby—"

"She'll be fine." He crawled in behind the wheel and started the engine shifting the Jeep into gear with a jerk.

They drove past a number of barns and continued to disappear into a grove of trees. When they parted, the scenery opened up to a field where horses and cattle roamed. They tore through the pasture, heading up a winding road, scattering the herd in all directions. Ahead of them was the skeleton of a house under construction perched high on a hill. They were heading straight for it.

As the road became rougher, Jessie held onto the oh-shit bar, the vehicle tossing her about. Wade pulled the Jeep to a stop before the structure and sat silently gazing over it with something close to pride in his eyes.

From the spacious foundation, Jessie could see it would be a large dwelling. It had a gorgeous view across the land, especially the sunset that streaked across the sky in orange, gold and red. "Yours?"

"Yeah." The door moaned as he pushed it wide and stepped out. He moved around the Jeep as she got out. Again she found herself in his arms, drowning in his kisses.

He moved his mouth across her as if he was thirsty for her taste. His arms held her tight, his body a slow caress against hers.

"Jessie." Her name was a whisper on his lips. "I want you."

"Here?" Her voice pitched in surprise. Out in the open where anyone could see them? The temperature had dropped even lower since the sun was descending. Her nose was so cold she'd need a nose mitten before long. Not to mention it was just the two of them.

"Here." Beneath shuttered eyelids, he gazed into her eyes with so much passion. No one had ever looked at her like that. The back of his hand smoothed across her cheek. "I've dreamed of making love to you here. Just the two of us, you—me."

They shouldn't. It wasn't what Jessie wanted.

Oh who was she kidding? It was exactly what she wanted.

Yet in her dreams she had pictured making love to only him a little differently. Jessie had to admit that she had the perfect seduction in mind, perhaps a glass of wine, a little foreplay before a warm fire, and then consummating the night in a soft bed. She had never imagined their first time would be on the ground, beneath a star-studded sky or in the backseat of a crowded Jeep.

Wade rubbed his nose against the side of hers. His lips were a whisper against hers. "Please."

Jessie's heart skipped a beat. She had never heard a plea in his voice as he sealed it with a soft, tender kiss that melted her.

How could she turn him down?

# Chapter Ten

The sun had slipped behind the mountains. A hazy moon hung in the sky as Wade stole another kiss before Jessie could turn down his request. In minutes darkness would fall and a million stars would twinkle above them.

A tremor of need raced through him that zinged straight to the bone. If he had to beg, he'd beg to make love to her, just the two of them in the wood frame of the home he was building for her—for them. He knew the smart thing to do was to climb back into the Jeep and make a beeline for the house, but desire like he had never felt before swelled inside him, stirring his emotions into a hunger he could barely hold onto. He hadn't known bringing her to this special place would affect him so deeply. The need to know that she shared what he felt, wanted him as much as he did her, was overpowering.

When she tugged on his shirt, slipped her cool palms beneath his jacket and shirt, he lost control and pulled her against him. "Man. I want you." He dipped his head to capture her lips again.

She made a soft sound as he crossed his mouth over hers again and again. Their tongues dueled, hands tearing at each other's jackets in an attempt to disrobe quickly. Goose bumps immediately rose across her bare skin as he pulled her sweater over her head. Through a lust-induced fog, Wade remembered the blankets he had packed in the Jeep several days ago when he went hunting for a new foal and her mother.

It was difficult, but he released her. "Give me a second." As he stepped away, she crossed her arms, rubbing them briskly. Wade hurried to the Jeep and retrieved the blankets. He threw them over his shoulder.

When he returned, Jessie had removed her shoes, unfastened her slacks, but still had her bra on. Without a word, he scooped her into his arms and carried her over the area where he had envisioned the threshold to their house would be. He had chosen an easterly facing area for their bedroom and that's where he set her upon her feet.

Time was ticking. Dinner would be ready shortly, so he quickly spread the blankets on the cement floor. Kicking off his shoes, he didn't hesitate to finish undressing as she followed suit. It was cold, but the moment of discomfort would be worth it knowing the warmth that awaited him as she scrambled beneath the top blanket. Barefoot, he moved toward her, remembering a condom at the last minute. A cool breeze whipped around his nakedness, almost killing the hard-on he wore. Trekking back to his jeans, he fished out the latex. His hands shook as he held the package and ripped the top off with his teeth. In mere seconds he was sheathed, beneath the covers and back in Jessie's arms.

"This is ridiculous, you know?" There was amusement in her voice. Her teeth were chattering. "We'll be lucky not to get caught."

Even that held an air of excitement as he crawled atop her, using his knee to separate her legs. It took everything he had in him to move slowly, not take her fast and hard. But it was important this moment be something they both remembered, cherished.

He inhaled the powdery scent of her skin and the hay scent on the blankets. "Would you like an audience, Jessie?" He kissed a path up her chest, in the hollow of her collarbones and along her neck as she lay on her back.

She turned her head, giving him more access. "No." Her tone had turned sultry. Her palms smoothed down his back, resting on the cheeks of his ass before her fingernails curled, biting into his skin. "I want you—" She paused for a heartbeat before she added, "Only you."

His chest grew taut with happiness. He had waited forever to hear those words. "Mine." The growl rumbled in his throat. "All mine." He pressed his lips to hers.

Jessie didn't contradict his affirmation, but then again he didn't give her a chance. Instead he chose to drug her with long, slow kisses meant to steal her breath and make her powerless against his assault on her heart. She returned his caress tenderly, so affectionately he smiled against her mouth.

*Mine.* Possession whispered through his mind.

She arched into him, wrapping her legs around his waist. "Fuck me, Wade. Do it now." Her sexy words and the urgency in her voice was his undoing. He angled his hips, felt his cock at her warm, wet entrance and thrust. Her body welcomed him.

As he slipped further inside, he moaned, "Tight." He hissed in a breath as a tremor raked through him. "Wet."

Look what she'd done to him. She had reduced his vocabulary to one syllable words. But damn she felt good.

With measured strokes, he moved in and out of her, his erection strengthening as blood rushed his groin. He loved the caress of his sensitive balls striking her ass over and over again. It was bittersweet pain that made them draw taut against the shelter of his body.

Her inner muscles clenched around him. "Wade," she said

on a gasp.

It was too soon. "Don't come, baby." Even as he spoke, the first rays of desire stung down his shaft. He could climax on a dime, but he wanted this moment to last forever.

Wade felt the shiver that shook her as she fought the inevitable. They were fighting a losing battle and he knew it. Throwing back the blanket that covered them, he rose to his knees and pushed his hands beneath her ass to raise her lower half off the ground. With a thrust, he slammed into her, striking the back of her pussy with such force they both lost it at once.

Jessie screamed.

Wade's head lolled back on a cry of ecstasy. Fire rushed down his cock, curling his toes as he held on tight. Neither one moved. Instead they both allowed the sweetness of the moment to overtake them.

How long it took before the embers of his orgasm cooled, Wade didn't know. The only thing he did know was that he was sated and happier than he had been in a long time. Jessie had dropped her shield. Tonight she had made love to him and only him.

Wade rolled to his side, hand beneath his head and a big smile on his face. He drew Jessie close to him and then pulled the blanket over them, tucking it around her. She released a deep sigh, content to lie next to him and stare up at the now darkened sky.

Making love had never been so momentous—so passionate—or so quick. His need and depth of caring had touched a part of her that no man had ever come near. It excited and frightened her.

Could he be the real thing? Someone who she could trust and believe in? What if she allowed him to be part of her life and he failed her, but more importantly failed Shelby?

His fingertips smoothed over her forehead as if he tried to erase the worry wrinkles she knew where etched there. "Don't pull back from me now. Not after rocking my world and giving me hope." His lips were warm against hers. "I love you, Jessie. I want to be with you. Make a home for us, here." He gazed around them. "This is all for you."

"Me?" The beat of tears burned behind her eyelids. She cleared her throat, pushing the emotions back, refusing to give them control over her. Jessie had to keep a clear head. It didn't matter that everything inside her was demanding she take a chance on him. It wasn't just her heart in jeopardy. Shelby's happiness had to be considered. With a yank of her arm, she started to pull away. She needed to put distance between them to think. "Thank you, but—"

His fingers closed around her biceps. "Please, Jessie. Give me a chance."

"We need to get back. Shelby will be wondering where I am. Your mom will be worried about us." It was true, but an excuse none the less.

"Mom will hold supper."

"She knows where we are?" Jessie asked. Did she also know that her son had proposed? That he built this house for her?

"I didn't tell her, but that doesn't mean she doesn't know. That woman seems to know everything. Has all my life." There was a hint of amusement in his voice though he didn't smile. This time when Jessie rolled away from him, he didn't stop her.

The minute the cool air brushed her skin shivers raced up her spine. "Wade." She spoke as she started to dress. "I have to think about Shelby. I still don't know if my father has left for good. Either way I plan to fight him for her." Again, tears threatened to fall. Damn them to hell. She wouldn't cry. "I can't let her live the life I lived." Wade was on his feet as she found her stockings and leaned against a stud to put them on.

"I know that." He jerked his jeans on. "But she'll need a father." He grabbed his T-shirt and pulled it over his head.

Sarcasm edged her laugh. "Not like Daniel Evans. Besides I've done all right without one." She knelt to tie her shoe.

"Not him. Me. I'll adopt her."

Jessie stopped tying her shoe and looked up. Was she hearing him clearly? "Adopt? You want to adopt Shelby?"

"If Shelby is part of your life, then she'll be in mine as well."

Jessie finished tying both shoes and rose. "Do you have any idea of the mess you'd be getting into? I have baggage and now a child." She pushed her arms through her jacket. "I don't even know if I can commit to one man."

Wade stepped before her. "We'll unpack your bags together. Here." He looked around them. "As for children, I'm great with them."

She said child—not children. Just the thought of bringing another innocent life into this world made her ill. "I can't have children."

"Jessie, I'm sorry."

"No." She shook her head. "I won't have children. I refuse to bring a child into this world who isn't loved and protected."

Relief rang in his laughter. "Darlin' you don't have to worry about that. Besides, I think I'll enjoy trying to change your mind." He slipped his hand behind her head, cupping her neck to draw her to his lips.

Just before their mouths met, she whacked him on the chest. "I'm serious."

"So am I." He sealed his mouth over hers.

It was probably her imagination, but she felt the promise in his kiss with each possessive caress. He held her firmly, a rock in her turbulent life. A glimpse of hope rose as they parted, leaving her feeling a little giddy. On her own accord, she leaned in for another kiss, but this time he refused her. "We'd better get going."

Jessie blinked. "Uh...okay." Disappointed, she watched as he gathered up the blankets.

He chuckled. "Sorry, honey. But I'd hate for my family to send out a search party. Maybe we can continue this later." He winked and she couldn't help the sigh that filled her.

"Come on." He grabbed her by the hand. Opening the passenger side door, he helped her in, tossed the blankets in the back and moved around the vehicle to get in.

The ride back to Wade's parents' house was over way too soon. Her head was spinning. Fears and doubts played havoc with her mind as she attempted to sort out the possibilities. As the engine died, she checked her makeup in the Jeep's mirror.

"You look beautiful. Well, except for this." He pulled a blade of hay from her hair.

"Oh my God. What if you mother suspects what we've been doing? Wade, I can't go in there."

Again he chuckled. "Who cares if she does?" He climbed out of the Jeep and came over to her side to let her out.

She pinned him with a frown. "It isn't funny." He reached over and pulled another piece of grass from her hair. She died a little inside. "Damn you, Wade Peterson."

"I'll show you to the bathroom." Devilment played in his eyes. "No one will even suspect that I've had my dessert before supper."

She released a huff, attempting to step around him, but he

stopped her, lavishing her with another breathtaking kiss. Jessie was still caught in its dreamy aftermath when Madeline opened the front door.

"There you are." Jessie leaped out of his arms like a child caught with her hand in the cookie jar. Heat rolled up her throat, spreading like wildfire across her cheeks. Either Madeline didn't notice it or she was being polite by not reacting. Instead his mother wiped her hands with the dish towel she held. "We were wondering if my son had absconded off with you."

Wade slid his arm around Jessie and pulled her close as if she belonged tucked beside him. "I tried, but she wouldn't hear of it. Where's Shelby?"

Madeline looked past them, scanning the land. "Well, that's another one who has gone missing."

Jessie felt her eyes widen as concern moved its way to the surface. "Missing?" She spun on a heel, quickly taking in the shadows looming in dim yard lights dotted about.

"I'm sorry, dear. I frightened you. What I meant is she and Tori headed out to the barn earlier to see the new colt and they haven't returned."

Shelby's laughter as she darted around the corner with Tori hot in pursuit made Jessie tense. Had her sister done something inappropriate? When Tori caught her by the waist, lifting her into her arms to twirl her about, Jessie realized they were just playing. She tried to remember a time in her life when someone had paid her attention and made her giggle like Shelby.

Nope. There wasn't even one opportunity she could recall.

Shelby was out of breath but still full of energy when Tori set her down on her feet. As if it was so natural, she ran to Jessie and threw her arms around her and Wade's legs. She gazed up and the happiness on the child's face warmed her heart.

She placed her hand on Shelby's head. "Having fun?"

"Yeah. The baby horse is so cute."

"Colt," Tori corrected, sauntering up to them. Her eyes met Jessie's and this time she extended her a genuine smile as she stopped next to her mother.

Madeline gazed at her daughter with so much pride. Had Jessie's mother ever looked at her in that way?

"Dinner's on the table." Madeline wrapped her arm around Tori's waist and together they walked into the house. Wade, Shelby and Jessie followed.

As promised, Wade showed her to the bathroom. Staring into the bathroom mirror, Jessie was relieved to see not a speck of hay in her hair or on her clothes. Her hair was in disarray, but that could be blamed on the Jeep ride. She ran her fingers through the tangled mass, washed her hands and then joined the rest.

As she stepped into the dining room, she drew everyone's eyes. They were standing around a big oblong oak table with intricately carved chairs. It appeared they were waiting on her before being seated, which made her a little self-conscious. Clint Senior smiled at her before he pulled out a chair and offered it to Madeline. His wife sat and he leaned down and kissed her softly on the cheek. Ty offered Tori a chair, but as she sat, he made the motion like he would pull it out from beneath her. She swatted him on the arm and he cringed before bursting into laughter.

Shelby watched the interplay grinning. Her smile deepened when Clint Junior offered her a chair. Wade assisted Jessie and then all the men took a seat.

The table was garnished with a large roast Clint Senior

began to carve. Juice oozed from the meat, releasing its mouth-watering fragrance. Mashed potatoes, gravy, fresh green beans and baked bread were passed around the table.

"Would you like some milk, Shelby?" Tori asked, holding a large pitcher.

Shelby sat up straight. "Do you have soda pop?"

"Milk is just fine," Jessie interjected and Shelby frowned as she fell back in her chair. Wade placed a comforting hand on Jessie's thigh. He nodded approvingly.

Dinner with the Petersons was definitely an experience. There was laughter, business and politics discussed. No arguing or fighting except for the occasional poke or jab Ty sent in Tori's or Shelby's direction, but it was all in the name of fun. The event was so different from the ones Jessie remembered of her family.

When dessert had been served and eaten, Clint Senior leaned back in his chair, holding his belly. "That was delicious, darlin'." He gave Madeline a wink that made her smile as she rose from the table.

"Thank you," she said, picking up her plate.

All at once, the entire family stood, retrieving their plates, glasses and silverware along with other dishes on the table.

Men who clean?

It was a unique concept, but Jessie liked it. But then again she did remember Clancy saying that Wade was a helluva cook and he did help with cleaning up when he had stayed for spaghetti. Looks like Madeline had taught him well. She and Shelby got to their feet and followed suit, carrying their plates to the kitchen.

A towel snapped and Madeline let out a squeal, turning around to swing at Ty as he danced around the kitchen.

"We'd finish faster if Ty wasn't here," Tori grumbled.

"You want me to leave?" Ty asked eagerly. "That can be arranged."

"No way, buster," Clint Senior said as he placed a clean glass into the cabinet. "If I have to help, so do you."

Wade shook his head, leaning into Jessie to whisper, "It's like this every night."

If that was true, then he was a lucky man. Dinners at her house had been just the opposite. TV dinners or any other eat and toss away meals. There was no laughter, no peace and unity, only silence or arguing that ended in a fight.

Amazingly, the dining room and kitchen were clean in no time and they were gathered in the living room again. Jessie could see why there were so many La-Z-Boy chairs, because each of the men took a seat, propped their feet up and fell immediately into relax mode, except for Wade who sat next to her on the couch. There was an end table with pieces of an unfinished puzzle on it. Madeline and Tori sat on the floor around the table and began to put it together. Shelby joined them. It was all so unfamiliar, but nice.

"Jessie, any new stock coming through the auction?" Clint Senior asked.

"We're seeing a few new ranchers out of Austin shipping their cattle and horses in."

"I'm keeping an eye on it," Wade assured his father.

Ty wagged his brows. "I'm sure that's what you're keeping an eye on."

"Behave," Madeline snapped over her shoulder, placing the final piece of the puzzle to complete a blue sky. Shelby had lost interest about fifteen minutes ago and crawled up on a big comfy chair, hugging a throw pillow to her chest. Jessie watched her sister's eyelids grow heavy, and before she could end her conversation with Wade's father, Shelby had fallen asleep. She looked so small and innocent lying there.

Jessie nodded in Shelby's direction. "I'd better get her home."

Madeline groaned as she got to her feet, placing her palm against the small of her back. She bent forward, stretching as her bones crackled. "It's the pits getting old." She flashed Shelby a tender expression. "Dear, why don't you leave her here? She's already asleep. Besides Tori promised her she could spend the day with her if you're okay with that."

Jessie didn't know what to do. Leave her sister with Wade's family or drag her out into the cold? Her life had gotten so complex in a matter of days. So many decisions and now she had someone else's welfare to consider. It seemed a shame to wake the child.

Yet how would she react waking in a strange home? What if she had another bad dream?

There was also the fact that Jessie had a lot of things to do tomorrow and having someone watch Shelby would be convenient. "Are you sure it wouldn't be an imposition?"

"Not at all," Madeline assured her.

Jessie rose with Wade beside her. Everyone else got to their feet. The moment was a little awkward, good-byes always were. "Thank you for dinner and being so kind to Shelby."

"It was our pleasure," Clint Senior extended his hand. Strong fingers wrapped around hers. In Jessie's job, she met a lot of men. She usually found it easy to pick the good ones from the bad. Wade's father was a good man. When Clint senior released her, she found herself walking into Madeline's arms. "You're both welcome here anytime."

Ty, Clint Junior and Tori said their good-byes as Wade

*Mackenzie McKade*

retrieved their jackets and her purse. It was strange, but Wade's family had a way of making her feel right at home. He helped her with her jacket and walked her outside. Bathed in moonlight, he looked so darn sexy standing before her.

"Jessie," his voice dropped to a sensual caress. "Can I follow you home?" He reached for her, jerking her hard against his chest, leaving their lips a breath away. His touch was feather-light across her mouth as he spoke. "I haven't had enough of you."

Jessie's pulse leaped. "You haven't?"

"Never." He closed the space between them, stealing her breath with a sinful kiss that promised a night of heaven in his arms.

# Chapter Eleven

As Jessie maneuvered her truck into her driveway her headlights flickered off of a vehicle. It was Clancy's truck parked off to the side of the house. "Damn. I forgot to call him."

Of course it didn't help that her cell phone was on vibrate and probably buried at the bottom of her purse. Switching the engine off, she unbuckled her seatbelt, opened the door and got out. Clancy was nowhere to be seen, but he had a key. Whenever she went out of town, he always fed and watered Jax.

Her friend waited inside while Wade was minutes behind her, definitely the makings for an interesting evening. Clancy had wanted to hookup tonight if she could arrange for a babysitter. After Madeline's invitation to her house for dinner and Shelby's excitement, Jessie had completely forgotten about contacting him. Couple that with what happened between her and Wade during her visit tonight, Jessie couldn't help wondering how the night would unfold. In fact, she had a strange case of nerves as she pushed opened the door and walked in.

Clancy lay stretched out on her couch, boots off. His hand hung over the side, scratching Jax behind the ear. The dog barked, jumped up and headed straight for her, sitting at her feet to stare up at her expectantly. Jessie set her purse down on the end table and shrugged out of her jacket, tossing it beside her keys; she reached down to pat the dog on the head.

With measured movements, Clancy got to his feet to face her. "Forget something?" She heard his concern which made her feel guiltier. While he had worried, she had been enjoying herself.

"I'm sorry. But—" Before she could explain further, the door swung open and Wade stepped inside. The first thing she noticed was the broad smile on his face. The next was the jingle of spurs strapped to his boots. Her gaze fell to his feet and snapped back up.

*Crap.* Wade must not have noticed Clancy's truck outside.

There were only two reasons Wade wore spurs, riding and playing. Wade wagged his eyebrows teasingly. He was ready to play, and by the surprise on Clancy's face, he knew it too.

Eyes focused on her, Wade hadn't realized they weren't alone. He reached for her, drawing her firmly against him. "Are you ready for a ride, darlin'?" When she didn't answer immediately, he frowned. "Something wrong?"

"Ummm..." Was all that came out of her mouth.

Clancy cleared his throat.

Wade jerked about, but he didn't release her. In fact, his grip tightened. Silence stretched between them. There had never been an awkward moment between the three of them, but Jessie felt it now. It hung heavy and foreboding in the air.

Clancy crossed his arms over his chest. She couldn't read his nonplused expression, but there was something defensive in his stance. Possession was etched in the hard lines on Wade's face as he held her like he wouldn't let go.

"Jessie?" Clancy finally spoke. When she didn't answer, he said, "Why do I get the feeling that our threesomes have come to an end?"

Both men pinned their questioning stares on her.

*Great.*

Jessie wanted to squirm, but made no move. Her answer should have been easy. It lay perched on the tip of her tongue. She had fought all her adult life to avoid the complications of a relationship. She didn't want a man like Wade who could consume her body and soul, nor did she want to become her mother.

Wade dipped his fingers beneath her chin so that he looked her square in the eyes. "After tonight I can't share you with another man, not even Clancy." The tension in his tone was hard to miss. Her heart skipped a beat.

She found herself saying, "I'm sorry, Clancy," before she realized it.

*Oh God.* What the hell was she thinking? Maybe that was the problem. She wasn't thinking. No matter how she cut it, she wanted Wade, wanted a chance to see how their lives would evolve and wanted to believe that fairytales do come true.

Clancy unfolded his arms and approached. He offered Wade his hand. Wade hesitated only briefly before he released Jessie to accept his friend's offer of goodwill. Although the moment seemed amicable, Clancy grew solemn. "Don't make me regret walking away without a fight."

"Not a chance." Wade glanced at Jessie with a tenderness that made her belly flip-flop. "I'll do everything in my power to make her happy."

Clancy looked from Wade to Jessie and then he pulled her into his arms. He didn't speak, only held her so close it stole her breath. Before he released her, he pressed his mouth against her ear. "I'm gonna miss you." His voice lowered to a whisper. "Goodbye, baby." There was an ache of sadness in his farewell. He kissed her softly on the cheek before he stepped away.

When he cleared his throat, she heard the emotions he struggled with as she fought her own. They had been each other's rock, anchor in this chaotic world.

"Take care of her." He started to leave, but hesitated. "Jessie—" His voice broke on her name. "You know where to find me if you need me or just want to talk." He stared at her for a second longer as if there was more he wanted to say, and then he silently turned and left. The click of the door behind him sent a shiver up her spine. Jessie was still staring at the door when she heard Wade's spurs jingle.

"He loves you?"

She spun around. "No. He can't." They were friends—close friends—but friends nonetheless.

Wade watched her intently. "How do you feel about him?"

"He's my best friend. We've gone through so much together."

"Nothing more?"

How could she answer his question? Yes. Clancy was more than a friend. For God's sake—they were intimate, but it was something deeper—soul deep.

Still she didn't feel the same about him as she did about Wade. Wade touched her in places Clancy couldn't come close to. The man turned her inside-out and back again. Even now her body was reacting to his. Her breasts were heavy. Her nipples stung.

Frustrated because she couldn't find the right words to express herself, especially now that all she could think of was Wade naked in her arms, Jessie shrugged. "I can't explain it. I love him, but it's not like how you think."

"Not like how you love me?"

"Yes. I mean—" Crap. She pulled at the neckline of her sweater. Did she just admit to loving Wade? Was it true?

He grabbed her hand before she could move away, pulling her to him so that they were chest to chest. "Why is it so difficult for you to admit you love me?" His warm breath brushed her face. Jessie felt as if she were drowning in his dark brown eyes.

"I don't want to love you." Now that made her sound childish.

A roguish grin hauled the corners of his mouth up. "I know, but you do." He stroked his nose against hers, giving her feather-light kisses everywhere but where she needed them— her mouth. She hungered for his taste.

*Kiss me.*

He teased her nibbling at the corner of her lips, but not giving her what she wanted—his mouth pressed to hers. The man was insufferable. "All right. I do."

"Do what?"

"Love you." The words sounded so right coming from herself. They slipped out with such ease they had to be true.

He smiled against her mouth. "Say it again."

Jessie slid his Stetson off, letting it slip from her fingertips to fall to the floor at their feet. "I love you." Rising on her tiptoes, she snaked her arms around his neck, exerting pressure to draw him nearer. "Now kiss me."

The moment Wade had dreamed of had arrived. Jessie had finally confessed her love for him. He was nearly exploding with happiness as he gave in to her desire.

When their lips met, it was explosive, fire to a fuse. Sparks flew, the sizzle hot and exciting. Their tongues moved against one another in a frenzy of raw passion. She tasted of heaven and the promise of a future.

"Naked," he growled.

Wade wanted nothing between them. Not clothes, another man or the past. He wanted her very soul bare and opened to him.

As the caress ended he buried his palms beneath her sweater, stroking her skin. She whimpered, reaching for his belt buckle. Just the feel of her touch made blood race to his groin, filling his balls to induce a throb he prayed he could rein in. He allowed her to unfasten his jeans and set his cock free before he moved her hands away to push her sweater up and over her head. A flick of his wrist tossed her shirt aside.

Full breasts peeked from her black bra. She was exquisite as her chest rose and fell quickly. Her breaths matched his, rapid and heavy. The beat of his heart echoed in his ears. A twist of his fingers and her bra popped loose.

"Wade," she moaned, shrugging out of the lacy material. Her nipples immediately grew taut in the cool air, small bumps forming around her rosy areolas. He dipped his head to taste her.

Jessie threaded her fingers through his hair, holding him close. He loved the forcefulness of her touch and the need in the small breathy sounds she made. Gently, he teased and sucked the peak hardening more against his tongue. Increasing the pressure, he slid his teeth across the sensitive skin, making a popping sound as he released her. A groan from somewhere deep in her throat was released.

She clenched her hands in his hair, pulling him up. The sting was breathtaking, but it was her excitement that set his blood to simmer. "I need to taste you. Now." The desperation in her voice thrilled him. Releasing him, she drifted to her knees, grasping his jeans to pull them down with his skivvies.

His cock arched against his belly. The tails of his shirt swept across the head, drawing a drop of pre-come. While velvet soft hands smoothed down his hips, stroking and caressing, her fingernails left reddened paths awakening his nerve endings. When her breath brushed over his member, it jerked, sending tiny rays of sensation shooting in all directions. He hissed, sucking air into his lungs and then holding it.

As her warm, wet tongue slid up his length, he released his breath in a single gush. "Jessie." Her hair whispered over his thighs, making goose bumps rise across his flesh.

Wade had died and gone to heaven—or was it hell as he struggled to keep his control in check?

Teasingly, she made circles around the crown of his erection. Tonguing the small slit, she moved to stroke beneath the ridge. He thrust his hips, encouraging her to take him within her hot cove. Yet she insisted on taunting and playing with him, refusing to give him what he ached for. He needed her mouth surrounding him, to feel her throat squeezing as she sucked him deeper and deeper.

The image forming in his mind made his entire body scream for her touch. His testicles throbbed, becoming more painfully engorged by the minute. Fisting his hands in her hair, he growled, "Fuck me, darlin'. Use that beautiful mouth to drive me wild."

Eyes glazed with desire stared up at him. Kiss-swollen lips parted, making him clench his jaw. He circled his fingers around the base of his dick and guided it toward her lips. She leaned into him. Heart pounding, he thought he'd die as she took him inch by pulsating inch into her mouth.

Wet and warm, she felt so good. Better than he had ever dreamed and without a condom. There was only skin against skin. It was the first time, but not the last.

"Damn—" She stole the rest of his words as she began a slow, sensual pace, moving up and down his shaft using her tongue and the suction of her mouth to do exactly what he asked—drive him fuckin' wild. He closed his eyes and let his senses go.

The small sucking noises she made were beyond erotic. Her touch was that of an angel. Tenderly, she cradled and massaged his balls, pulling gently on the sac as she sucked, smoothing her tongue over the vein on the underside of his cock with each pass. When he thought she couldn't take any more of him, she took him deeper.

Wade's eyelids sprang wide as his testicles slammed hard against his body with a throb that bordered on pain and pleasure. He placed his palm on her forehead and eased in a terse breath.

"Darlin', stop." He couldn't move as she looked up at him. "I'm about to explode."

The smile she gave him caused her throat to contract. It didn't help she took that moment to swallow. The tightness and squeezing of her throat nearly blew the head off his control. He shuffled backward and she released her hold on him.

Lord he couldn't breathe. Bending at the waist, his hands on his thighs, he lowered his head, fighting the burn and the need to let go of the fragile hold he had on his climax. Standing perfectly still was the answer, that and not thinking about the woman who knelt before him.

"You okay?" She asked with a hint of amusement. He heard her rise.

He glanced up at her and she was indeed grinning. "Oh, you think this is funny, do you?" He tried to move forward but his jeans pooling around his ankles prevented him from reaching her as she hastily backed away.

Sweet laughter burst from her mouth as she clapped a hand over it.

Damn. She was gorgeous standing there in nothing but her dress slacks and shoes.

"Laugh now, but when I catch you we'll see who is laughing." He jerked up his pants so he could raise a foot and pull off his boot. Tossing his shoe aside, it landed with a thud as he worked quickly to remove the other one.

Jessie giggled. Without delay, she took off for the hall, her heels clicking against the floor.

Was this the first time he had heard her sound so carefree?

Wade took only the time needed to remove the rest of his clothing, extract the belt from his jeans and unbuckle his spurs from his boots before he headed after her. The linoleum was cold on his feet. There was a chill to the air, but soon she would be in his arms and reigniting the fire that simmered within him.

Just inside the bedroom, he stopped, mesmerized by the sight of her. Naked and laying upon a mountain of pillows she looked sinfully wanton against the silky white sheets. She crooked a finger, beckoning him to her side.

"God. You're beautiful," he said, wasting no time to close the distance between them.

"Those for me?" she asked.

In one hand, he raised the spurs and belt with the shiny buckle. With the other hand, he circled his fingers around his cock. Slowly he slid his palm over himself. "Yeah and so is this." He was rock-hard and dying to slip between her long legs, exploring the pleasures of her body.

"Mmmm..." She stretched, drawing his attention to her full breasts, and then the little patch of dark hair at the apex of her thighs. "I can't wait." Jessie bent a knee, exposing the pink flesh of her sex. Through thick eyelashes, she gazed up at him. "Saddle up, cowboy."

Wade wasted no time doing just that. He set aside the spurs, reached for his belt to make a loop. Jessie's chest rose and fell rapidly as he slipped the belt around her wrists, securing them to the headboard. Damn. She was sexy bound for him. He might just love her all night long.

Picking up the spurs, he climbed upon the bed and kneeled between her splayed legs. It was the perfect position to tease and play with her. A spur in each hand, he traced them down her arms, watching goose bumps pebbled across her skin.

"Hmmm..." she hummed, closing her eyes, eyelashes soft crescents upon her cheeks.

He pulled the spurs lightly down each of her sides, from armpit to hips, and watched her wiggle as the spikes tickled her. She was so fucking sexy. "You like that?"

Eyelids half-shuttered, she gazed up at him. "You know I do."

He also knew she enjoyed the illusion of being restrained. When she was in the right mood, she even enjoyed actual bondage, which thrilled him. What he would have given to have his bondage gauntlets. There wasn't anything hotter than silk rope against her tender flesh. Just the thought made his cock thicken and jerk with excitement.

Adding a little pressure, he made crisscrosses over her midriff, leaving a path of pinpricks. Tracing the spurs over her engorged breasts, he paid special attention to her nipples.

"Wade," she breathed his name. Her lust-filled eyes were unmistakable.

He dragged the spurs through the dark hair at the apex of her thighs and then farther. "Yes darlin'?"

She squirmed, moving her hips side to side, when the cold metal touched her folds. "Make love to me."

Something inside his chest tightened. His control was nonexistent when it came to Jessie, especially when she asked like that. He tossed the spurs aside and they jingled as they struck the floor.

"My hands—release them." She smoothed her tongue between her lips. "I need to touch you."

*Oh yeah.* He could do that. Just the thought of her silky palms on his skin made him hotter than a firecracker ready to blow.

Wade leaned over, straddling her to unfasten the belt around the bedpost, when something warm and wet slid along his cock. His hands as well as the air in his lungs froze.

"Mmmm..." she cooed, circling the crown of his dick with her tongue.

"Baby—"

"Release me," she hummed against his sensitive flesh.

*Oh hell yeah.*

He wasted no time untying her hands.

Jessie's cool palms smoothed across his hips, cupped his ass, before she pulled him to her. "Hold onto the bedpost." Her voice was pure silk, sliding over him to make his hands shake as he gripped the headboard. When she flicked her tongue over the small slit, his fingers tightened.

"Darlin'," Wade growled in warning. If she continued teasing his cock, he would be a goner. Before he could continue, Jessie wrapped her lips around him, plunging him into a maelstrom of sensations.

Her mouth was hot and wet, while he had cold chills racing up his spine as she started a slow, sensual pace. Up and down, her tongue moved along the bulging vein in his shaft. The exquisite pressure she exerted was nearly his undoing. He held on, but barely.

It was difficult to speak, but he managed a weak, "Tight. Wet," as he sucked in a much needed breath. God she felt so good sliding up and down while her tongue danced over him. Blood rushed his balls, filling them with a pulsing ache that stole the air from his lungs leaving him winded. "Oh fuck," he wheezed, a tremor shaking through him. His ass cheeks clenched. "*Jessie.*"

Her grasp grew taut. She took him deeper into her mouth, increasing the suction to drive him out of his friggin' mind. He dropped his head between his arms, trying to gather his control.

*Breathe, dammit. Breathe.*

Jessie flicked her tongue against the slit and then rimmed it.

He wasn't prepared when red-hot rays tore down his cock. Sparks burst behind his eyes. The skyrocketing explosion of his climax couldn't be stopped even if he had wanted. He threw back his head. Tears misted his eyes as he released a strangled cry.

One after another, streams of come bathed the back of her throat, but she didn't stop fucking him with her mouth. Unmercifully, she wrung every drop from him, leaving him weak and disoriented.

When the sensation turned from pleasure to discomfort, he shuddered. "Jessie, enough."

She released him and he peered down between his arms to catch the mischievous grin on her face.

He raised a brow. "So you think that's funny?"

Her smile deepened and she nodded, flicking her tongue out once more along his cock to make him flinch.

This side of Jessie he had never seen. The carefree, playful woman aroused him to no end. He wanted to make her happy—keep her smiling for eternity.

He moved away from the headboard, easing down beside her, before he took her into his embrace. Laying there in his arms, she felt so right. She belonged next to him.

"God, I love you," he said as she tucked her head beneath his chin. Maybe he shouldn't bare himself to her, but it was hard not to declare his feelings at a moment like this.

There was no denying it—he loved her.

"Marry me." The words burst from his lips.

"Wade— I—" She fell silent.

He released her, putting enough distance between them so that he could gaze into her eyes. If she didn't love him, then Wade wanted her to prove it to him.

Her smile had faded. She was biting her bottom lip like she did when she was nervous. No—not nervous, scared to death by the fear in her eyes.

"Talk to me," he said, smoothing his palm along her bare arm. *Come on, baby, talk to me.*

Jessie didn't pull away from him.

*A good sign.*

Instead she licked her lips and swallowed hard. "Marriage isn't for me." She shrugged. "Besides I doubt a fairytale romance exists."

Wade brushed her hair from her face. "Honey, that's because life isn't a fairytale. It's hard work. If I've learned anything from watching my parents it's that couples disagree. It's a series of give and take, of compromising and respect for

225

each other."

"How do you know our life together will be like your parents?"

"I don't," he admitted. "No one knows what the future holds. But I can promise to love and care for you and Shelby."

"But what about my father?"

Wade caressed her lips with his. "We'll face that hurdle when it arrives—together."

"But—"

He silenced her with a finger pressed to her lips. "No worries. I'll take care of everything." It was a promise he anticipated keeping. That sonofabitch would never hurt Shelby or Jessie again.

She blinked away the tears. Strangely he had never seen her cry. "Wade—" She released a weighted breath. "We don't live a conventional lifestyle."

"Thank God." he laughed. "Darlin', what happens behind our bedroom door is between us."

She flashed him a skeptical eye.

"Here." He rolled her onto her back and eased his large frame over hers so that his cock was nestled between her thighs. "Let me show you."

# Chapter Twelve

Jessie's eyelids fluttered open, greeting the light of a new day shining through her bedroom window. Dust bunnies danced in the brilliant ray spreading across her bed. There wasn't much different from any other morning she woke except for one thing—she wasn't alone.

A silly grin spread across her face as she inhaled the scent of sandalwood and a night lost in Wade's arms. The musk of their loving hung heavy in the room, a perfume that made her pulse leap with joy.

In the past, when she allowed herself to dream of waking in his arms, it hadn't compared to the real thing. It felt wonderful to have him spooning her from behind, so warm—comforting. His heavy arm circled her waist, while a very impressive morning hard-on was pressed against her back. Even his light snoring against her ear was welcoming.

Jessie burrowed her head into her pillow. She closed her eyes, remembering the decadent night. After their talk abruptly ended, he had made love to her two more times, each time more tender and precious. No one had ever made her feel so special—so cherished.

Yet how could he be so confident in their life together?

Call her a pessimist, but from her experience nothing was forever.

*Dammit.* She wanted forever.

The thought disappeared as quickly as it had appeared when Wade smoothed his palm up her ribcage to cup a breast. A wicked finger played softly over her nipple.

"Good morning." His sleepy voice was deep and sexy, causing her skin to come alive, but it was his lips to her neck that sent chills up her spine.

He had no idea how good a morning it was for her. "Morning." Last night he had given her the gift of hope—something that had been missing from her life—something she had longed for. She wanted more than anything to hold onto his belief.

It hurt that she couldn't commit to marrying him, not yet.

In a moment of weakness, she had agreed to give their relationship a chance. His happiness had been infectious. He spoke of the house he was building for them and their future. It was exciting, but scared the shit out of her. Before she fell asleep last night, she had prayed that she had made the right decision, not only for her but Shelby.

Jessie pushed her fingers through his tousled hair and drew him down for a kiss.

When they parted, he released a growl and tossed back the covers. Taking her by the shoulders, he rolled her upon her back. Through half-shuttered eyes, he swept his heated gaze over her naked form. His drop-dead expression of male appreciation made her nipples draw taut, sharp tingles radiating through them.

"Damn, woman, you're beautiful, and you're all mine."

Jessie did feel beautiful beneath his scrutiny. She loved the way he looked at her as if he had eyes for no one else. Not to mention the sound of being his thrilled her.

Of course, there was nothing like two men's attention focused on her. But Wade did things to her mind and body that no man had ever come close to. He made her want a family and a home—to take a chance on him.

His grin deepened. "You look good enough eat."

The bed moaned beneath his weight as he crawled to his knees. Using one of them to part her thighs, he moved between her legs. Slowly, he eased his body upon hers, pressing his firm erection against her folds. Skin to skin, her arousal soared. As he began to rock back and forth, sliding and teasing, her moisture anointed him.

*Mmmm...* On the glide of his hips, if she tilted her hips just right he would be buried deep inside her.

Jessie released a sigh. That's exactly what she wanted.

The blare of the alarm clock next to her bed destroyed the moment. She flinched. Her gaze darted to the neon green screen.

Six o'clock.

She had a meeting with a rancher this morning.

"Wade." She gave his shoulders a shove. "I've got to go."

He slid on his side and she slipped out from beneath him.

"Where?" he asked.

Jessie scooted across the bed to stand. The linoleum was cold on her bare feet. "Work." She moved hastily across the room to the dresser and pulled out the top drawer that contained her bras and panties.

"Call in sick. I've got other plans for you."

That sounded like heaven. But no can do. "Can't." She glanced back at him.

Propping a palm beneath his head, he bent a knee, his erection jutting from a patch of golden brown hair. "Come on, darlin'." His hungry gaze followed her every move.

Jessie loved the way he devoured her body with just a look. It heated her blood and made her ache to crawl back in bed with him. She had a strong, virile man whispering her name, taunting her to make love to him one more time, and she was rushing off to work.

*What a waste.*

Extracting a black bra and thong from the drawer, she paused.

*Maybe?*

*No.* She had to go. Putting off the inevitable only made it worse. Her thighs were slick with her juices. Her breasts were heavy for his touch.

"Lay back down beside me." He patted the bed. "I'll do naughty things to you that will leave you screaming my name."

There was no doubt in her mind he could live up to his promise, but she had already wasted as much time as she dared. "I can't." She donned her bra and thong, before heading for the closet.

"You know you want to. Please, baby? One night in heaven isn't enough with you." He sounded so sexy, so downright appealing, begging her to come back to bed.

It was hard to deny him, but Jessie had to.

Spying a black pair of jeans, she jerked them off the hanger, and then reached for a thin red sweater. After grabbing her matching boots, she spun on her heels and ran straight into Wade. He wrapped his strong arms around her, pulling her hard against his chest to hold her tight.

"I don't want to let you go." There was a sense of unrest in his voice, as well as in his big brown eyes.

Jessie knew she ran hot and cold. He was probably afraid

that she would change her mind about giving their relationship a chance. She had to admit she'd thought about it a time or two, but she wanted this too.

Perching on her toes, she kissed him softly. His beard and mustache tickled her lips. "How about lunch?" she said, hoping that it would reassure him. "Maybe you could bring Shelby."

The tension in his face seemed to drain a little. He loosened his hold, but didn't release her. "About eleven-thirty?" he murmured against her ear as he nibbled on her earlobe.

"Hmmm..." She couldn't think as his tongue rimmed her ear. "Uhhh... Make it twelve." He blew warm air over her moist skin. A shiver raced up her back.

"Twelve it is." He kissed her neck, the caress turning passionate as he began to suck.

"Stop that." She giggled, trying to pull out of his arms. "I'll never get to work if you continue that."

"That's my plan." He chuckled. Stealing a quick kiss, he released her. The moment was bittersweet.

"What am I going to do with you?" Jessie asked, smoothing her hand over his cheek.

"Love me." He turned his face into her palm and pressed his lips to it.

*I do* was on the tip of her tongue, but the words never came. Why? She didn't know. Instead, she dropped her hand and turned away, but not before seeing disappointment register on his face.

*Dammit.* Jessie couldn't help it if she was burdened with emotional baggage. It did her no good to apologize for it—it was what it was. She headed back to the dresser to retrieve a pair of socks.

While she set everything down upon the bed, Wade

disappeared into the bathroom down the hall. With a tug, she wiggled into the jeans, pulled the sweater over her head, and then sat to don her socks and boots.

She was heading out the bedroom when Wade came out wearing his jeans and nothing else. "There's coffee in the cupboard. Food in the fridge." The fine line of hair down his abdomen that led to his groin looked so hot. She had the urge to trace it with her tongue.

Wade picked up his shirt and slid his arms through the sleeves. "I'll pick something up on the way home."

"Okay. Well..." She paused. What she wouldn't give for one more tumble before she left, but it wasn't to be. "Guess I'd better get going." Without another word, she turned and walked out of the bedroom.

Jax met her halfway down the hall, wagging his tail. "Hey boy." She scratched him behind the ear. He barked, turning to run into the kitchen. "You hungry?"

He barked, his front feet coming off the floor.

Her pace increased. After she fed the dog, she headed for her truck. In minutes, she was pulling out of her drive and onto the road.

The sky was clear, the morning air cool and clean smelling. Wade fished his truck keys out of his jean pocket as he saw the taillights of Jessie's truck disappear around a corner.

He pulled the front door closed. An extra tug of the doorknob ensured it was locked. The keys and spurs in his hands jingled, reminding him of Jessie naked and an expression of ecstasy on her face. Their night of pleasure had come to an end sooner than he had planned.

Come the weekend, she was all his.

The thought of her wrapped in his arms for two long days and nights put a bounce in his step. As he headed for his truck, his pace suddenly slowed.

Shelby.

*Damn.* He'd almost forgotten about the kid.

Reaching for the truck door, he jerked it open. Jessie wouldn't be his the entire weekend. He slid in behind the wheel, inserted the key and the engine roared to life as well as his radio.

Wade had never dated a woman with a child, mainly because of his sexual desires. He liked a woman willing and ready when the itch tickled him. Shifting the truck into gear, he accelerated and the truck began to move. Throw kids into the equation and, well, there was no spontaneity.

It's not that he didn't like children, it was just the opposite. He wanted children—several. He just hadn't planned on them this soon. Instead he had looked forward to Jessie and his relationship growing stronger. Having a child around would be new to him as well as her, but he was looking forward to it. He'd do anything to have her in his life.

As he maneuvered onto the main road, a man in a suit driving a white BMW laid on his horn. He tipped his hat. Everyone was always in a hurry. But not him, he puckered his lips and began to whistle softly to the song playing on his radio.

He was proud of Jessie. She had made it clear that her intentions were to take care of Shelby and to keep their father out of the picture. With a bit of luck, the man would never return to San Antonio.

Maybe later Wade would swing by Guy Sandoval's office and see where Jessie stood in gaining custody of Shelby. He had met the attorney through Dieter. Wade's hum turned into a shrill note as he thought of the days the three of them spent raising hell. An odd threesome: a lawyer, cop and cowboy, but the women had loved it.

Those days were gone. A smile pinched his mouth. He was going to be a family man. Well, that is if he could convince Jessie to marry him.

Shelby and his mother were cutting roses as he pulled his truck in front of the house. It warmed him when Shelby grinned and ran to meet him. Opening the door, he stepped outside and immediately had two little arms wrapped around his legs. As quickly as she hugged him, she released him.

"We're picking flowers for breakfast," she said, beaming up at him. "I have gloves."

Wade couldn't help laughing. "I can see that." She must have worn a pair of Tori's gloves, because they looked to be two sizes too big.

The pride in the little girl's eyes glistened. He was amazed at the resemblance she and Jessie shared. Their eyes were identical, even their hair color.

"Hi, sweetheart." Madeline waved her gloved hand holding a bunch of flowers. In the other hand, she held a pair of shears. "Missed you last night." She winked.

It was his mother's subtle way of letting him know his presence didn't go unnoticed. He had the good sense to blush, heat rising up his neck.

Madeline chuckled. "Shelby, why don't you put these flowers in the vase we found earlier?"

Shelby perked up. "Okay." The child accepted the flowers his mother extended to her.

Wade remained quiet until the child was out of earshot. It was obviously his mother had something to say. "Spill it, Mom."

"Son." She paused, her brows furrowing with concern. "Do

you know what you're getting into here?"

Did he?

Not exactly.

"I'm winging it," he responded lightheartedly, but felt anything but. He knew there would be hurdles, maybe even times it felt like quicksand sucking him under. He'd be a fool to say he wasn't scared shitless. Yet Jessie was worth whatever was thrown in his path.

Madeline pulled off her gloves. "These two come with a lot of emotional baggage. Are you ready for the issues that might arise?"

"Mom, I love Jessie." Wade would fight the demons he had to just to be with Jessie.

Madeline nodded. "Okay then. If you need me—"

He pulled her into his arms and kissed her softly on the forehead. "You'll be there," he finished her sentence.

"I just want you to be happy." She gave him a hug.

How did he get so lucky? His mother was priceless. Hell. His entire family would put their lives up for him, as he would for them. Emotion lodged in his throat. He wanted to share his family with Jessie—wanted them to love her as much as he did.

He cleared his throat. "I know. Now what's for breakfast?"

Madeline shook her head. "Come on. Tori's got French toast on the skillet."

As they walked into the house, the scent of sausage cooking made his stomach growl. He inhaled, realizing how hungry he was after a night of loving.

"Better wipe that grin off your face before Ty sees you or he'll give you a rash of teasing," his mother suggested with a grin of her own. Of course, she was right. His brother never missed an opportunity to harass a family member or complete stranger.

The kitchen was abuzz with Tori at the stove, his father gathering plates from the cupboard, Ty chasing Shelby around the table, and Clint retrieving a pitcher of milk from the refrigerator.

"Ty, stop that," Madeline barked just as his brother scooped Shelby into his arms.

"Ah-huh. You thought you could get away from me," Ty jested, tickling her.

She wiggled and laughed. "*Waaade*...help me. Save me."

"She's already looking to you to be her protector." Madeline's hushed tones were for his ears only, but his sister heard nonetheless. She flashed him a concerned look as she carried a plateful of French toast to the table.

Wade couldn't say that the notion wasn't disturbing, but what was—was. He took the steps necessary to close the distance between him, Ty and Shelby. With a great show of heroism, he wrangled her out of Ty's arms, holding her close to his chest. He wanted the child to feel safe, even if it was in fun.

Arms tight around his neck, Shelby stuck her tongue out at Ty. The shock on his brother's face had everybody bursting into laughter. The little brat fit perfectly in this family. Strangely Wade couldn't see it any other way.

*Well hell.* The kid had weaved her way right into his heart. The thought of Dan Evans returning made him hold her a little closer—a little tighter.

# Chapter Thirteen

Dressed in an expensive gray suit, Guy Sandoval sat behind a mahogany desk listening intently. The lawyer's inquisitive gaze was pinned on Wade as he finished his story about Jessie's dilemma.

Male interest made the corners of his friend's mouth rise. "This *chica,* she is beautiful, yes?"

Wade rolled his eyes catching a glance at the velveteen picture of a matador hanging on the wall. He should have known the Spanish playboy would be interested in the woman first, the problem second. Okay, maybe that wasn't fair. Guy had a reputation of being ruthless when the situation warranted it. He was as successful in the courtroom as he was with the ladies.

"Yes," he finally offered, but refused to share any more personal information about Jessie. Call it jealousy or what you will. The less this man knew of her the better.

"Hmmm..." Guy pinched his nose and closed his eyes momentarily as if his eyes hurt. In fact, he looked a little haggard. Knowing the Latin lover, Guy probably had a long night with not one but two women in his bed. "Did her papa express his intent not to return?"

"No." Wade sat his booted foot across his opposite knee and then removed his Stetson to hang it on the toe of his shoe.

"Evans told the child he was going to look for a job. He never returned."

Guy shook his head. "Sorry bastard." He picked up his coffee cup and took a drink. "How long has this man been gone?"

"Just a couple days."

Setting the mug down with a clink, Guy asked, "Any chance of him returning?"

That was the problem. "I figure he'll haul his sorry ass back into town when he needs something." Unexpected anger rose. Wade could only imagine what pain Jessie and Shelby had suffered beneath Evans's parenting.

Guy eased back into his leather desk chair. "You know my specialty is corporate law."

And he was good at it if the stories Dieter had told Wade were true. He was hoping that his friend knew someone who could help him. "Yeah, but I thought perhaps you could offer some advice."

Guy took another sip of his coffee. "From what I can remember about family law in Texas, the statute states that the court may order termination of the parent's rights if they find by clear and convincing evidence the parent has voluntarily left the child alone, or in the possession of another, without provisions for support for a period of six months."

"Six months? That long?" The lump in Wade's stomach felt like it thickened. "Waiting will drive Jessie crazy." Not to mention him.

"The law is the law. Right or wrong, the court would rather keep a parent and child together than separate them. If your *chica's* sister is in imminent danger then the courts would respond quicker, but she is not if I understand you correctly. With a flighty papa, the court's hopes are that he will come

238

around and do the proper thing."

"Fat chance of that." Wade's sarcasm made Guy's eyes widen.

"I know." He nodded sympathetically. "Let me check with a friend of mine who deals in family law. If he feels he can help, I will hook you two up."

Wade removed his hat from his boot and rose. "Thank you." He extended Guy his hand and they shook.

"My pleasure. Now when do I meet this *chica* of yours?" Again that devilish smile made Wade cringe inwardly.

Wade released Guy's hand and squared his hat on his head. "Never." He paused. "Maybe at the wedding."

Guy drew out a long, weighted sigh for Wade's benefit. "The women will be so disappointed to see the *vaquero* is no longer available." A gleam brightened his eyes. "More for me." He winked.

Oh yeah. This cowboy had no need for another woman. Jessie was all he needed or wanted.

As he let the glass doors shut behind him, the sweet scent of the myrtle trees lining the sidewalk rose. Wade made a beeline for his mother's office, right down the street. She had offered to entertain Shelby while he met with Guy. It was almost twelve, time for lunch with Jessie. A sense of happiness filled him.

Man. He had it bad for her. Just the thought of the woman made him giddy.

Wade frowned. Giddy?

What the hell? But that's exactly what she did to him.

He was so intent on having her that he had hired a few men this morning to work on his house. He wanted the thing ready when she finally gave in and agreed to marry him.

When he pushed the door open to his mother's office, Shelby was surrounded by stuffed animals and toys. They must have just arrived, too, because the girl looked like a child in a candy store, mesmerized by her setting.

"Madeline, can I touch them?" Her voice held a note of awe.

It broke his heart to think that Shelby's childhood had been so limited that a couple of stuffed animals would thrill her. His mother must have felt the same way. The concerned expression on her face as she said, "Yes," mirrored his.

Shelby moved slowly toward a pink bunny-rabbit. She reached out, felt its softness, and pulled it into her embrace. Her eyes twinkled as she looked at Wade. Still holding on tight with one arm, she dragged her palm over several other animals, and then sat at the small table to tinker with the rollercoaster toy atop it. The maze of corrugated steel with colorful wooden balls was a favorite of every child's. At least, every time he visited his mother, the kids seemed to be intrigued.

"Jessie called earlier to see how Shelby is doing," Madeline said as they watched the child. "Did your visit with Guy go well?"

Wade shrugged. "I don't know, Mom. It appears to be a waiting game."

Madeline placed her palm on his arm and squeezed. "I know, son, but it's worth the wait." They both gazed at Shelby and he knew it would definitely be worth the wait. If it was within his power, he would see that glow on Shelby's face each and every day. But for now they had to go.

"I hate taking her away from the toys, but we have to meet Jessie at noon."

"Shelby, would you like to have Mr. Bunny?" Madeline asked.

Shelby stared from Madeline to Wade. "Can I?"

"Thanks, Mom." Wade pulled her into his arms, gave her a quick hug before he said, "Come on, shortcake. It's time for lunch."

A knock on the door forced Jessie's attention off the stack of papers on her desk. The clock on the wall announced eleven fifty-five. Wade and Shelby were here. As she pushed from her chair, the door swung wide.

Her heart stuttered. She nearly fell back in her chair as her father strolled into her office. For a moment, she couldn't speak. When she found her voice, she said, "What are you doing here?"

"What?" Dan placed a palm over his heart as he walked farther into the room so that she turned and followed him with her glare. He fiddled with a bridle she had hanging from the wall. "You're not happy to see your dear ol' dad? I thought you'd be thankful I came to take that brat off your hands."

*Oh God. No.*

Jessie swallowed hard. Her heart started racing a mile a minute. She couldn't lose Shelby now that she'd found her. But Jessie couldn't let her father see how much her sister meant to her.

"I'm thrilled to see you," she lied, placing her palms on her hips to control the tremor that seeped into her hands. "Skipping out and leaving me with your baggage wasn't a very fatherly thing to do."

Surprise registered on his face, giving her a sense of satisfaction. The sonofabitch hadn't expected her response. What he had in mind wasn't apparent, but he hadn't counted on her to readily give Shelby up either.

"When are you two leaving?" Jessie added. When a startled gasp came from behind her, she whipped around to see Wade

241

standing there, holding Shelby's hand. In her other arm, she held a pink furry rabbit.

Jessie didn't know if the redness in Wade's face or his angry expression was meant for her father or her as he glared at them both. But it was the pain in Shelby's eyes that made Jessie's mouth go dry.

How much had the child heard?

The child's bottom lip trembled. Her chin wobbled and her eyes went moist. Before she could explain, Shelby pulled her hand out of Wade's, turned and ran.

"Shelby!" Jessie faced her father. "You bastard." He just smirked as she revealed her hand. He knew her act had been a façade, but at what cost?

Jessie spun on a heel to go after Shelby, but Wade had beaten her to it. She was oblivious to the people she passed as she sprinted out of the office and through the auction house, following Wade outside. She nearly ran into him as he stopped, his gaze darting around in search of Shelby.

"Where is she?" Jessie asked as her own gaze scanned the corrals.

"I don't know." He turned on her like a pit-bull, grabbing her by the arms to give her a little shake. "What the hell was going on in there?"

"He showed up. I thought—"

*Fuck.*

Jessie hadn't expected Shelby to overhear her. She jerked out of Wade's grasp. "Does it matter? We need to find Shelby."

Again, Jessie scoured the horizon, but Shelby was nowhere in sight.

Spying Poyo on a horse, she yelled his name. "Have you seen Shelby?"

He shook his head. That's when she saw something pink laying on the ground in one of the corrals. Lord. There had to be at least a dozen horses. Their hooves stomped, driving the stuff animal Shelby had held into the muck.

Jessie's breath caught. Her eyes widened in horror as she reached out and grabbed Wade's shirt.

His gaze followed hers. "Oh. My. God."

Without another word, they both moved at once. They walked slowly, but with an air of urgency, afraid that they would spook the animals. Their hooves were like knives, sharp and deadly, with a thousand pounds of muscle above them.

Through misty eyes, Jessie searched for Shelby.

*Please*, she silently prayed. *Please let Shelby be all right.*

For the first time in a long time, tears clouded her sight. She swiped at them, trying to clear her vision, but they fell like rain, as if a dam of emotions had been set loose. Jessie choked back a breath. She couldn't think straight. She had to find Shelby.

"She isn't here," he announced, looking at her strangely when she laughed. It was nervous laughter—relieved laughter, but where could Shelby be?

Jessie grasped for control wiping her eyes on her sleeve as she wrestled with her emotions. "Poyo, gather the men. I want everyone looking for the child," she ordered, swallowing a much needed breath.

"You okay?" Wade asked.

"Fine." But when her father appeared beside her, she lost it. Years of resentment, anger and fear bleed from every pore in her body. She spun around to face him, doubled up her fist and swung.

Bone met bone, grinding to snap his head to the side with a

crack that sent his cowboy hat flying. Jessie's full-on right had caught him off guard. He blinked, staggering. His knees buckled. He fell on his ass to stare up at her in disbelief.

Pain splintered through her hand, but she had never felt such relief in all her life.

"Bitch," he growled, moving slowly to his feet. "You'll pay for that."

From out of nowhere, Wade appeared. He placed his body between Jessie and her father.

She couldn't see Wade's expression, but she heard the malice in his voice when he said, "Touch her and I'll kill you."

Her father must have believed him because he took several steps backward, before he said, "This doesn't concern you, Peterson."

"The hell it doesn't." Wade's tone deepened to an eerie calm. "You have hurt my girls for the last time."

Something in Jessie's chest tightened. She didn't take the time to evaluate her feelings. Instead, she circled her fingers around his biceps and felt tension, tight and restrained, beneath her touch. He didn't acknowledge her.

"The child is mine. I can do anything I want with her," her dad snarled.

Wade didn't make a sound. He moved so quickly that neither Jessie nor her father knew what happened except that Daniel Evans now lay on his back, Wade atop him with his hands around his neck.

Her father's eyes bulged as he grabbed onto Wade wrists, struggling. Wade's expression was like ice, chilling and callous. Slowly he exerted pressure. Her father gasped. Wade was cutting off his air. In seconds, he would crush the bastard's windpipe.

"Wade. No." Even as Jessie attempted to stop him from killing her father, she couldn't help wanting it to be her fingers around the sonofabitch's throat. Her voice trembled. "Dad, you need to walk away while you can."

"I won't—"

"Or I'll have you jailed," she added quickly.

As Wade eased his hold, her father choked sucking air into his lungs. "On what charge?"

"Murder."

His eyes widened. "Murder?" he coughed, trying to rise, but Wade held him firmly beneath his grasp. "You're out of your fuckin' mind," he wheezed.

"You think?" Nervously, Jessie forced what she hoped was a shrewd expression upon her face. "I know." She inched a brow up.

"You know what, bitch?" he spat.

Wade tightened his hold and her father squirmed, fear rimming his eyes until Wade eased up again.

"That you supplied Shelby's mom with the drugs that killed her. For all we know you forced her to take them."

"The hell you say." The shock on his face melted into a sneer. "No one is going to believe that brat."

"Maybe—maybe not." Jessie looked him square in the eyes. "Are you willing to take that chance? You were the only one home with Shelby's mother. You discovered her dead."

Jessie could feel his anxiety rise. It thickened the air. But she wasn't finished, no, she had just began.

"Your long record of substance abuse as well as mental and physical abuse won't bode well for you. Especially when I stand up there and tell the jury of the hell you put Mom and me through."

Unstrained laughter burst from her lips. It came from some deep, dark place inside her. Wade and her father pinned her with the strangest look, but she couldn't help it. Something broke inside her—shattered into a million pieces.

"You're finished here." She fought to regain her control, succeeding, but barely. "There isn't anyone else for you to taunt and destroy. Wade, release him. I think he's ready to leave town now."

But Wade didn't let him go. "I'll have papers drawn up by noon tomorrow for you to sign."

"Papers?" her father asked weakly.

"Giving us the rights to adopt Shelby." As Wade released him, he placed his knee in the middle of her father's chest and the man groaned in pain. "Remember, Guy Sandoval's office tomorrow at noon. If you're late, our next stop will be the police."

Daniel Evans wasted no time getting to his feet. He picked up his hat, never looking back as he high-tailed it to his truck.

Jessie turned to Wade, speechless. They had won for now, but there was more at stake.

"Shelby," she breathed. "We have to find her."

# Chapter Fourteen

The sun was sinking in the west. Wade looked up at the streams of red, orange and yellow that streaked the sky and marked the hours which had gone by and they had still not found Shelby. Not to mention, with each minute that passed, so did Jessie's confidence. The woman was a mess, unwilling to go home or leave the auction house just in case Shelby returned.

After scouring the vicinity for the third time and coming up empty-handed, he had contacted the police. At least six marked patrol cars were parked in the Carmel parking lot, while several more could be seen driving up and down the nearby streets.

He had also placed a call to his family. They were amazingly supportive and genuinely concerned. Ty and Tori were on horseback searching the immediate area, while his father and Clint had taken to the streets in separate vehicles.

In the distance Wade saw his mother wrap her arms around Jessie, trying to console her for the umpteenth time, but her tears appeared unending. She blamed herself for Shelby's disappearance. He could hear her sobbing, her sorrow breaking his heart.

*Fuck.* Wade pushed his fingers through his hair and then placed his hat back on his head. He felt useless.

Where the hell could the child have gone? She wasn't out of his sight but for a second.

The thought that she might have been kidnapped had entered his mind and sent a chill to his bones. He hadn't mentioned it to Jessie, but the police thought it a possibility as well.

The toe of his boot kicked a rock, sending it skipping across the ground, as he tried to erase the image in his head. He had saved her from her father only to have her end up in someone else's hands.

Desperation stole the air in his lungs as he exhaled, and then pulled in a deep breath. He couldn't think that way. Still, it was a chaotic nightmare as friends, family and even strangers roamed the area. He was touched by their caring. Even Dieter and Guy had joined the quest to find Shelby. But the extra activity had the animals fidgety which only helped to fill the air with a sense of unrest.

"You okay?" Clancy asked as he came to stand beside Wade. He took his hat off and slammed it against his leg several times.

"I don't know where else to look." Wade heard sorrow in his voice. That was not going to work. He'd hoped to mask his disquiet for Jessie's sake. But damn, it was hard. His skin felt like it was crawling. He had to do something—anything.

Clancy looked in Jessie's direction. "I've never seen her like this—ever." Anxiety tugged at his brows as he placed his hat back upon his head.

Clancy's revelation worried Wade more than he wanted to admit. Clancy was Jessie's confidant. Throughout the years, he should have seen Jessie at her lowest point. If she worried him, just how bad off was she?

Wade had tried to hold her—soothe her—but she had pushed him away. There was no time to speak to her or figure out just what happened. He didn't care then or now. He knew there had to be a good explanation. Finding Shelby was his foremost concern.

"I don't know what to do for her," he admitted. It tore him in two to see her this way.

Clancy shrugged. "Guess we'd better find her sister."

As they turned to leave, a bloodcurdling scream cut through the gentle breeze.

The knot in Wade's stomach twisted. He didn't think, only reacted, running toward the child's outcry with Clancy hot on his trail.

When Wade turned the corner of the building, Poyo had Shelby strapped to his side by an arm. She was kicking and squirming as he cursed softly in Spanish.

"Let me go," she yelled, struggling with all her might. For such a little girl, Poyo was having a helluva time restraining her.

Wade had never been so relieved in his life. "Where did you find her?"

Poyo grunted as she nailed him with a foot to his shin. "Peeking out of the grain barrel." The man yelped when she sank her teeth into his arm. "*Cogida!*" He released her, holding onto his arm.

As soon as Shelby's feet hit the ground, she was off.

"Shelby!" Wade ran after her. This time she didn't get away from him. He grabbed her arm, pulling her to a stop, but that didn't take the fight out of her. She was a little hellcat, thrashing and flailing her arms about.

"Let me go," she cried again as tears rolled down her dirt smudged face. The sweet scent of grain covered her, as well as several oats scattered about her clothes.

Had the kid been hiding there all along? There was six fifty-gallon drums all covered with lids. Did no one think to look inside? He sure as hell hadn't. In fact, he had passed this way at least half a dozen times.

Shelby attempted to jerk out of his hold, but he held on tight. Even when she tried to kick him, he didn't let go.

"Shelby, calm down. Honey, please."

Her eyes were puffy when she glared up at him. Her cheeks reddened and she was cold to bone. Sorrow etched in her forehead make his chest ache, but it was the forlorn sound in her voice as she whimpered, "She doesn't want me. Let me go," that chilled him to the bones.

Wade dropped to his knees stilling holding on to her. "Ahhh... Shortcake, that isn't true."

"Shelby." Her name was a whisper on Jessie's lips as she stopped six feet away from them. "Oh God." She took one step and stopped. "I'm sorry. I didn't mean it."

Shelby buried her face against Wade's shoulder. He picked her up and then stood. The child refused to acknowledge her sister as he closed the distance between them.

"Shelby." Jessie pressed a palm to her mouth as if she fought back her own sobs. Silent tears streamed down her cheeks. She raised a hand to place on the girl's back, but she stopped midair. Slowly her arm fell to her side and she retreated.

"Let me talk to her," Madeline offered. She took Shelby from Wade's arms and the child went willingly, snaking her arms around his mother's neck. Madeline ruffled her hair, little specks of oats peeking through the dark strands. "You gave us quite a scare."

"Can I live with you? Please," Shelby mewled.

Sadness darkened Jessie's eyes. She stumbled backward

as if her sister's plea had been a slap to her face.

Wade didn't want to separate Shelby from Jessie, but Shelby wasn't ready to forgive her sister—not yet. It was probably best not to push the child. "Mom?"

"Why don't I take Shelby home with me? I'll feed and clean her up. You'd like a bath, wouldn't you?" Madeline asked.

She didn't answer, her face now buried against his mother's shoulder.

"Wade, perhaps you can bring her clothes. Maybe she'll be in the mood to talk later." His mother didn't wait for him to answer or for Jessie to object. As Madeline walked away, he saw her reach for her cell phone, probably calling his dad to pick them up.

Clancy and Wade approached Jessie at the same time. She was shaking and it wasn't due to the weather that had turned cold as night had fallen. With moonlight on her face, she looked up at Wade and her bottom lip began to tremble.

"Hold me," she murmured before falling into his arms.

It was a bittersweet moment for him. She had chosen him over Clancy. Her tears dampened his shirt as he embraced her.

Clancy refused to leave her side. The anguish in his eyes was almost as palpable as in hers, making Wade hurt for the two of them. Both of them were bound by the past, fighting to be released. Perhaps today was a new beginning for Jessie and Shelby. But what about Clancy?

"Take her home, Wade," Clancy said. "I'll take care of things here. Just call me later—let me know if things are all right."

Wade nodded.

As he and Jessie turned to leave, Guy approached them. "Is there anything I can do for you?" he asked Jessie.

"Honey, this is a friend of mine. Guy Sandoval," Wade said.

"It's nice to meet you." Jessie sniffled back the last of her tears.

"The pleasure is mine." Guy bowed over her hand and then kissed it softly before releasing her. "Is there anything I can do?"

"I need you or your friend to draw up custody papers. Daniel Evans will be by tomorrow at noon to sign his parental rights over to us."

Guy perked up looking from Wade to Jessie. "Does this mean there is a marriage in the near future?"

There was a moment of silence that Wade didn't know how to address. His threat to Evans had been off the cuff. Jessie had never agreed to marry him. He doubted after the events of today that she would even consider it. He was just about to explain and ask that the custody be placed in Jessie's name alone, when she said, "Yes."

Wade's heart stuttered. Did he hear her correctly? He gazed down at her and she gave him a weak smile.

"Are you sure?"

"Yes. I want Shelby to have a real family."

"Hot damn." Wade tore her off her feet and twirled her around. Another big hug before he released her.

Guy slapped him on the back. "*Felicitaciones.* I will contact my friend tonight. The papers will be ready by noon. Until tomorrow."

"Thank you," Jessie said.

Wade and Guy shook hands. When he was out of earshot, Wade pulled her to him. "For a woman who has just announced her engagement, you don't look all that happy."

Jessie's face was drawn. "Shelby hates me."

"No, honey, she's hurt. Your words crushed her. What was

going on when we arrived?" He looped his arm over her shoulders and started to guide her to his truck.

Several people came up to them and extended their congratulations for finding Shelby. When they stood before his truck, Jessie said, "I knew he was taunting me. He wanted to see what I'd do if he told me he was taking Shelby away. I played along—it back fired." She sighed. "I've made such a mess of things."

Wade opened the passenger door and Jessie climbed inside. "So do you think Shelby is right?" he asked, holding the door wide.

"Right?"

"Do you think Evans killed her mother?"

"Oh that. Anything is possible, but I made that part up." A weary smile found its way upon her face. "I had to try something. He was going to take Shelby."

*Clever.*

Wade wedged himself between Jessie and the open door. "Judging by your father's reaction, you struck a nerve."

A glimmer of hope sparked in her eyes. "Do you think he'll go through with signing the papers?"

Wade smoothed his knuckles across her cheek and leaned in for a tender kiss. "Yes." If not, he had full intentions making good on his promise. "I think after tomorrow you'll never see him again.

Jessie exhaled as if the weight of the world had been lifted from her shoulders. "That would be fine with me."

Wade patted her on the knee. "What do you say that we swing by your house and pick up clean clothes for Shelby?" He moved away, shutting the door before he rounded the truck and got inside.

After he secured his seatbelt, he inserted the key and cranked the engine. "I can't believe that whippersnapper was hiding right in front of our eyes, probably laughing at us each time we passed her."

Jessie slipped her seatbelt on. "Shelby did say she was a good hider."

He reached over and gave her hand a squeeze, and then he brought her palm to his lips. "We'll have to remember that."

Shelby was a precocious child that surely would keep Jessie and him on their toes for a long time to come.


Jessie couldn't believe how nervous she was as they pulled up in front of the Peterson's home. As Wade turned off the truck and got out, she remained seated, startling when he opened her door.

"Honey?"

She grabbed the sack that held Shelby's clean clothes. "I'm scared." It was the truth. Her heart was racing. Her palms were sweaty as she rubbed them on her jeans. "Let's keep our engagement quiet for now."

His disappointment was obvious as his face hardened.

"There's too much going on right now. I don't want to overwhelm Shelby," she tried to explain. "We probably shouldn't mention the custody papers either—not until we know for sure." She licked her dry lips awaiting his response. She needed him to understand—needed his support.

After a pregnant pause, he said, "You're right." Extending her a hand, he helped her out of the truck. She was glad when he didn't release her. Instead he weaved his fingers through hers and led her to the door.

From the doorway, she heard the television playing. Her stomach rumbled as the scent of a savory meat dish touched her nose. When had she eaten last? She'd missed breakfast because she was late for work. With the events of today she had missed lunch as well as dinner.

"Hungry?" Wade asked.

"I want to see Shelby." Eating could wait.

From the archway of the living room, Jessie could see Shelby lying on the couch, her head in Madeline's lap as she ran her fingers through the child's hair. She was wearing a large T-shirt that swallowed her up. When Jessie and Wade entered, Shelby perked up, but then turned her back to them.

Madeline gave Shelby a little nudge. "Remember what we talked about." Wade's mother scooted out from beneath Shelby and rose. She straightened the baggy T-shirt she wore with khaki pants. Barefooted, she padded across the room. "Wade, why don't you help me in the kitchen. My guess is the two of you are starving."

When Shelby and Jessie were alone, Jessie moved closer to the couch, sitting the bag she held on the end table. Her every move felt like it was being scrutinized as the child glared at her.

It was obvious their discussion wouldn't be easy.

Jessie drank in a breath of courage. "Shelby." Her voice cracked and she cleared her throat. "I didn't mean what I said earlier."

Shelby grabbed a throw pillow and held it to her chest like a shield. "You don't want me."

"That's not true." Jessie inched closer careful not to crowd her. She wanted to touch her sister so badly it made a knot form in her throat. "You may not understand, but Dad was threatening to take you away. I had to make him feel as if it didn't matter—I didn't care. But I do care, Shelby."

Shelby's bottom lip quivered. "I don't want to go with him. I want to stay with Wade and Madeline."

Of course, she would want that. The Petersons were the only people who had made her feel safe since her arrival. Jessie sure hadn't.

"You don't want to come home with me?" she asked anyway.

"No." Shelby's eyes misted, big blue pools of sadness.

"I miss you. That great big bed is awful lonely." Jessie blinked, trying to make light of the moment.

A singled tear fell down Shelby's cheek, and then another raced after the first.

Jessie's nose stung as her emotion began to build. "Sweetheart, don't cry." Her words did just the opposite seemingly breaking the dam holding back the girl's tears and she began to weep. Jessie wasted no time closing the distance between them and taking her sister into her arms. "Shhh... Baby."

Through moist eyelashes, Shelby looked up. "Is Dan going to take me away?"

"No." It was a promise she shouldn't have made, but she didn't know what else to do. Besides she would fight their father with every breath of her soul to keep her sister with her.

Disbelief was apparent in Shelby's wary expression. "The police made me go with him."

Jessie tapped her on the nose. "Not this time, shortcake."

Shelby laughed through her tears. "I like it when you call me shortcake—Wade too."

The light scent of powder was apparent when Jessie pressed her lips to the child's forehead. "Let's go home."

Shelby swallowed hard. "Okay."

A joy Jessie had never felt before touched her. This was right. Saying yes to Wade's proposal was right. Now if things went as expected tomorrow her life would be perfect.

"Hey, what's all this laughter?" Wade asked entering the living room, Madeline close behind him carrying a brown paper sack.

"We're going home," Shelby announced jumping to her feet to run into his awaiting arms. The excitement in her voice, as well as how comfortable he appeared holding her, warmed Jessie's heart.

At that moment, she realized he would be a great father—and husband.

Madeline's gaze met Jessie's. The woman winked knowingly.

Jessie mouthed, "Thank you." Wade's family had been so supportive, his mother invaluable in breaking the ice between her and Shelby.

Madeline crossed the room and embraced Jessie. "You're welcome, dear. If you need me, you know where to find me." Before she released Jessie, she added, "Take care of them both."

Jessie thought about the words Madeline spoke. When the woman pushed the sack into her hands it barely registered. What did sink in was that Madeline would soon be her mother-in-law and she was entrusting her son to Jessie.

Had Wade told her about their engagement?

*Holy shit.*

She would be a wife soon. Not to mention a big sister and responsible for the care of a child.

Wade bounced Shelby on his hip. "Mom made us some sandwiches to take with us." Her light laughter was like white noise in Jessie's foggy head.

She pulled her attention to him. "What?"

He nodded toward the bag she held. "Sandwiches."

"Sandwiches?" She stared at the paper sack like an idiot, before jerking her head and saying, "Thank you."

Madeline tugged on the hem of Shelby's T-shirt. "Our little girl didn't eat much at dinner."

Wade furrowed his brows watching Jessie closely. "You okay?" Amazingly, he was in tune with her every emotion since she had dropped her barriers and let him into her heart.

When he reached out and touched her arm she felt his strength and caring. It radiated in his eyes and his tender expression filled with affection reflecting back at her.

Taken back by the depth of his feelings for her, Jessie took a much needed breath. "Yes." She was okay. In fact, she was better than okay. She smoothed her fingertips along his jaw line.

Gorgeous.

He was perfect.

Why had it taken her so long to admit that she loved this man?

"Jessie?"

Jessie's chest tightened. Her skin prickled with joy.

*I love Wade Peterson?*

"Jessie?" Shelby repeated dragging Jessie from her revelation. "Can we go home now?"

"Home?" She felt the silly grin that tugged at the corners of her mouth as she gazed into his eyes.

*I love you.*

Wade gave her an uncertain look.

God. What she'd do to kiss him. Better yet, make love to

him all night long. Home sounded wonderful to her. "Sure, Shelby. We can go home now."

After Shelby dressed they said their good-byes and stepped outside. Wade hoisted the child on his shoulder and carried her to the truck and opened the door. He sat her on the seat, securing her seatbelt, and waited until Jessie climbed in beside her. Before he shut the door he pressed his lips to hers.

*Mmmm...* He tasted so good.

She couldn't wait to get him alone, to feel him naked against her. A tremor assailed her as an image of her wrapped in his arms rose.

"Cold?" he asked, maneuvering the truck onto the street.

"No." It was more like horny, but sex would have to wait. She had to think of Shelby first. The child leaned into her growing quiet. As they turned down her street, she noticed Shelby had fallen asleep.

"She's had a rough day." Wade looked at the child with a softness on his face that made Jessie love him even more. He would make a great father. "I'll carry her into the house and put her to bed."

When he pulled the truck to a stop Jessie grabbed the paper sack and got out. She moved quickly toward the house to unlock the front door. Jax barked and she heard his footsteps sliding across the floor as he came to greet her. Holding the door open with her foot, she blindly searched for the light switch. With a flick of her finger, light spilled across the room.

"Hey boy." She patted the dog on the head.

Wade and Shelby passed through the door and Jessie closed it tight, relocking it. While he disappeared into the hall, she headed toward the kitchen to feed Jax. She sat the sandwiches Madeline had provide them on the table, before heading for the pantry to retrieve his food.

Jessie was pouring dog food into a bowl on the floor when Wade entered the kitchen. "Hungry?" she asked.

He gazed at Jax's food. "For that, no." Then his eyelids grew heavy. "For you, yes." He circled his fingers around her arm, pulling to draw her to her feet. "I want you." His nose gently rubbed against hers. "I need you naked." His lips caressed hers with each word. "Now."

When he slipped a hand beneath her shirt to cup a silk-covered breast, her pulse began to race. He thumbed her nipple making it bead.

"We can't." She gasped as his wicked fingers slipped beyond her bra. His palm warm against her skin. He pushed her shirt up and dipped his head.

His mouth found her aching flesh. Hot. Wet. He flicked his tongue several times before latching on and sucking for earnest.

Jessie slid her fingers into the coolness of his hair. Her head lolled back as her eyelids fell. It felt so good. He tugged scraping his teeth over the sensitive nubs causing tingles to radiate her now heavy breasts. The rays of sensation shot downward and moisture pooled between her thighs.

She wanted him. But a cold nose against the back of her hand reminded her that they weren't alone.

Jessie licked her parched lips. She opened her eyes to see Jax standing there, looking up at her as he wagged his tail.

*Damn. Damn. Damn.*

But it wasn't the dog that she was worried about. "Wade. No. Shelby."

He groaned, but stopped immediately tugging down her shirt. "When?"

She slipped her hand beneath her shirt to pull down her bra. "When what?"

He adjusted his hips. "When will you marry me? I can't go around like this for long."

She glanced down confirming what she expected. He was as hard as a rock.

Jessie chuckled. But the truth was she hadn't even thought about when they would tie the knot. She'd only been engaged for less than a day.

Yet he did make a point.

Neither one of them was good at waiting for what their bodies demanded. Even now her blood sizzled. The pulse between her legs hadn't died; it grew stronger as he gazed at her with such longing.

"Your call," she said.

"Really?" A sinfully wicked grin pinched his mouth. "You'll leave everything up to me. Date? Time? Place?"

His smile should have been a warning, but the truth was she didn't know anything about weddings. She hadn't allowed herself to dream the impossible and now it was actually happening. "Sure."

It should have concerned her when he slapped a half-assed kiss on her lips. "I'll see you tomorrow at Guy's office around noon." He turned, but spun around on the toes of his boots. "Mom will pick Shelby up from the auction house around ten. She'll entertain her while we're busy with your father."

Father? Jessie cringed. She'd almost forgotten him or was it wishful thinking?

"Are you leaving?" She didn't want him to go. Hell. She didn't want him to ever leave her.

"Yep." Then he reached for her and she went willingly into his arms. "Too much temptation here, if I don't leave now I'll have my way with you whether you agree or not." This time he kissed her like a man in love.

Slow. Passionate. His caress made her legs go rubbery and her heart stutter.

When he released her Jessie lips were still puckered, still longing for more.

# Chapter Fifteen

It was a beautiful day. The sun was shining. Birds sang in the lacy pink myrtle trees that lined the sidewalk in front of Guy's office. Wade breathed in their sweet fragrance. It was fifteen to twelve and Daniel Evans was nowhere in sight. On the other hand, Jessie was beating the pavement toward him.

"Is he here?" she asked breathlessly, pulling at the collar of her vest. Her gaze darted around nervously.

She looked like an angel dressed in boots, jeans and a cotton shirt.

His angel.

"Not yet."

"He isn't going to show."

He tugged on her long black hair she wore loose. "What a negative Nellie you are today." Yet the thought had crossed his mind as well. He'd kill the sonofabitch if he ruined today.

Jessie bit her bottom lip. "What are we going to do if he doesn't show?"

He caressed his finger over her lip. "Stop that. He'll show."

Her eyes widened as she peered over her shoulder. "Ohmygod. He's here."

Wade turned around to see the sour expression on Evan's pinched face.

He walked straight past them to the glass doors. "Let's get this done. I've got a ride to catch."

Wade didn't know if it was excitement or nerves that made Jessie grab his arm and hold on tight. As he tossed his arm over her shoulder, he felt the tremor that rushed through her. She raised her chin as if doing so gave her courage to follow Evans into the building.

A cute little redhead sat at the receptionist's desk as they entered Guy's office.

Hmmm... She hadn't been here yesterday.

Wade was just about to introduce them, when she smiled sweetly. "Mr. Sandoval is waiting for you. He said to go right in."

Evans jerked the door open and stomped in. Clearly he wasn't happy about the situation. The receptionist followed Jessie and Wade in closing the door behind her. She took a seat off to the side, but not before she switched on a recorder.

"Thank you, Tess." Guy winked. "Tess Allen is my paralegal. She will witness and notarize your signatures." He stood, moving from around his desk to shake Wade's hand. "So nice to see you again, Jessie." He leaned over and kissed her softly on the cheek.

"Fuck this. Either we sign the papers now or I'm out of here," Evans snapped as he crossed his arms over his chest. There was a blush on his face growing deeper with each second that passed.

Guy raised a perfectly groomed eyebrow. "So you are signing your parental rights to Shelby over to your eldest daughter on your own accord, without coercion or force?"

Evans glared at Jessie beneath his cowboy hat. It was the first time he had looked at her since his arrival.

Wade felt her bristle beneath his arm. But she pinned her

father with her own steely glare.

"Yeah. I wouldn't be here if I wasn't," Evans grumbled.

"Then we will begin," Guy said smoothly. "Tess has tabbed in yellow every place that requires your signature, Mr. Evans. But first, may we see some identification?"

Evans pulled a wallet out of his jean pocket and fished out his driver's license.

Guy took it from him and then turned to his paralegal. "A copy please."

Tess stood, crossed the room and took the identification from Guy. Although she was professionally dressed in a modest suit, her hips swayed seductively as she moved to the copier. Wade got the feeling that swing was meant for Guy, because the man's interested gaze never left her ass.

The smell of ink rose when the machine whined and started. A light flashed, dying out as quickly as it shone. Tess picked up the copy, extracted the license and returned it to Evans. He snatched it out of her fingers, cramming his ID back into his wallet and then his pants.

Wade didn't miss Guy's subtle grin as he held up a pen. "If you will, Mr. Evans."

Evans snarled, taking the pen, before flipping to the first yellow tab and scribbling his name. It was amazing how quickly someone could give up his fatherly rights and then turn and walk away forever, but that's exactly what Evans did. He finished in record time not letting the door hit him in the ass as he high-tailed it out of there.

The tension in Jessie's shoulders seemed to disappear when the door slammed behind her father. "Is he gone? Really gone?"

Wade nodded.

She turned throwing her arms around his neck. Her laughter was one of relief and joy. "I can't believe it."

"Do I get some of that?" Guy asked, but Wade refused to release her.

"Not on your life, buddy," he said. "This one is all mine."

He liked the sound of that. There is no way he would let another man near Jessie. If she got restless, he'd just have to find some other interesting ways to entertain her.

"Tsk. Tsk. It isn't like you to not share," Guy taunted as Tess sidled up next to him. He placed a finger beneath her chin, raising her lips to his. He didn't kiss her, only smoothed his mouth over hers teasingly. "This one is always ready to play."

Jessie frowned, nailing Wade with a firm look as her arms tightened around him. "Don't even think about it."

Wade chuckled, loving the jealousy that dotted her cheeks.

"Never, darlin'. From now on I'm a one-woman man."

"I like the sound of that." She leaned into him kissing him softly. "Should we go tell Shelby our news?"

Damn. Wade glanced at the clock on Guy's desk. He'd forgotten the time. It was already fifteen to one.

"Your mom said to meet them at Trellis Gardens when we finish up here." Jessie shook her head. "Funny place to have lunch, especially with a child. I probably would have chosen McDonalds."

Trellis Gardens was a bed and breakfast that catered to romantic interludes and special occasions. Then again, it was New Year's Eve.

Guy gave Wade a knowing glance as he let Tess go and quickly changed the subject. "I'll have these documents filed immediately."

Tess began to gather the papers, stuffing duplicates in a

manila envelope, which she extended to Jessie with a warm smile.

Jessie released Wade and accepted the envelope. When the papers were in her possession she pressed them to her chest as if they were precious. "Guy, I don't know how to thank you."

His eyelids dropped half-mast as he approached her. He raised her hand turning it palm up. He bowed over her fingers, his brown gaze stroking the beauty of her face. "Just promise me if this cowboy ever does you wrong that you'll give me a chance." He took his good sweet time pressing a kiss to her wrist, lingering longer than was comfortable to Wade.

He cleared his throat and extended Guy his hand, forcing him to release Jessie. "We'd better go."

Guy chuckled. "Later, my friend."

"Yeah. I'll see you later." Wade placed his palm in the small of Jessie's back and guided her out of the office.

When they were outside she threw her arms around him and planted a great big smack on his lips.

"What was that for?" He liked it, but it was out of character for her.

"Everything. Thank you." She stepped away. "Shelby is safe. Dad will never be able to hurt her."

*Or you.* If the man even showed his face around town Wade would have his ass.

"Let's take my truck," he said. "We can come back for yours later."

"Okay."

As they walked down the sidewalk, he snaked his arm around her shoulders. She fit perfectly by his side. When his truck came into view, he took out his keys and pressed the button to unlock it. Anxiety slithered across his skin as he opened the door and she hopped in.

Damn. He hoped she didn't kill him once they got to Trellis Gardens. One thing that he did know about her was she didn't like surprises and he had a helluva big one waiting for her.

When they pulled up to the swanky white building wrapped in elegance, Jessie said, "I hope Shelby hasn't broken anything. Ever been inside this place?"

Yes. This morning, but instead of the truth, he said, "No."

"Me neither."

The valet opened her door, as Wade got out of the truck. He tossed another young man in a freshly pressed uniform the keys. Instead of walking toward the main entrance he headed to the cottages that surrounded the actual restaurant.

Jessie pointed back to restaurant. "Ummm... Wrong way. I think that was the entrance."

"No. I think mom said they would be on the patio. This is a shortcut."

"Shortcut?" Suspension etched wrinkles in her forehead. "I thought you said you've never been here before."

Well, he blew that one.

She stopped dead in her tracks. "What's up?"

Wade pulled a cleansing breath. "You said I could choose the date, time and place. Today. Three o'clock. Here."

Jessie released an uneasy chuckle. "You're kidding, right?"

He shook his head.

Her eyes widened. "But— I mean— Really?"

"Really." He didn't dare approach too closely just in case she chose that moment to deliver him a right. Evans had found out how deadly her fist was.

"How? We don't have a license."

"It pays to know people in high places. Guy can make things happen quickly. It doesn't hurt to have someone on the police force on your side either." Dieter had close connections to the owner of Trellis Gardens. His old girlfriend had promised the patio for two hours before the New Year's celebration began.

"I can't believe this. Is Shelby here?" she asked.

He nodded. "Mom too. They'll help you get dressed."

Panic spread across her face. "Dress?" She took several steps backward. "Wade, I don't have anything appropriate for a wedding."

"Clancy has taken care of that. He took Shelby shopping this morning."

"What? Clancy? You left my dress up to a rowdy cowboy and a six year old?"

Well, when she put it like that it didn't sound like the best decision he had ever made.

"The groom isn't supposed to see the dress. It's tradition," he added quickly.

She narrowed her gaze on him as her palms went to her hips. "Please tell me your mother went with them?"

He shrugged. Perhaps he hadn't thought this through.

"Okay." She exhaled an exasperated breath. "Let's go see what they've done."

Why did she make him feel like a disobedient child? Hell, all he tried to do was surprise her and it was blowing up in his face.

Jessie cracked up laughing. "You look like a beaten dog. I'm sure everything will be just fine."

"You're not mad?"

She moved before him and placed her palms on his chest. "How can I be? I love you."

"Can you repeat that?" A big grin tugged at his mouth.

She thumped him on the chest. "Don't press your luck. Now, lead the way."

When they entered the patio, her step faltered and she gasped. "Oh, Wade, it's beautiful." He heard the awe in her voice.

"So you like it?"

"I love it."

But she hadn't seen the dress yet.

Wade's mother said the dress and cake were two of the most important things in a wedding. He had two more opportunities to really screw this up.


Jessie couldn't believe her eyes. The garden looked like something out of a fairytale. Orchids, roses and a variety of other fragrant flowers gave color to the lush greenery and trees giving an almost tropical feel in the middle of Texas. It was a slice of heaven on earth.

She was still breathing in its loveliness when Wade grasped her elbow. "Come on, darlin'. Let me show you to our cottage."

The bungalows were earthy tones, blending in with the vegetation. A cobblestone walkway and a small sign identified the way to each small house. He appeared to know exactly where he was heading as he veered off to the right.

"We're staying here tonight?" She could only imagine what the rooms where like in a place like this. Not to mention it must have cost a bundle. There were finely dressed workers moving discreetly about. The outside lighting could have doubled as chandeliers, frosted glass dangling from the silver posts. She'd lay a bet it was pure grandeur at night. Such a romantic place and Wade had made it all happen.

"I knew you couldn't get off work without notice. I figured we'd stay here tonight, and then arrange a real honeymoon when we have Shelby settled. Mom said she'd watch her when the time is right."

Jessie was beside herself. Everything was happening so fast. Marriage. Adoption. What else lay in store for the new year that lingered before her?

As they moved through the patio, excitement as well as anxiety slithered across her skin. This was so not her. She was cut from the land. A cowgirl. This setting was for a girlie-girl. But that wasn't her biggest worry.

Could she be a wife? A mother? She had enough trouble just taking care of herself and Jax.

With each step she grew more nervous.

What if she failed?

No. Failure was not an option.

Jessie wasn't like her mother, and she sure as hell would never let Shelby and Wade down.

Perspiration beaded her forehead. Her hands felt clammy as she wrung them together.

As they stopped before one of the small homes, Wade asked, "You okay?" He watched her intently. "You look like you might run."

Jessie didn't even pretend she didn't know what he was talking about. This was a major change in her life. Although it felt right, she was scared to death. "I'm okay."

"Well, this is where we say good-bye until three o'clock. Mom gave me strict directions to drop you off and skedaddle. But I think I'll wait until you're inside."

He turned the doorknob and she entered. Before she could say good-bye he shut the door behind her. That's when the real chaos began.

"Jessie," Shelby squealed running up to hug her around the waist. Her sister was beaming from ear to ear. "Are you happy?"

Madeline sauntered into the room. She appeared interested in hearing Jessie's answer too as she cocked her head.

"Yes. I'm very happy." She smiled reassuringly at Madeline.

"I helped." Shelby beamed from ear to ear.

"I bet you did."

"Can I show her the dress? Clancy and I picked it out. Oh, Jessie, it is *soooo* pretty." The child chattered like a squirrel.

Madeline must have seen the panicked look in Jessie's face, because she said, "Why don't we give your sister a little time to get her bearings? How do you like the cottage?"

Jessie gazed around the breathtaking room. White lacy sheers covered the windows with black velvet valiances and matching ties. Elegantly decorated, the furniture had to be from the Regency period. The cabinet and dwarf table were intricately carved and a wood-trim floral black and white loveseat sat before a marble fireplace. Off to the side was an intimate table and chair set for two. Mirrors adorned the walls making the room seem bigger then it was. Vases of flowers powdered the air with a sweet subtle scent.

"Can I show her the dress now?" Shelby fidgeted back and forth where she stood. "I got a dress too."

"You did?"

"Yeah. Want to see it?"

"Of course, I do." Jessie steadied herself. There was no telling what she would be wearing down the aisle as her sister dragged her in the bedroom by her hand.

Jessie stopped short of falling over her feet. The gown

hanging before her was breathtaking.

Elegant, but not pretentious. The strapless, satin A-line cut was narrow at the top, fitting close to the ribcage, with smooth, elongated lines that extended from the waist down. Antique lace scalloped the bodice and hem with just enough color to enhance and not take away from the purity of the dress.

She couldn't help reaching out to touch it. It was so soft—so beautiful.

"Do you like it?" A familiar voice had her pivoting on her toes.

"Clancy, it's gorgeous."

He was gorgeous.

She had never seen him in a suit, much less a tuxedo. The Stetson he wore gave it a Western flair that worked. Yet there was something wrong. His smile didn't reach his eyes. In fact, he didn't appear happy at all.

"It's you," he whispered. Closing the distance between them, he kissed her on the cheek.

A giggle jerked their attention to Shelby.

"No thanks to this brat. She wanted to buy a ball gown."

Jessie would have hated a ball gown. This simple but tasteful dress would have been exactly what she'd chosen if she had done the shopping.

"It's lovely isn't it?" Madeline asked. "We better get you ready or you'll miss your own wedding."

"Could you give me a moment with Clancy?" There was something about him that worried Jessie. She couldn't quite put her finger on it.

"But—"

"Come on, dear. Your sister needs a moment, and then you can show her your dress."

When Wade's mother and Shelby left the room, Jessie cupped Clancy's face in her hands. "Are you all right?"

He placed his hands over hers and drew them down holding them against his chest. "I'm fine. What about you?"

"I don't think I could do this without you." She started to tear, but refused to. There was enough emotion in his eyes to sink a battleship. Instead she tried to lighten the moment. "Would you be my maid of honor?"

He burst into laughter softening his face. "I'd love to, darlin' but your groom has already asked me to walk you down the aisle, and then take my place as best man."

She hadn't thought about walking down the aisle, especially unescorted. She threw her arms around him and held on tight, once again fighting tears. "Thank you. I can't think of anyone I would rather have walk me down the aisle."

"I would rather be standing in Wade's place." His off-handed comment surprised her. She didn't know if he jested or what.

"Clancy—"

"Don't say anything. Just give me a kiss."

His caress was tender, heartfelt, but brief.

"Get dressed. Wade awaits his soon-to-be wife." He gave her one more lingering look and then turned and left.

The next hour and a half was a blur. Hairdressers, manicurists and of course, Shelby, who was in her element. Her little fingers and toes were polished pink to match her dress of chiffon. She twirled for the umpteenth time before the mirror to watch the material flow around her. Jessie knew exactly how she felt as the image of a bride reflected back at her as she stood beside Shelby.

In the mirror she saw Clancy approach. As she turned

around, his jaw dropped. When he regained his composure, he said, "You clean up nicely Jessica Evans." He paused for a moment before he added, "You're exquisite."

"What about me?" Shelby pressed for a compliment.

He glanced at Shelby. "Well, you're just the prettiest thing I've ever seen. If you ladies are ready I'll escort you to the patio."

Turning his attention back to Jessie, he started to place her shoulder-length veil over her face when she said, "Leave it. I don't want to miss a thing."

He nodded, extending them his arms. Shelby grabbed a little basket of flower petals and a bouquet of snowy clusters of hyacinths and cattleya orchids with a shimmering black vintage jacquard ribbon. She handed the bouquet to Jessie making her realize this was really happening.

She was getting married.

As she linked her arm within his she looked around the room. "Where's Madeline?" The woman had been a lifesaver. She seemed to know when to help and when to ease back and give Jessie breathing room, and she was a miracle worker with Shelby.

Lord. The kid ricocheted off the walls as if she were high on drugs, but Jessie knew it was happiness. It had a way of making a woman feel as if she were walking on clouds and that's exactly how she felt.

"Her husband came to retrieve her." Clancy was careful of their dresses as he led them out of the cottage.

The warmth of the day was dying and she felt it on her bare shoulders. Soft music was playing as they entered just behind a trellis of white climbing roses. A woman who introduced herself as the wedding planner met them there.

"You look lovely. I'm Helen Cortez. I'll be queuing the

procession."

Shelby tugged on the woman's black jacket that matched her thigh-high skirt. "Do I look pretty too?"

Helen smiled warmly. "You do. I especially love your black hair against that pink."

Shelby beamed beneath the compliment.

Jessie inhaled a shuddering breath. She couldn't believe that in minutes she would become Mrs. Wade Peterson. It had a certain ring to it that made her bubble up inside with happiness.

Clancy patted her hand. "You okay?"

"I'm doing the right thing, aren't I?"

"I'm afraid you are. But if you want to change your mind I'll run away with you right here—right now." Jessie could see the truth reflecting in his eyes and it saddened her.

She wet her dry lips. "I love him."

"I know." Disappointment was evident in his voice.

The music subtly changed to a light airy tune. "Flower girl." Helen motioned to Shelby. "Go."

Shelby looked like an angel. Yet her face pinched tight as she concentrated hard on taking a step and dropping a petal. At this slow speed it would take an hour for her to make it to the end of the aisle.

Jessie didn't care. This was her sister's day as well as hers. They both needed to feel special and loved. She couldn't wait to tell her sister about the custody papers.

Jessie thought of Wade, the fact that he stood behind the trellis waiting for her. Chills rushed over her skin as her chest tightened.

The bridal song began and Helen ushered her and Clancy forward. "Now."

The swish of her gown against his leg was the only thing she heard as they moved around the trellis and faced a small assemblage. She was thankful Wade hadn't invited a large group of people.

Several individuals from the auction house were in attendance, including Carrie. The entire Peterson family was present, as well as several of their closest friends. But it was Wade who stole her attention.

Their eyes met. Everyone seemed to disappear but the two of them. The moment was magical as she made her way down the aisle.

When he took her hands any misgivings she had vanished. He looked at her with such love that she moved closer, needing to hold onto him forever.

The minister began to speak. When he asked for the rings, Jessie froze. Clancy gave her a reassuring look, then moved forward and placed two rings into the man's hand.

Wade had thought of everything.

The exchange of vows and promises was quick. The ceremony was over before she knew it. The best part was when the minister said, "You may kiss the bride."

Strong arms surrounded her as Wade drew her into his embrace. "Mrs. Peterson," he said with a foolish grin, before he dipped his head and captured her mouth.

Jessie melted against him, surrendering to his caress as she slid her arms around his neck.

His kiss was slow and seductive, sweeping her off her feet. Lost in his caress, it took a moment to realize he was actually lifting her.

"I love you." He hugged her close, and then twirled her around.

She threw back her head laughing. When he sat her upon her feet, she whispered, "I love you too."

In seconds they were barraged with well wishers. But it was Clancy who got to her first. He held her so tightly he momentarily cut off her air. "If you ever need me you know how to find me."

"Clancy, I'll always need you. I love you," she said softly. Her words made him smile.

That was the end of their conversation as she was handed from one person to another. Time passed quickly. Helen was amazing, keeping them on schedule. Dinner was hors d'oeuvres and drinks as the wedding planner ushered Jessie and Wade onto the dance floor for their dance.

As they swayed to the music, he asked, "Are you happy?"

"Yes. You?"

"Honey, you have no idea." He hugged her. His hand pressed to the small of her back drifted lower. "You look so beautiful. I can't wait to get you out of that dress."

Jessie didn't recognize the girlish giggle that rose from her throat. She reached for his wandering hand and raised it. "Stop that. There is a small set of eyes pinned on us."

He glanced at Shelby standing at the edge of the dance floor and motioned her to them.

A happy expression spread across the child's face. She ran to Wade and jumped in his arms.

"Come here," he growled taking Jessie back into his embrace, and then the three of them danced.

When the song ended, Helen was right there. "We need to do the toast and cut the cake. It's almost six."

Waiters delivered glasses of champagne as once again Wade, Jessie and Shelby with her flute of apple juice stood in front of the assemblage.

Clancy stepped forward and raised his glass. He bowed his head. For a moment, Jessie wondered if he would be able to deliver, when he raised his gaze to meet hers.

"What can be said about two individuals who have touched my life in so many ways? Wade. Jessie. I hope your lives are filled with love and happiness, that the storms be minimal, and that the rainbows are plenty. To you and your little addition." He tipped his glass toward Shelby.

Cheers rose amongst the crowd. Jessie sipped her champagne, while Clancy chugged his, before reaching for another.

*Oh Clancy.* Her heart was breaking. She wanted to reach out to him—comfort him, but now wasn't the time or place.

Would he ever find a woman who could heal him as Wade had her? And if he did, would he even give her a chance?

She leaned into Wade seeking his strength. He pressed his mouth to her ear. "Sweetheart, he'll be okay."

"He's hurting because of me." She choked back emotion.

"I know, but he's strong." He ran his palms up and down her arms. "You're cold. Everyone is preparing to leave. How about you and me escape to our room?"

The sullen mood that had swept over her wasn't fair to Wade. This was their wedding night.

Jessie scanned the area. "Where's Shelby?"

"She left with Tori. Shortcake thought she was spending the night with us. It took a bribe of riding lessons to get her to leave."

"But we haven't talked to her about the custody papers."

Wade eased her against his hard body. "Honey, it can wait until tomorrow. Tonight is our night." He captured her lips. His seductive kiss promising a night of heaven.

*Mmmm...*

He was right.

# Chapter Sixteen

Finally, they were alone. Well, almost.

An attendant in a black suit and tie, a starched white shirt and a badge that announced him as Bob, stood before the cottage door. He bowed and opened the door, stepping aside to allow Wade and Jessie entrance.

Wade took the moment to slide his arm beneath her knees and raise her into his arms. She made the cutest sound of surprise. Her wedding gown puffed all around them, blocking his view. But nothing would stop him from carrying her across a threshold, even if it wasn't their new home.

She hugged his neck, amusement in her voice when she spoke. "I thought carrying a bride over a threshold was a myth."

"Nope. Family tradition. I plan to do it again once our home is complete."

Her laughter was light and airy.

God. She was beautiful.

He couldn't believe that she was his—all his. The things he planned to do to her tonight and every night from now on could only be described as downright sinful. His wicked thoughts as to what to do first, ravish his bride's lips or strip her naked, were interrupted when Bob began to close the door.

"How a wonderful night, Mr. and Mrs. Peterson."

"Mr. and Mrs. Peterson. I like the sound of that." Wade took a step deeper into the room noticing that the staff had tidied up and left them a present.

Several vases of long-stem white roses were placed throughout the room, while red petals were strewn upon the floor.

"How beautiful." Jessie inhaled. "They smell so good." The fragrance wasn't overpowering, but just enough to set the stage for a night of romance.

A warm fire flickered in the fireplace adding to the ambience, but it was the decadent display of food on the small table that caught Wade's eye. Whipped cream, a chocolate fondue, fruit and more champagne chilled in a bucket of ice. Everything he needed to make the night memorable. He enjoyed food play and if he devoured Jessie in the process so be it.

"That grin on your face worries me," she said, but the sparkle in her eyes revealed the opposite.

He nodded toward the table.

"Mmmm... Looks like they thought of everything."

Not everything. Wade had stayed up most of the night making her something special. "I have a surprise for you." That is if the staff followed his directions and placed the box on the bed.

Releasing her knees, he held her close so that she slid down his body. He doubted that she could feel how hard he was beneath the layers of material she wore. But she would soon feel his rigid cock between her thighs. He had plans to show his wife exactly how much he loved her tonight and every night from now on.

"How could you top what you've already given me?" Her voice was tender, her touch soft as she caressed his lips with hers. For the first time she let her guard down and he saw love reflecting back at him humbling him.

Her skin was cool as he brushed his palms along her bare arms. "I'd give you the world if I could." He'd fight her demons and rescue her from pain if it was within his power.

"I know." She closed the distance between their mouths again, but this time she kissed him with a hunger that fired his blood. Her tongue dueled with his as her fingers curled in his tuxedo jacket.

Wade cupped the back of her neck forcing her to arch into him as he stole the reins of control from her. He wanted to leave no part of her untouched, no doubt in her mind who she belonged to.

"Make love to me, Wade." It was a cry of passion that wrapped strings around his heart and pulled tight.

He wasted no time in bending to her will. Smoothing his palms over her waist, he found the buttons at the back of her gown and began to pluck them free. Even before he was finished, the dress gaped, giving him a view of the satiny bra beneath.

When the silken material fell at her feet, she stood before him in her veil, a strapless bra, panties that rode high on her hips, thigh-high nylons and stilettos. A garter belt circled one thigh completing her sensual appearance.

Wade's cock pressed hard against the zipper of his pants as he ran his finger along the garter. "Is this for me?"

She shifted her weight, palms on her hips, as she struck a provocative pose that made his heart skip a beat. "Everything you see is for you."

Heart thumping, he extended her a hand and helped her step over the mounds of satin and lace. "I like that. Now I have a surprise for you." He weaved his fingers through hers and led her toward the bedroom. Her heels softly clicked against the marble floor.

The lights were dim as they entered. Over two dozen candles burned, flickering shadows off the walls and the amazing diamond ring he had gifted her. More rose petals lay about and another bottle of champagne cooled on the dresser next to a large full-size mirror.

He stopped before the mirror, leaving her to retrieve the box lying on the bed. Without a word he handed the present to her.

She smiled up at him, before she removed the lid to look inside. A giggle surfaced as she extracted a pair of snowy white bondage gauntlets made of leather, lace and golden D-rings. She also held a roll of satin ribbon in her hands.

A gentle pulse began in his groin, but skyrocketed when she gazed up at him through feathered-lashes. "Will you put them on me?"

*Oh hell yeah.*

He took one forearm bracelet and she slipped her arm into it. The thin leather lacings were tougher than they looked as he crisscrossed the stitching to secure them. If he wanted to, he could tie her up and she would be completely under his control. Yet tonight he wanted the effect of her bound in ribbon—his own personal gift to open up and devour over and over again.

When the final gauntlet was in place he took the roll of ribbon from her and began to secure one end to a D-ring. She placed one forearm above the other in front of her and stood silently, watching him intently as he slid the cool fabric across one of her breasts and over a shoulder. Her nipples tightened and goose bumps rose across her arms and abdomen as he pulled the string back to another D-ring.

Every time the stark white ribbon slid across her velvety skin his cock pushed against his zipper. His breathing began to elevate. He knew she would be a mixture of purity and sin in her white lingerie and the sexy gauntlets and ribbon—and he was right.

Again and again, he caressed her skin with the ribbon to bind her so she couldn't move. When he was finished he put distance between them so that he could gaze at her beauty. Then he stepped behind her allowing his fingers to follow the paths of the ribbon crisscrossing around her breasts, chest, abdomen, hips, and legs. He couldn't help slipping a finger in front of her panties to stroke the dark curls of her pussy and delve into her heat. She was warm and wet when his finger parted her folds and slipped inside.

"Wade." Jessie swayed gently unable to touch him with her arms pinned to her side. "Please."

He pumped his finger in and out slowly. "Please what, darlin'." She was so soft and fuckin' hot, bound for his pleasure.

"Fuck me, Wade. Put your cock inside me and drive me wild."

Dirty talk was one of his weaknesses.

Without hesitation, he stripped off his jacket tossing it on a nearby chair. "More." He didn't need to tell her what he wanted. She knew.

"I want you, Wade." Her lips parted on a moan. "I can't wait to feel you between my thighs, your mouth on my breasts."

His hands shook as he unfastened his suspenders, releasing one too quickly to snap him on the chest. "Ugh."

He saw the glint of laughter in her eyes, but instead of chuckling she directed his attention to her lips as her tongue moved sinfully along her bottom lip.

"Maybe I'll fuck you with my mouth again." She inhaled, her chest rising to make her breasts more inviting. "Would you like that?" Her voice was simmering hot, stroking him with each word.

"God yes," he groaned.

His fingers had become all thumbs trying to unfastening the little buttons.

*Fuck it.*

He grabbed a hold of each side of his shirt and pulled, popping buttons to fall to the floor. That was going to cost him, but he didn't care.

"I can't wait." She squirmed as if her body was burning up like his. "Please. Take me now." There was urgency in her voice that thrilled him.

*Shit. Shit. Shit.*

Whoever invented belts should be horse whipped. He pulled and pulled, finally releasing the damn thing so that he could unfasten his pants. The second his firm erection burst free a pang shot through his groin doubling him up and making him groan.

He sucked in a breath as he fought the climax that threatened him. "Baby, as much as I love your dirty talk, if you continue I'll lose it before we even began."

Funny how she was the one tied up, but he felt helpless under her power, especially when she said, "Release me and I'll help you undress. Then I'll ride you all night long...cowboy."

That was it. He went to the dresser, looking for the scissors he asked one of the staff to include tonight for him. They were in the top drawer as he opened it and took them out and returned to his new bride.

Snip. Snip. She was free in no time and made good on her promise.

Jessie placed her palm against his chest guiding him

backwards until his legs struck the bed. She gave him a push and he fell upon the downy comforter.

He loved the seductive gleam in her eyes as she reached for his boots and pulled one off and then the other. His socks followed, before she reached for his pants. With one swift tug she pulled off his pants and skivvies. He lay naked before her. His cock arching against his belly waiting for the moment she bathed him in her warmth.

Shredded ribbons hung from her wrist gauntlets. Her veil flowing down to her shoulders gave an awesome effect, not to mention the thigh-high nylons.

Lord. He was dying here.

"Come to me, baby," he coaxed her. But she had other things in mind, like leaning forward and going down on him.

A breath caught in his throat as her mouth slipped over his cock. Hot. Wet. So fuckin' good, he couldn't speak for moment. When he finally did his voice was as rough as sandpaper. "Damn. Woman."

She made a soft sound as her head began to bob.

Wade speared his fingers through her hair helping to guide the slow and steady pace. She stroked and teased him with her tongue, smoothing it along the crest of his cock, and then down the underside. Up and down, again and again. The wet sounds of her mouth moving over him and her hungry moans were driving him friggin' out of his mind.

He sucked in a tight breath as rays of sensation shot down his erection. "Jessie." He cringed. Fighting the inevitable, every muscle in his body tensed. "Oh God, woman, stop."

She complied, but she wasn't through with him.

Jessie reached for the scissors where he had dropped them on the bed. She didn't hesitate cutting the crotch of her panties, so that they hung loosely on her hips.

"Scoot further on the bed." He did as she directed, and then she straddled him. "Cowboy, I intend to ride you hard. All. Night. Long."

She lowered her hips, building his anticipation to feel her warmth wrapped around him. With a tilt of her hips she found the head of his cock and inched it inside her pussy.

Wade grasped her hips, slowing her pace to make the moment last.

"Tight," he said through clenched teeth. Damn. She felt tighter than she ever had. Warm and inviting, she was all his.

When he filled her completely, she began a gentle sway. The rocking motions pushed him deeper so that he struck the back of her sex. She gasped at the same time as fire lanced down his cock.

*Not now.* He had to hold on.

Yet even as the impossible thought entered his mind, a throb began in his balls. The steady compression pulled his testicles tight against his body ready for the moment of ecstasy.

Their eyes met, an expression of love reflecting back at him to heat his arousal. His fingers pressed into her hips. He couldn't lose it now.

She looked so beautiful in the throes of passion. Her blue eyes were dilated beneath heavy eyelids. Her lips were parted, her tongue sweeping across the bottom one. But it was the way she sought her pleasure as she increased the pressure and the speed of her movements that almost shattered his control.

"Feels so good," she murmured. Face flushed, her breathing became short, quick pants. "Wade. So deep. *Ahhh...*"

The walls of her pussy contracted, squeezing him and forcing a hiss from between his teeth. "Easy." He was too close to climaxing. It wouldn't take much to throw him over the edge.

Evidently, Jessie was past the point of no return too. She leaned her palms on his chest, grinded her hips against his, and then threw back her head on a cry.

Over and over, her body milked his cock until there was nothing he could do but release his hold and join her.

Lights burst behind his eyelids. Heat waves rolled over his skin. Every muscle locked as his climax shot down his shaft bathing him in hot and cold sensations that made him tremble.

Jessie was lost in the love she felt for Wade as she collapsed atop him. Ear pressed to his chest, she heard his rapid breathing, felt the steady beat of his heart.

He plucked at the clasp of her bra and it came loose in his hands. Where he disposed of the thing she didn't know or care. All she knew was that she loved the feel of her nipples rasping against his chest. His skin was moist, slick against hers.

He kissed the top of her head. "I love you."

"I love you too." It was amazing how easy the words of affection came to her now. Peace she had never felt before surrounded her like a blanket as she snuggled closer. Wade had given her that precious gift. Now if only they could give Shelby the same feeling of harmony and contentment. "When should we tell Shelby about the custody?"

He stroked his palm down her back resting his hand on her ass. "We can tell her tomorrow if you'd like."

"Tomorrow?" Thoughts of her sister beginning to disappear as he ran a finger down the crease between her cheeks. "How long do we have this room?" She wiggled her butt.

He chuckled. "Check out is at eleven, but I can call and ask for a late departure."

"I think you might have to do that. I seem to remember seeing a can of whipped cream that looked awful tempting."

He rolled her upon her back draping his body over hers. She laughed and for the first time felt it deep in her chest. "Make love to me, Wade." He closed the distance between their lips and began to do just that.

All night long he worshipped her body. Took her to places in her soul she had never been. As they lay in each other's arms, the clock struck midnight.

"Happy New Years, darlin'," he whispered in her ear.

She moved atop him feeling his strength as his arms surrounded her. She looked deep into his eyes and saw a future filled with love and happiness. "Happy New Years."

It was a new year offering a new beginning and Jessie would take all it had to offer—starting now.

# About the Author

A taste of the erotic, a measure of daring and a hint of laughter describe Mackenzie McKade's novels. She sizzles the pages with scorching sex, fantasy and deep emotion that will touch you and keep you immersed until the end. Whether her stories are contemporaries, futuristics or fantasies, this Arizona native thrives on giving you the ultimate erotic adventure.

When not traveling through her vivid imagination, she's spending time with three beautiful daughters, three devilishly handsome grandsons, and the man of her dreams. She loves to write, enjoys reading, and can't wait 'til summer. Boating and jet skiing are top on her list of activities. Add to that laughter and if mischief is in order—Mackenzie's your gal!

To learn more about Mackenzie McKade, please visit www.mackenziemckade.com. Send an email to Mackenzie at mackenzie@mackenziemckade.com or sign onto her Yahoo! group to join in the fun with other readers as well as Mackenzie! http://groups.yahoo.com/group/wicked_writers/

He's going to give her the Christmas gift of her dreams…
in triplicate.

# Unwrapped
## © *2007 Jaci Burton*

When Justin Garrett accidentally views Amy Parker's private online journal, he sees the cold corporate exec in a brand new light. It seems the icy, unapproachable Amy has fantasies. Fantasies that both appall and intrigue her.

No one knows the real Amy Parker, and she's satisfied to keep it that way. A woman with kinky tastes wouldn't cut it in the straight-laced law firm where she's fought her way to partnership. And she certainly refuses to let an underling use her to advance in the firm. Justin Garrett might be brilliant, gorgeous, and sexy as hell, but he's firmly restricted to her fantasies and that's where he'll stay.

While working together on a corporate acquisition in Hawaii over the Christmas holidays, Justin sets out to make Amy's secret fantasy come true—a night of passion with two men who adore her. And he knows the ideal other man to help Amy unwrap the perfect Christmas gift.

But first he has to melt her heart and convince her he sees her as a woman, not a rung to climb on the career ladder. In fact, by giving Amy exactly what she's always wished for, Justin hopes to climb right into her heart.

*This title contains the following: explicit sex, graphic language, ménage a trois, a trip to Hawaii and maybe a glimpse of Santa on a surfboard.*

*Available now in ebook and print from Samhain Publishing.*

*Is it love? Or sabotage?*

# Between a Ridge and a Hard Place
## © 2008 Annmarie McKenna

After a year of being ignored as a woman by her boss, Morgan steps up her game—and strips down. What better way than a miniskirt to capture her hardheaded boss's attention? The butt floss she can do without, but hey, if the ploy works...and it does, with spectacular results. Now if only she can keep him interested permanently.

Ridge can't believe it when the woman he's quietly lusted after for a year shows up dressed...or rather, undressed...to drop any man to his knees. Instead of worrying about winning a bid after losing the last two under strange circumstances, he whisks her to his place to demolish any notion she might have of changing her mind.

Then it becomes clear why his company is losing bids— there's a mole planted in their midst. Ridge suddenly has to question Morgan's sudden transformation from faithful P.A. to office vixen.

Is she the woman he's been waiting for? Or a corporate saboteur sent to take him down?

*Warning: contains several graphic love scenes. You know, on the bed, on the couch...whichever is closest at the time.*

*Available now in ebook from Samhain Publishing.*

*Vengeance is what she sought...eternal love is what she found.*

# Fallon's Revenge
## © 2006 Mackenzie McKade

Young and inexperienced, Fallon McGregor is an immortal with one thing on her mind. Revenge. She'll do anything to destroy the demon that killed her daughter and made Fallon his flesh and blood slave. One step ahead of her tormentor, she knows her luck is running out. She needs to discover the mysteries of the dark—and fast. When she meets Adrian Trask she gets more than she bargains for in tight jeans and a Stetson.

Adrian will share his ancient blood and knowledge with Fallon, but he wants something in return...her heart and her promise to stay with him forever.

But Fallon doesn't have forever. Once her nemesis is destroyed she will seek her own death. Tormented, she must choose between a promise made and the love of one man.

*Available now in ebook and print from Samhain Publishing.*

# GET IT NOW

## MyBookStoreAndMore.com

GREAT EBOOKS, GREAT DEALS . . . AND MORE!

Don't wait to run to the bookstore down the street, or
waste time shopping online at one of the "big boys." Now,
all your favorite Samhain authors are all in one place—at
MyBookStoreAndMore.com. Stop by today and discover
great deals on Samhain—and a whole lot more!

WWW.SAMHAINPUBLISHING.COM

# GREAT
# CHEAP
# FUN

## Discover eBooks!

THE FASTEST WAY TO GET THE HOTTEST NAMES

Get your favorite authors on your favorite reader, long before they're out in print! Ebooks from Samhain go wherever you go, and work with whatever you carry—Palm, PDF, Mobi, and more.

Samhain
Publishing ltd

WWW.SAMHAINPUBLISHING.COM

LaVergne, TN USA
01 March 2011
218360LV00002B/7/P